Child
of where
Two Oceans Meet

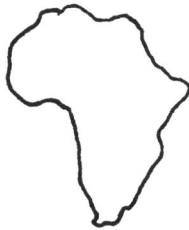

CYNTHIA ELIZABETH SULLY

woodsmoke on an open fire
lion on a savannah plain
distant drums on a moonlit night
crashing waves on rugged shores

... TEMPUS UMBRA ...
CARPE DIEM
time is a shadow
seize the day

Order this book online at www.trafford.com/08-0516
or email orders@trafford.com

Most Trafford titles are also available at major online book retailers.

Editor: Cynthia E. Sully

Cover Design/Artwork/Designer/Photographer: Steve Tronson

The book cover design is by Steve Tronson of Cape Town, South Africa, former photographic editor, (now retired), of one of South Africa's popular motoring magazines. He is a multi-talented man. Of note, are his Tronsigns humorous Christmas greeting cards, which are much sought after... Father of two grown sons, he resides with his wife Myrle, (the author's sister), in Edgemead, South Africa.

Note for Librarians: A cataloguing record for this book is available from Library and Archives Canada at www.collectionscanada.ca/amicus/index-e.html

Printed in Victoria, BC, Canada.

ISBN: 978-1-4251-7661-7

We at Trafford believe that it is the responsibility of us all, as both individuals and corporations, to make choices that are environmentally and socially sound. You, in turn, are supporting this responsible conduct each time you purchase a Trafford book, or make use of our publishing services. To find out how you are helping, please visit www.trafford.com/responsiblepublishing.html

Our mission is to efficiently provide the world's finest, most comprehensive book publishing service, enabling every author to experience success. To find out how to publish your book, your way, and have it available worldwide, visit us online at www.trafford.com/10510

Trafford
PUBLISHING   www.trafford.com

North America & international
toll-free: 1 888 232 4444 (USA & Canada)
phone: 250 383 6864 ♦ fax: 250 383 6804 ♦ email: info@trafford.com

The United Kingdom & Europe
phone: +44 (0)1865 487 395   local rate: 0845 230 9601
facsimile: +44 (0)1865 481 507   mail: info.uk@trafford.com

10 9 8 7 6 5 4 3

Child
of where
Two Oceans Meet
a tale of africa

published by

Trafford
PUBLISHING

The magnificently beautiful Cape Peninsula at the Southern tip of Africa was called by the English seaman — Sir Francis Drake – "the fairest Cape in all the world." The region is a paradise of Eden's beauty. Called many names over the centuries – TAVERN OF THE SEAS – CAPE OF STORMS – CAPE OF DREAMS and by the Portuguese sailors of a bygone era – CABO TORMENTOSO…

Along the south western Cape coastline are the modern bustling ports of Cape Town, Port Elizabeth and East London. Cape Town – the Mother City is the oldest city in South Africa. This is my homeland… This is the country called SOUTH AFRICA.

AUTHOR'S NOTE

This book is a work of fiction. The characters in this novel are fictional though there are references to actual persons and historical events throughout its pages...C.E.S.

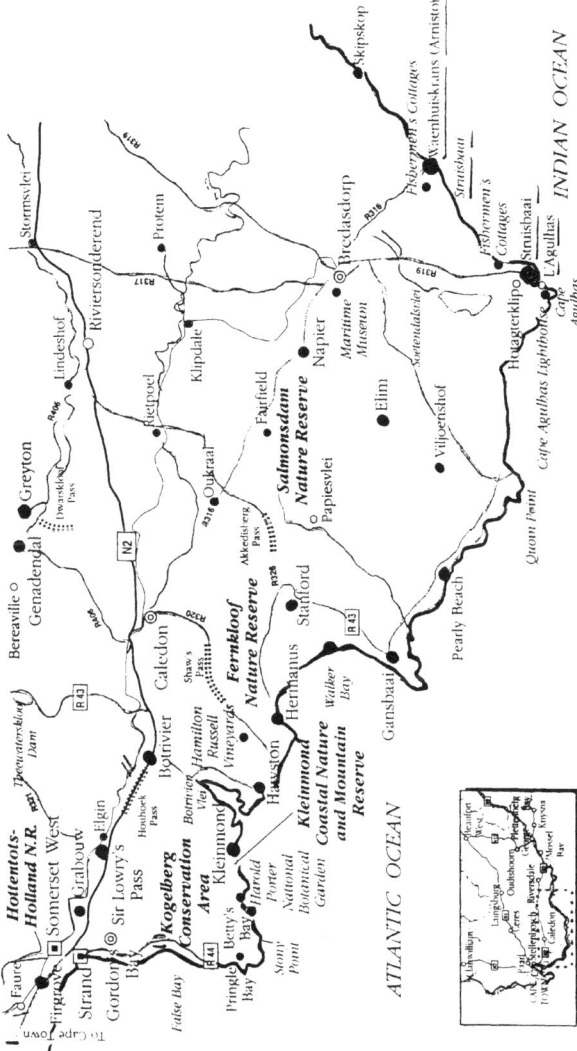

... the setting for the story ...

DEDICATION

...to all those continuing to fight for truth, justice and freedom in a world where these issues continue to plague those who will listen to their consciences acting upon what their hearts know is the right thing to do and have stopped hiding their heads in the sand like ostriches...

...for all those GOGOS (GRANDMOTHERS) of Africa, who brightly shine like candles in the wind to raise those children whose parents have died from HIV-AIDS, wars, famine and poverty... so there may be strength, hope and laughter and the Tribes will sing again... SIMUNYE... we are one GOD BLESS AFRICA and HER TRIBES...

...to my own beloved grandchildren...
Gabriella Adrienne Lima – Umanqulwana
Lucas William James Handford – Ibhele
Anna Rose Sully – Uvemvane
Mathias Owen Sully – Imvu-yamanzi

...you have known the love of your grandmother – Uzekamanzi – Ukhulu (zulu)/ Umakhula (xhosa)

ACKNOWLEDGEMENT

…to my sister Myrle Tronson who enabled me to have this – my book – published through a legacy from our father – William Samuel James Collins…

CHILD OF WHERE TWO OCEANS MEET

This tale you are about to read is that of a woman of Africa.
The initials of her names spell out the word

"F.R.E.E."

Fleur
Rowin
Elizabeth
EUGENE

Her Zulu nanny whispered these words to her, when
she was a very little girl to comfort her ...

Wemsheli Wame. Thul'u laleli intombazane

(speak to me softly – stay silent – listen small girl)

Fleur-Rowin stood for the ideals she was brought up to
believe in

FREEDOM
HOPE
STRENGTH
LAUGHTER

SHE LEARNED TO PRAY FOR THE FREEDOM
OF THE TRIBE EVERY NIGHT, FROM A VERY
TENDER AGE. SHE WAS A TRUE CHILD OF
AFRICA WHERE THE COLOUR OF YOUR
SKIN SHOULD NOT MATTER ...

… with eyes wide open – gaze upon Africa's splendid vista. Breathe deeply of her intoxicating smells. Hear her sounds as they greet your awakening senses…

Discover dance, poetry, music and song, all an integral part of ritual festivals in South Africa. All are essential elements in the celebrations of events connected with every aspect of life.

From the twanging, strident sound of the handheld mbira and beating of traditional drums under the light of a full moon, people gather readily to enjoy the communal pure pleasure of dancing, with drinking and courtship side attractions. When you feel the earth vibrate and tremble with the chanting and rhythmic footpounding of several hundred men, you will know why the Zulu tribe aptly liken this to "crashing waves on the seashore." The belief in charms, spells and witchcraft, continues to walk alongside the teachings of the former missionaries. The rituals and traditions of the African tribal peoples goes back to time immemorial and are inbred with each new generation, for Africa is an ancient land…

Through the dust and heat of Africa, one truly feels the passion and wild, as yet, untamed splendour and beauty of this great land. Walk her earth. Drink from her pristine streams and before you leave South Africa – taste her wines. Some of the finest wines to be found in the world come from South Africa.

Its viticulture began with the first vines transported to South Africa by the French Huguenots, who had fled persecution in their native France to settle amidst the magnificent mountains of the Cape in 1688. With them, they brought not only their ancient and fine winemaking skills, but their unique culture as well. They settled mainly in the Cape's Fransch Hoek (French Corner) district. Even today, the town remains very distinctly "French" with its superb cuisine and the surnames of the families living there. Fransch Hoek also boasts an impressively beautiful monument to its pioneering early French settlers.

The Holy Trinity is symbolized by the three arches of the Monument. The woman standing in the centre of these arches, holding a Bible, together with a broken chain, is representative of religious freedom and she also rejects oppression with the casting off of her cloak. The fleur-de-lys pattern on her raiments reflects her gracious nobility.

Freedom of spirit is symbolized by the earth-globe on which she has placed her feet. All of these features surely must indicate what SOUTH AFRICA should be all about today...

After you have visited South Africa, if curiosity has drawn you there, when it comes time for you to leave, the Tribes will say to you:

"Kiss all four walls of your room as you walk through the portals of this African place, for then you will return one day to Mother Africa's bosom. Take with you a shell from her beaches and a small stone from her hills when you leave, so Mother Africa may call to you softly on the wind and you will return to her ..."

Africa **WILL** draw you back like a magnet. (Perhaps this is why I have returned to her shores so many times). As you say "farewell" – the Tribe will say to you:

hamba kashle (go in peace)

and your reply should be:

hlala kashle (stay in peace)

Under God's heavens, here on His earth –

WE ARE ONE: SIMUNYE ...

... so you may envisage the setting for my book ...

herewith, a very brief synopsis of a little of South Africa's history, which is pertinent to the story you are about to read.

You will find yourself travelling through time, as waves crash against rugged cliffs and caress sandy beaches in undulating rhythms of the ebb and flow of tides ...

Rain will touch your body and southeasterly gale force winds will whip your hair across your face and you will feel both pain and euphoria as you spend time in the company of an enigmatic soul. May the wild passion of Africa accompany you each night as you watch a sunset ...

As you travel along and turn each page, you will be in the area of Gordon's Bay (just outside of South Africa's large, bustling cosmopolitan Mother City – Cape Town), and the story will unfold along the south coastal seaboard, all the way down to Mossel Bay, near Capt Saint Blaize. You will walk those same sandy beaches our heroine – Fleur-Rowin Elizabeth Eugene and her friends walked and where you will watch with her the wildly tumultuous surging together of the two mighty oceans, as huge waves crash foaming waters against the rocks and shore. Feel the oceans meld as one; like two lovers caught up in the mad initial ecstasy of unbridled passion; when sanity is temporarily lost timelessly in oblivion, somewhere almost surreal – Atlantic meets Indian ...

∻

My book is a tale – part truth – and part fiction. Where do these two collide? You, reader, will have to decide where that truth actually began and where fiction ended it, and to wonder: "did all these events really take place? Did they really happen?"

Experience the insane corrupt madness of a government hell bent on controlling its nation through interminable decades of a brutally vicious apartheid system, which almost destroyed the very fibre and existence of a nation's people in this passionate land. Though battle scarred and weary, South Africa emerged victorious through an amazing transition when apartheid WAS finally dismantled. This is an extraordinary story of ultimate triumph, renewed hope and forgiveness, when laughter returned to the Tribes. Now, Africa faces another scourge – that of HIV-AIDS.

Most of South Africa consists of a high central plateau, flanked to the south and east by hugely magnificent mountain ranges, among them the Hottentots Hollands, the Outeniquas of the Cape Province and the majestic Drakensburg Ranges of the KwaZulu-Natal Province. Between the mountains and the sea is squeezed a fertile coastal "terrace." To the west, the land runs out in a bleak, near desert fringe, abutting the Atlantic Ocean. The chill waters of the Benguela Current on the west, have their counterpart in the warm Agulhas Stream of the Indian Ocean to the east.

The historically famed Cape Agulhas Lighthouse was erected in 1848 at Africa's southernmost point, confluence of two mighty oceans. This particular coastal area is known as "The Graveyard of Ships" – for its waters are extremely treacherous with jagged rocks laying just beneath the surface. The rugged shoreline is home to a myriad of historical fishermen's cottages and beyond Agulhas, is a tiny resort town – quaint Struisbaai – which boasts one of the longest areas of neverending splendour – nine miles of pristine beach, notably, said to be the longest stretch of beach in the southern hemisphere. Walk the beach sands of purest white, dazzling in their brightness. Feel the untamed beauty of the area.

Cape Point on the tip of the Cape Peninsula – where Cape Town stands, is too: breathtakingly beautiful and regal in splendour.

∴

As a separate continent, Africa was born some 180 million years ago. A huge flattened bowl of the subcontinent became separated from the landmass of "GONDWANALAND." It then saw very long temperate periods, when the rest of the earth was locked in ice. The central plateau, for millions of years was a teeming marsh, where dense fern forests abounded with pre-historic life. Earth became warmer and mysterious

Africa became the sun-baked continent of today. The old pre-historic animals died out. New creatures took their place. The lion – King of Animals – the elephant, springbok, zebra, impala, buffalo, and kudu, roamed the dry savannah upland plains. Hippo shared the mud banks, pools and rivers, with one of the few survivors of the reptilian past – crocodile.

In time the animals were joined by a "new creature," at first, very much in minority. The scattered first groups of early men emerged in historic times as Bushmen and Hottentots, hunters and herders in harmony with the wildlife. Then began an invasion of their land to the north, with the appearance of dark-skinned BANTU-speaking NGUNI peoples from Central Africa. As they settled along the eastern seaboard, yet more intruders arrived, this time from the sea. At the end of the 15th century, Portuguese caravels picked their way down the west coast against the mighty power of the Benguela Current driven by dreams of a passage around Southern Africa to the wealth of the far distant orient. In the year 1488, Bartolome Diaz rounded Cape Agulhas to become the first European to sail the Indian Ocean. He was followed by yet another Portuguese explorer – Vasco de Gama in 1497. The former – Diaz – left many stone crosses (padraos) behind at the various places he dropped anchor along the Southern African shoreline. These crosses can still be seen today. For a century and a half the Portuguese plied their trade around the coast of Southern Africa. It was only in the mid-17th century that a permanent settlement was undertaken. It was the work of a small party of Dutch settlers from Holland – servants of the Dutch East India Company, under their commander Jan van Riebeeck – who set up a small revictualing station on shore – mainly to overcome the dreaded disease of scurvy suffered by the sailors and ships' passengers. The City of Cape Town now stands on this very shore, which lies in the shadow of the magnificent brooding Table Mountain, with her awe-inspiring peaks flanking either side – Devil's Peak to the left and Lion's Head, with Signal Hill in the foreground to the right and behind these peaks and following the rugged coastline – the peaks of the Twelve Apostle range. Following the Dutch, who had arrived in 1652, came the British with their English East India Company, with a second and more permanent occupation by the British in 1806. Both Portuguese and British were fascinated by the Bushmen and Hottentot peoples, who were now constantly warring with each other. The Bushmen later moved northwards to the arid desert regions of the Kalahari Desert and South West Africa, now known as Namibia, which is totally independent from South Africa and self-governing. There were many settlers to South Africa during the intervening years carrying Protestantism and their culture to the country. Disagreements began to arise between the different language groups, but mainly between the Dutch settlers and the English speaking groups. Disagreements, still sadly, in evidence today. Disenchantment arose from so many things to do with the stringent governing laws from Britain, land rights and claims, cultural traditions and languages. The "boers" decided to move into the interior of South Africa, far away from the coast. "Trekking" or moving northwards and eastwards. The very famous, historical "Great Trek" began from 1835-1843. The most famous trekkers (pioneers): Retief, Potgieter, Pretorius – after which many of South Africa's towns and cities were named. The Afrikaans language was born out of the "Trek" and is a dialect of mainly Dutch/German linguistics and is today just one of many official languages in South Africa. The predominant languages are still English and Afrikaans, which all races learn in school, together with the various Bantu languages. Most South Africans are fluent whether they are black or white or "in between." The black races have the upper hand language wise: they speak their own tribal dialects as well; the Xhosa and the Zulu languages being the most predominant, as these two tribes are the largest of the black tribes living in South Africa.

From the Great Trek was born the South African War or the Anglo-Boer war. This war basically was over land rights of the boer and the rights of the British to lands in South Africa. The war lasted from 1899 to 1902 and one finds many monuments worldwide to the many soldiers who perished during these tragic years – countries such as Australia, Canada, New Zealand, India and Britian, all sent and lost precious soldiers to the fighting.

The history of South Africa is extremely interesting and fascinating but it would take an enormous tome to cover its vastness. I have briefly attempted to cover some of the more pertinent events leading up to the history of the present day.

∻

The discovery of diamonds in 1866 and gold with the first finds of real importance made during the 1870's. Discoveries which played a major role in South Africa's economy and history. This wealth in abundance was much fought and sought after…

On May 31/1910 – all the territories of South Africa amalgamated to become the Union of South Africa and part of the British Commonwealth.

Though racial segregation had been in effect in the Country for hundreds of years, it was not YET decreed by LAW.

In 1948, a General Election was held with only ONE section of the population permitted to vote – WHITES ONLY. BLACKS were totally EXCLUDED. The unfair and extremely archaic laws of the country had come into play… The present ruling United Party (led by Second World War leader – General Jan Smuts), was soundly defeated at the polls. This defeat was an enormous shock, for Smuts was a most popular and also well-respected figurehead worldwide. He was at the zenith of international recognition, yet could not win the majority vote at home, in his beloved South Africa. During World War II, Smuts had supported the Allies headed by Great Britain and enlisted South Africa in the fight against Nazi Germany, but the National Party of South Africa had totally refused to support him and blatantly and very publicly sympathized with the enemy – the radical Nazi Regimé of Adolf Hitler.

The National Party leader, who had won the 1948 elections, Dr Daniel Malan (a former news reporter and Dutch Reformed Minister), had led the Afrikaner party, who were critically dominated by arrogant bitterness, to victory. They were heavily and radically centered around the 'swart gevaar' (black danger). They fought successfully, instilling fear, on twin slogans: "Die koelies uit ons land, (the coolies out of our country – 'coolies' – the Afrikaners derogatory term for East Indians and Malays)," and "Die kaffir op sy plêk, (the nigger in his place – 'nigger' their derogatory term for black people)." Malan's party members were violently anti-English and obsessively opposed to English-speaking South Africans, who HAD treated the Afrikaners as inferiors for decades. The Afrikaners hatefilled bitterness toward the Africans, was shocking in intensity and these diehard members of the National Party believed wholeheartedly and completely the black South Africans were threatening in no uncertain terms, the ultimate prosperity and purity of their precious Afrikaner only culture.

NOTE: The Africans despised the National Party with a not unfounded vengeance and had NO loyalty towards General Smuts and his United Party either.

APARTHEID – a radical **NEW** word for an **OLD** established ideal, was Dr Daniel Malan's soapbox. This cleverly consolidated the former haphazard segregation of the past centuries. Apartheid's premise was: whites were and always would be far superior to Africans, Indians or Coloureds. The Nationalist slogan: "Die wit man **MOET** altyd baas wees, (the white man **MUST** always be boss)." They stood for white supremacy in all of its unfairness, suppression, horror and harshness. Even the Afrikaners Dutch Reform Church supported this apartheid regimé, with religious teachings which so vociferously proclaimed Afrikaners were and are God's own chosen people and all Blacks were and always would be nothing more than a contemptuous subservient subspecies: (inherent and fundamental words indeed). For them, this apartheid and their Church walked hand-in-hand. English as a language would now take second place to Afrikaans (which the English-speaking derogatorily called 'kitchen-dutch'). The National Party slogan purported their mission loudly and very clearly: "ons eie volk, ons eie taal, ons eie land" (our own people, our own language, our own land). Their radical doctrines ultimately created such discord, hatred and so much chaos and heartbreak for the African nation over the years, it was likened to the nazi-ism of Germany. Smuts decried vehemently the harsh ideology of apartheid. (He realized the terrible dangers ahead, saying this apartheid is "… a crazy concept, born of prejudice and fear" – how true his words would come to haunt South Africa).

∴

The National Party continued in power and in 1960, under the leadership of Prime Minister, Dr Hendrik Verwoerd (formerly the Minister of Bantu Education), it was decided South Africa needed to break away from the Commonwealth of Great Britain – time for South Africa to become entirely independent. On May 31/1961, a referendum was held and the Republic of South Africa came into being. The scheming machinations of Verwoerd and his National Party created in South Africa, an apartheid regimé, with far-reaching tragic consequences. Verwoerd was named the "Father of Apartheid" and he had the support of his party and the Afrikaner population behind him. Hendrik Verwoerd died an extremely brutal death – he was assassinated in 1966. He was stabbed to death by an obscure and rather unknown, white parliamentary messenger, who had no apparent reason, other than insanity for his actions.

∶∼

Apartheid continued with years and years of hardline tyrannical rule, but the winds of change were blowing, reaching gale force proportions likened to a howling Cape south easterly wind.

Many lives were lost – all in the name of freedom, justice and equality. There were brutally vicious killings and torture of the black people. Political parties who were in anyway anti-government were banned. Black leaders worked underground against the apartheid system and openly as well. Many blacks fled South Africa in fear for their lives… and the winds continued to blow.

Sanctions against South Africa were in place by many countries opposed to what was happening in South Africa.

∶∼

… and then one of South Africa's greatest men – Nelson Mandela – after more than a quarter century of imprisonment behind bars was released in 1990 (his fight against racial oppression won him the Nobel Peace Prize), South Africa went through an amazing transition. Led by its black leader, Nelson Rolihlala Mandela, the abolition of the abhorrent apartheid regimé was about to come to an end. Misery would change to euphoria. Midst this euphoria, when other political prisoners were released along with Mandela, there was a tragic sadness for those terrible, lost years behind bars all for the true belief that **ALL MEN ARE FREE – TO LIVE – TO WORSHIP – TO BE – ALL MEN ARE EQUAL**. The final dismantling of the untenable apartheid system took its toll upon all the peoples of South Africa, but MORE so on its black peoples, for it was not without terrible pain, bloodshed, suffering, families destroyed and uprooted, and for many death – that a hugely ransomed price was paid for South Africa's freedom.

∿

The last leader and head of the National Party was F.W. de Klerk, elected after the resignation of P.W. Botha (due to ill-health. Botha an extremely belligerent man, was nicknamed the Crocodile…) De Klerk was also South Africa's last white prime minister. (He too, was awarded the Nobel Peace Prize). He, together with Mandela worked at dismantling the intricate machinations of the former regimé. This did not happen overnight, but on the evening of May 2/1994 – de Klerk made a gracious speech – conceding the white minorities defeat. They were turning over power to the black majority (with bargained for concessions of course).

South Africans of **ALL RACES** had gone to the polls. All stood in the long lines together, whatever their colour or creed… The incredible images over the four-day voting period, were burned into the memories of South Africans and into the memories of nations worldwide. April 26/1994 was the first day of voting. South Africans voted for the Party **THEY** wished to see rule their country. Emotions ran high…

At last, **HOPE, STRENGTH, LAUGHTER,** would be part of South Africa's future. When the results of the voting began coming in, it was obvious to all, that the formerly banned ANC (African National Congress), would form the new government.

∿

On May 10/1994, midst great jubilation, the ceremonial inauguration would take place on the hallowed grounds at the huge amphitheatre formed by the majestic Union Buildings in Pretoria, (South Africa's capital).

The legislative assembly of the now *former* National Party government, the beautiful old sandstone buildings, would mark the site for history in the making, as a "rainbow" gathering of different "colours" and peoples of other nations would join together to witness the installation of the Republic of South Africa's very first: democratic, non-racial government.

De Klerk was the first to be sworn in on the podium, as second deputy president; with Thabo Mbeki sworn in as the first deputy president. When it was Nelson Mandela's turn to be sworn in as president, he pledged to obey and uphold the new and binding constitution and to devote himself to the well-being of the Republic and all of its peoples. In the final conclusion of his speech, he uttered these words:

> "… *we have at last, achieved our political emancipation. We pledge ourselves to liberate our people from the continuing bondage of poverty, deprivation, suffering, gender and other discrimination. Never, never and never again shall it be that this beautiful land will again experience the oppression of one by another. The sun shall never set on so glorious a human achievement. Let freedom reign. GOD BLESS AFRICA.*"

∻

Thousands and thousands of people went through such unimaginable sacrifice. So many gave of their very lives in the cause of freedom and justice against apartheid. Their courage and suffering can never be repaid and we must always remember NOT to forget…

It will take generations upon generations to heal the terrible wounds of apartheid. The hurt suffered has been gouged deep. The scars cover the wounds and will remain like a scourge upon the land for a very long time.

So many people were forced to lead a twilight existence of secrecy, pretence and rebellion for their beliefs in that right to freedom and the premise and promise, that all people are created equal. Some people buried their heads in the sand like ostriches, denying that which was so apparent to them, pretending not to have a conscience, but for those of all races who desperately attempted to fight for what they believed in – they – concluded that the long battle was worth all the sacrifices made. They never lost hope and their indomitable spirit could not be broken, even though their bodies may have been. For you see – hope and freedom must walk hand in hand.

The honour of the Tribe was vindicated on the backs of those who perished and on the backs of those who were imprisoned unjustly.

The "NEW" South Africa would bravely face the odds but much would be uncovered in the months ahead...

There would be investigations into all the apartheid system stood for: the TRUTH AND RECONCILIATION FINDINGS began and went on for many months, with many people coming forward to testify to the horrible atrocities committed. Much was revealed in all its sordid ugliness and the Tribes of South Africa wept tears of blood and wailed for the freedom of the Tribes and the black nation pardoned and forgave the terrible injustices.

The walk and the road ahead is a long and rocky one, with many pitfalls along its way. Sadly, there is much greed and corruption as South Africa struggles with a multitude of problems...

... but apartheid is no more and its terrible regimé could not break the spirit and the pride of its black people.

AMANDHLA

CHAPTER ONE

THE LETTER

... today, I must write to a special man I have grown so fond of, for the African tides of destiny may separate us forever...

Rowin sat up late finishing off the paperwork required for the exporting of several of the Estate's excellent wines to Canada. The vast Estate was now under the custodianship of the third generation of Eugenes although the lands had been farmed for almost two hundred years. "Belle-France" had proven itself in a variety of farming activities from wheat and alfalfa, to its South Africa mutton-merino stud sheep, but it was the wine-making skills of its owners, past and present which had placed "Belle-France" very firmly on the map. A rich variety of soils, slopes and various elevations created perfect conditions to produce the highest quality noble grapes... Their books showed a history of an unbroken wine tradition for over a century. Like many other viticulturalists in the area, they had weathered the scourges of drought, economic depression and phylloxera over all the years. The Eugene women, had together with their two brothers held the reins equally. Thus far, none of the lands had been sold off or sub-divided. Usually, the paperwork was done at the Estate office, but Rowin had wanted to get home and had undertaken to complete the task of tediously completing the many documents required to export their wines.

Finally, she had completed her task; yawning and stretching like a cheetah; pushing her swivel chair back, she stood up. Shrugging her stiff neck and shoulders, she wished Paul was there to give them a rub.

Picking up the documentation and looking around at the attractively decorated small office, she thought to herself how much the artist-signed African prints of leopard, cheetah, elephant and giraffe pleased her. She walked over to the white painted wooden mantelpiece, her hand idly rubbing two brass candlesticks (family heirlooms from County Cork in Ireland, brought over in 1893). There was a time when she would not have displayed them, let alone touch them. They still reminded her, all too vividly, of the terrible night at the "Belle-France" family home. Afterwards, her step-mother Felicity refused to have them in the living room and they were packed away, after the authorities had returned them when the criminal investigation and court hearing were over, no longer required as evidence to support the criminal case. On Rowin's wedding day, Felicity had wrapped them up as a gift and presented them to her step-daughter. This was a most maliciously cruel act on Felicity's behalf, but it was also so very typical of Felicity. She had always felt very threatened by Rowan and constantly resented her husband's special love for his eldest daughter. She also blamed Rowin for spoiling her (Felicity's), own wedding day, feeling Rowin had upstaged her.

Rowin refused to let Felicity's action mar her day and had quietly asked her old Nanny Hildy to repack the candlesticks and put them away for the time being. The candlesticks were brought out again on the day one of South Africa's political activists – Stephen Biko – had died in prison on September 12th of 1977. He fought for his peoples' beliefs against the apartheid regimé and paid with his life. It was Rowin who gently unpacked those candlesticks and placed new white candles in the holders and lit them at sundown and they burned until dawn of the next day. She lit new candles on each anniversary of Stephen Biko's death. This was her way of remembering so many things in the cause for justice and freedom.

Stephen Biko had died in that dreadful prison in Pretoria – a martyr to the cause – and each anniversary Rowin always said the same words: "I am broken and I wonder why?" She had known him and would always, always remember not to forget. Hildy Biko was part of her family and part of Stephen's family. All were of the same "tribe."

·∿·

Rowin so enjoyed this delightful place – her cottage – at Arniston. The first cottage had been presented to her by her father on her twenty first birthday. She had later acquired two other adjoining cottages and made all three into one large sprawling home, allowing for gracious ambience and comfort. Her home, for her, could only be decorated in one particular style (except for her bedroom), and this was AFRICAN. There was a multitude of leopard-print fabric covered chairs and cushions; African wild animal pictures in matte black frames; kisii stone figurines of hippo, lion, cheetah and zebra; Zulu woven baskets – both large and small; carved dried gourds and beautiful, intricate African beadwork. Her most treasured possessions were a six foot carved ebony wood mask, which hung on the entrance wall and an exquisitely carved ebony wood elephant, with long curved tusks of ivory. Her Aunt Joanna had presented these to her on her wedding day. (These had been Joanna's wedding and twenty first birthday gifts from her own parents). The ivory tusks worried Rowin somewhat, for she was an ardent conservationist of the protected animal species. Elephant and cheetah were her favourites of all the wild creatures.

Rowin loved her home for it was full of charm, its atmosphere was warm and comfortable and her visitors never wanted to leave its confines. Of course its wonderful view of the mighty Indian Ocean added to the beauty of the place, in all weathers. Her three 'joined' cottages had been declared National Monuments the previous year and a brass plaque had been placed on the wall adjacent to the front door, indicating the year the cottages were built. She was tickled pink when this had happened with much pomp and ceremony and the village had turned up for the occasion. She had generously thrown a braaivleis celebration for all one hundred people attending. Rowin stood in her office, keys in hand, realising she had been daydreaming. She would have to hurry back to the Estate office to get the export documents into the courier bag in time for delivery.

∿

Fleur-Rowin usually slept late, rarely arising before nine-thirty am each day. But then she went to bed far later than the average person… The bewitching hour of midnight would see her in her high four-poster bed, reading a carefully chosen literary tome for she was an avid reader. She always had a deeply scented bubble bath before retiring for the night and often accompanied her ablutions with a tall glass of chilled white wine, one of the Estate vintage wines, preferring the slightly sweeter cultivars of the hock variety. There were always candles in her luxuriously appointed en-suite bathroom – a myriad of glowing, glittering wicks, reflected in the bevelled glass mirrors as she lay back against the white terrytowel bath pillow. She loved to luxuriate in her bath and reflect upon the events of her busy day.

Tonight though, she was more than a little disturbed as she prepared her bath. Deciding she needed to relax both mind and body, she tipped some lavender scented crystals into the fast running hot water, combining this with just a dash of her favourite neroli and sweetpea blend of oils. The bathroom was bathed in a delicate fragrance, most pleasing to the senses. The aroma wafted through to her bedroom, creating an aura of delightful peacefulness. Her full-length swiss embroidered white lace nightgown was draped across the chaise-longue in the reading alcove of her room. She had chosen her nightgown carefully, expecting Paul to stay overnight, but just after lunch, she had called him and asked him not to make the long trip out to her cottage from Bantry Bay, a suburb of Cape Town, along the Atlantic coastline.… Her day had held a strange unreality to it…

∴

The morning had seen Fleur-Rowin up earlier than usual, as she wanted to cut roses from her garden at dawn, before the day became unbearably hot. She had secateurs in hand, and light gardening gloves on her hands, when she heard the postvan drive up at 7:00 am. The coloured postman waved to her and she greeted him with her cheery "Good Morning. You're early today. You don't usually get here with the post until at least

11:00 am." He chuckled: "You know today my eldest daughter is getting married, but the mail still has to be delivered. I'll be finished in under an hour. You of course know my daughter well. She used to work in the Estate wine office until she moved to Cape Town to live closer to her fiancé. She has been living with my mother for the last three months. Erica said you were kind enough to offer to supply the roses for her wedding. Are those the ones which you have cut?" Rowin nodded. She had already filled two large flower-baskets with the exquisite pink and white full-blown blooms. She asked: "Do you want to take them with you now? I was about to take them inside and immerse them in ice cold water to keep them fresh for this afternoon." Jan Theron replied: "No, no, I'd rather come back for them in about an hour. A big thank you Ms Eugene. The roses are too beautiful for words. Erica will be so thrilled. Your Estate is well known for its wonderful roses and wines. This is the first of my children to get married. It's hard on a father when his favourite child leaves and he has to give her away to another man. She has a good man though, a teacher with a good job in Bonteheuvel. But it's still hard." Rowin smiled and nodded knowingly and agreed, "Yes, indeed, but it's hard for a mother too, when the children leave the nest. You know Jan, as long as our children find happiness and contentment in life, and they live with fine ideals of honesty and fairness and rely on the good Lord to guide them, they can't go wrong. We, in this wonderful country of ours, have gone through so much to be where we are today, that each happy moment needs to be cherished. We must always hope and dream for our children and ourselves, for there is much to be thankful for."

She waved to Jan as he drove away.

Rowin gazed at the lovely roses with their intoxicating perfume, and added some butterfly-lavender to the baskets, remembering with nostalgia her own wedding day almost forty years previously, on a bright, sunny September morning…

Rowin had placed the bundle of mail Jan Theron had put into her outstretched gloved hands, upon the top of the stone sundial. The bundle contained three of her subscription magazines, a couple of bills, two thank you cards from charities she supported and a letter in an 'airmail' flimsy envelope. She picked up the latter, startled for an instant as she read the return address:

"Christian Mark Eastwood/Poste Restante
Alice Springs, Australia…"

Rowin's hands began to tremble and a fine beaded line of perspiration broke out on her upper lip. She had a great need to sit down, for her legs had turned to jelly. Instead, she retrieved the rest of the mail, secateurs and the baskets of flowers and walked inside allowing the coolness of her kitchen to envelope her. She placed the mail upon the large kitchen table, ignoring the fact that this had tipped over the bowl of sugar.

She carried the roses and lavender into the scullery, placing the blooms into buckets of icy water. Her hands continued to tremble and felt clammy in the gloves and she was breathing in short, sharp gasps. She was overwhelmed with a surge of fear and panic. She stood for an absurdly long time in the scullery, eventually pulling off her gloves impatiently. She pulled herself together and returned to the kitchen, and poured herself a large glass of her favourite juice – passionfruit, which she sipped very slowly, calmer now, feeling the cool liquid course down her throat. She poured a second tumbler of the juice, adding ice. The juice refreshed her parched throat. Thoughtfully, Rowin walked to the kitchen window, gazing at the calm ocean below, before washing her hands and face at the sink. After a moment, she collected both drink and letter. The letter seemed to burn her fingers and she let it fall to the floor, partially spilling her drink as she did so. She muttered to herself: "Oh, darn it. I'm being silly and stupid. It's only a letter"… Fetching a cloth, she mopped the liquid up, and took the remainder of the drink and the letter outside. She was barefoot, as she walked slowly down to the beach, a stones throw from her back door. Reaching the edge of the water, she allowed the tiny wavelets to wash over her toes. It was low tide and the gulls were wheeling and screeching overhead. The small sandpipers ran along the sand as she approached. The day was now hot, not a cloud in sight, the skies a radiant blue and the ocean a glittering, sparkling aquamarine.

Rowin was delaying opening the letter. The sun tickled her naked shoulders, for she wore a bright, strapless, red, white and blue sundress.

Finally, she ambled back to the large boulders where she liked to sit. Sighing, she made herself comfortable perching upon her favourite rock and drew her knees up to her chin, letter and glass still in hand. The day was pristine, soporific in the intensity of its heat. She put the glass down on the rock next to her, clutched the letter to her breast momentarily, then curiosity got the better of her...

As she read the words, the look upon her face, was one of consternation. There were seven airmail sheets, written by hand. She recognized Christian's strong heavy script, but there was a certain shakiness to the closely written lines...

Rowin sat for a long time, after re-reading the letter. Her heart was heavy and she felt unbearably sad. With a deep sigh, she stood up. Her legs felt heavy and leaden. She walked unseeing back to the cottage. Rowin's thoughts were far away when the loud rap of the brass doorknocker startled her.

Jan Theron was standing on the doorstep, ready to collect the roses for his child's wedding. He looked at Rowin and enquired: "Are you alright Ms Eugene? You look as though you have seen a ghost." Rowin nodded and tried to smile. A rather tremulous attempt at first and then with a superhuman effort, for she did not want to spoil this exciting day for Jan, she laughed and shook his hand. "The roses are ready. Take them in the buckets. We'll just pour some of the water out first. Oh, by the way, there are two cases of our best Estate wines for the wedding. One case is red and the other white. Please pass on all of our best wishes to the bride and groom. Enjoy all the excitement and blessings upon everyone."

Jan thanked her profusely. Rowin was a popular figure in the Arniston area and well known for her generosity, especially to the coloured and African folk living in the district.

The two of them carried everything to the postvan and she waved him off for the second time that morning.

∵

… Fleur-Rowin had a momentous decision to make. This would be a decision which would affect many lives. First, she rang her two children – Sebastian and Raine-Fleur. She talked on the telephone to them for over an hour. Next she called her sister – Mia Tansy. It was almost lunch time before she decided upon her course of action. Her next call would be to a very special person in her life. Would he understand when she asked him not to come out to Arniston today after all? She knew he would be bitterly disappointed. But would he understand?

They had only known each a few short months. Did she have the right to expect perhaps more than Paul really wanted to give her? Before Christian's letter had arrived, she had begun to feel very secure in the wonderful relationship she had with this comparatively new man in her life. Now, she felt in such turmoil, all over a letter…

The jangling sound of the telephone ringing interrupted her imaginings. She had almost decided not to answer, then made a grab for the receiver. The welcome voice of her sister, Mia Tansy's voice, on the other side of the line: "Hi Rowin. You left me a message to call you. What's up? You sounded very perturbed and you didn't leave me any details. We were down at Gordon's Bay visiting Granny Coral yesterday and decided to stay overnight, as we'd all partied a little too much and drank lost of vino."

Rowin answered her sister: "Mia, you'll never guess in a million years who has decided to contact me. Christian. I've had a most disturbing letter from him. He's still in Alice Springs and it would appear that our children know nothing of what has been going on over these last months. Can you believe that after seventeen years, Christian has finally contacted me? I'm in quite a state over the contents of his letter and am in a quandary as to know what to do. I don't want to discuss this over the phone. Are you able to come over right now? And can you come by yourself?"

Mia's reply was questioningly curious: "Rowin, at least give me some idea of what's going on. Yes, I can come over now. Put the coffee on and I'll bring some of my mother-in-law's cherry cake with me."

"Mia, please don't ask me any questions until you get here, but please hurry. I really need your input and your shoulder to cry on would be comforting too. Drive carefully, they are repairing the bottom road near the turn-off to my place."

Rowin replaced the receiver and sat for a while longer at her desk. Mia would be there shortly...

Rowin picked up her fountain pen. Hesitatingly, she began her letter to Christian.

... and Fleur-Rowin cast her mind back to places from long, long ago. Memories both good and bad and those in-between came flooding back with frightening intensity. All clamoured like a million voices babbling and demanding to be heard, to be listened to.

Rowin placed her hands over her ears, so intense were her thoughts, as she attempted to calm her rapid breathing. She inhaled and exhaled slowly to tame the inner churning of her racing, beating heart. Momentarily, panic overwhelmed her, as pain haunted her soul. She cried out in agony and sank to her knees on the floor of her bedroom.

∾

As a small child, she had refused to ever allow herself to cry. Now, all those pent up emotions and the suffering she had endured needed to be assuaged, so she gradually allowed herself to succumb to her emotions, as they ravaged her mind. She allowed herself to feel poignancy and she allowed herself to feel anger, but she would not allow herself to despair. Slowly her sobs ebbed like the receding ocean tides. She arose from the floor and walked unsteadily over to the Queen Anne writing console in the bay window of the room. She sat down heavily in the comfortable upholstered chair which matched the beautiful desk. Both angled in such a way, to allow the writer to enjoy the picturesque vista of the mighty Indian Ocean and the rolling never ending white beaches at Arniston. The sun was a bright ball in the morning heavens and the raucous gulls were diving into the briny waters catching the small fish just below the surface waves. She leaned to open the windows wider, allowing the breeze to filter into the room. She tied back the sheer voile curtains and watched the antics of the small coloured children chasing a brightly coloured beach ball, until a gust of wind caught the air-filled ball carrying it up into the air, as unseen tendrils lifted it higher and higher and then suddenly dropped it onto the ocean water where a wave caught at the ball, returning it once more to the beach. The children dashed into the water, yelling and shouting their excitement, having retrieved their precious plaything...

Now somewhat calmer, Rowin allowed herself the time and luxury of calmly putting her former troubled thoughts in order, avoiding the chaotic moments of a short time ago, when hysteria had almost destroyed any sensible reason. Rowin was normally, very much in control of herself, but the rather disturbing letter had rendered her downward spiral into opening her Pandora's Boxes, which contained her memories locked away from somewhere in the past...

She gazed unblinking for a moment, shrugged her tense shoulders and unclenched her hands. She poured a tumbler of water from the cutglass jug on her desk and sipped it slowly, forcing the nausea she felt to retreat. The cooling liquid eased the acrid taste of bile in her throat.

Her room was her retreat and she had decorated it in a French provincial, but somewhat nautical theme too, befitting the stunning seaside situation of the cottage. She had chosen shades of buttery cream, and a yellow – called Morning Sunshine and Forget-Me-Not blue. Antique nautical prints hung on the walls, together with sketches her aunt Joanna had done of Bath, in Somerset, where she had lived for a year before she'd married her husband Peter Robinson.

There was a small oval table next to the chaise-longue which had a myriad of family photographs upon it. All wonderful memories of happy times with her family. She had packed away all the photographs of Christian, for she could not look at them without feeling such sadness. The sadness had replaced her intense anger, which had been her 'companion' for many months. She pushed back her chair and walked over to her large closet, reaching down to the far back, she tugged at a large cardboard carton, pulling this toward her, she lifted it clear of the floor rails of the cupboard doors. Kneeling down, she broke the taped seal on the carton and slowly opened the flaps. Wrapped in bubble-plastic was a coloured, framed photograph of Christian, holding the hands of Sebastian and Raine-Fleur (their children). The three of them were standing on the beach at Cape Agulhas, in front of the rocky sentinel which indicated both oceans on either side. They were all laughing happily. The children must have been five and three years old. Rowin had taken the photograph and had it enlarged and framed as a Christmas present for Christian. A sob caught at the back of Rowin's throat. How very happy they had been. Twenty three years together. What went wrong? She still could not answer that burning question, even after seventeen years on her own. Resolutely, she continued to unpack the box, looking at each framed photograph in turn, willing herself to have the courage to face her past and to face her present. Her emotional reverie was interrupted by the arrival of Mia with a plate of cherry cake in hand.

The two women went through to the kitchen and perched on high stools at the built-in window table. This commanded a view of the other fishermens' cottages, dotted along the coastline and running into the interior section of the Eugene estate lands.

After pouring two cups of coffee, Rowin handed Mia the letter from Australia. Mia quickly scanned the pages, sipping her coffee as she did so. Neither of them said a word until Mia finished reading. She looked at her sister: "Rowin, I think you need to go to Christian in the circumstances. I know it has been aeons since you've had any contact, but perhaps this is now the time to get some answers to those questions which have haunted you for years. I always felt the two of you were meant to be together for all time. I know you've always said you would never ever be able to trust him again. Rowin, the only person you need to trust is yourself. I know you now have Paul in your life, but you really have known him for only five months. If your romance is meant to be, it will 'be.' But then again, if you and Christian can still sort things out, perhaps he's the man you should be with. No, no, don't shake your head like that. And stop looking so angry. You know I will always tell you plainly what I think. Get on the phone now, to the travel agency and book a flight to Alice Springs. Show Paul the letter and see how he reacts. Don't waste any time. It's no good procrastinating. Both Sebastian and Raine-Fleur have indicated to you they will go to their father as soon as possible. It would be a good idea if you got there a few days ahead of them. What do you think?"

Rowin looked at her sister and nodded. Mia fetched the telephone directory and dialled the travel agency's number in Cape Town for Rowin. Within a few minutes, Rowin's flight was booked to Australia.

She would leave in six days time...

Now, she had to talk to Paul. She would drive through to Bantry Bay the next morning and stay overnight with Paul and they would spend time to discuss what was about to transpire over the next weeks and possibly months.

After her sister had left, Rowin called her children to tell them of her decision. They agreed to give her a few days on her own with their father, before they arrived. They would also be bringing their spouses and their children with them.

∴~

... As Rowin changed her sundress to a pair of denim shorts and striped yellow and white t-shirt, she thought firstly, of Christian – the man she had married almost forty years ago (and subsequently divorced). She had adored him and loved him so much. (He was the only man she had ever been with intimately). Then she thought of Paul – her friend, lover and confidanté. She loved him too – a very 'different love' for theirs was a mature love, though very passionate and so amazingly spontaneous. After so long on her own (many suitors had courted her and attempted to seduce her without success), when she gave herself to Paul it was with a wild passion which had been bottled up for far too long. There was so much joy and togetherness, such wonder, and laughter, midst their moments of companionable silence when simply holding hands was enough or when a look from across a room said everything. Their relationship was deep and intense. They allowed one another to be entirely their own person, appreciating their differences and neither wishing nor attempting to change the other – and accepting imperfections which are evident in every relationship.

Rowin walked outside to the sundeck, deciding to read for a while and take in the glittering sunset. She found it difficult to concentrate and the words on the pages danced in front of her eyes. She had poured a glass of icy white wine, sipped this slowly savouring its bouquet, relishing the fruity earthiness of the liquid.

Thinking about her planned meeting the following day with Paul, filled her with trepidation. It was not long before she returned indoors deciding upon an early night. She ran a scented bubble bath. After stepping into the water, she sank back against the terrycloth bath cushion and closed her eyes. She did not remain in the tub for long, suddenly weary and in need of sleep. To her surprise, she slept well and awoke refreshed. She had expected to toss and turn and when stressed, dream usually, the old haunting dreams from childhood.

Paul had called her from Bantry Bay. He had to deliver fifty of his books to a bookstore in Napier – no need for her to drive all the way through to Cape Town after all.

They arranged to meet at the Zulu Kraal Restaurant for a late breakfast at 11:00 am, and then both would take separate cars and drive onto Gordon's Bay, before heading to Bantry Bay.

Rowin felt she needed to spend some special time with her Paul, as she sometimes jokingly called him. He was delighted. He simply could never get enough of Rowin's company. He confessed to his son: "This little 'inkosikazi' has spun a web around this old guy ..."

~

The day was gorgeously beautiful, as Rowin dressed in khaki shorts and matching safari jacket. She wore brown leather thonged sandals on her feet. Even at sixty-three, her legs were still beautifully shaped and tanned a deep golden honey shade. She added a leopard patterned scarf to her outfit and threaded an imitation leopard skin belt through the tabs of her shorts. Quickly, she packed her overnight bag, adding at the last minute, her white nightgown put out the previous night, plus her favourite

'Safari' perfume. She retrieved Christian's letter from her writing desk, popping this into her brown leather sling-bag. She had about two hours left to kill, before the drive to Napier and decided to continue her reply to Christian begun earlier. Upon completing her lengthy letter to her "was-band" (she hated the term ex-husband), she began a letter to Paul. She intended to leave this for him to read on the day she planned to fly out to Australia… Half-way through her second letter, she realized she would be late if she did not leave immediately. She would finish this second letter later.

Locking the doors to the cottage, she fast-walked to her land-rover and climbed in, before realizing she had forgotten her sunglasses in her office… Back inside she went, annoyed at herself. She had also neglected to close all the windows and turn on the security system. Under her breath she muttered: "Fleur-Rowin, you need to calm down and concentrate on matters in hand. Your mind is a sieve right now. Not good lady. Take a deep breath and smell your roses…"

She sat back against the car seat, then put her head on the steering-wheel, saying: "Oh, Lord, what am I doing?"

On reaching Napier, she went straight into the small post office and requested a Special Delivery Courier envelope. Placing her letter inside the envelope she sealed and addressed this to Australia, where it would arrive two days hence.

∾

Paul was already waiting for her at the restaurant and with a huge bear-hug and a kiss on her cheek, he smiled his welcome to her. They ordered their late breakfast of devilled kidneys on toast with crisply crumbled bacon on top, orange juice and champagne "Mimosas' and caught up on all their news. Rowin decided not to tell Paul about Christian's letter until they got back to his maisonette in Bantry Bay. She did not want to spoil this lovely time with him at one of their favourite dining places.

Paul was very attune to Rowin's moods and sensed almost immediately there was something troubling her. He knew too, she would not tell him anything until she was good and ready to do so. He would attempt to be patient.

After their delicious repast, Rowin announced: "Paul, I have a surprise for you. I'm coming through to Cape Town for three days to stay with you. Are you alright with this?" He nodded his head and hugged her.

∴⁓

Their three days together had sped by far too swiftly. She took her leave of Paul, not wanting to go and had almost cried when he kissed her tenderly. She drove back via Caledon, Bredasdorp and Napier and felt quite a pang of nostalgia as she went passed the 'Zulu Kraal Restaurant.' It was always lovely to get back to her own special slice of the universe.

Her father, now ninety-four years old had intimated he would be visiting her before she flew to Australia and she was looking forward to his visit. He was staying with her sister and brother-in-law at Cape Agulhas. Felicity had not accompanied him. The two of them had moved into a retirement village in the beautiful resort of Hermanus. The move had been quite emotional for William Eugene, for he loved his home at "Belle-France" and he had relinquished the reins reluctantly to his grandson, Rowin's son, Sebastian. He trusted Sebastian implicitly and had trained him well, imparting as much knowledge as he possibly could to this very capable young man, who looked so like his beloved grandfather.

Rowin was proud of both her children and they had married partners who were very supportive. Mia would drive their father over later that evening in time for supper.

Rowin opened up the house, letting the fresh air flow in and went outside to pick roses for the dining room table. She took pork pies and quiche out of the freezer to thaw and had picked up fresh tomatoes, spring onions, lettuce and avocadoes to make a salad to go with the light supper. Mia's husband, Sven Bjornsen would also accompany his wife and father-in-law. Paul was not sure whether he would be able to get there. (They all enjoyed his company immensely).

William Eugene would look after Rowin's home whilst she was away, with the help of Mia and Sven's daughter, as her husband was away on a university course. (Rowin was extremely fond of her niece, Susannah).

∴~

Only two days to go. Rowin's suitcases were already half-packed, stacked on her bedroom floor, along with her large, roomy travelbag. Flying first-class this time with South African Airways, she dreaded the flight and what lay in store for her at her destination. She had a stop in Perth, before flying onto Adelaide, where Christian's sister, Barabara would meet her. Barabara – like her parents before her – was a Bush Doctor, operating between Alice Springs, Adelaide and Cairns. Rowin would hitch a lift with Barabara to Alice Springs in the light bush plane. Rowin had never visited Australia before now, although her former sister-in-law had flown several times to South Africa on holiday.

∴~

Rowin enjoyed her time with her father, finding him in excellent fettle for all his many years. He was, in old age, a handsome man with a shock of white hair and his blue eyes still twinkled boyishly. He was always far more at ease when Felicity was not around… He would not be going to the airport and he wished his eldest daughter well, as he hugged her goodbye, cautioning her to listen to her heart. Mia Tansy had driven Rowin to the airport, dropping her off at the First Class

Departure Entrance. She knew she was far too emotional and would weep uncontrollably if she went inside with her sister. Paul was waiting though … He helped Rowin lift her luggage onto the baggage conveyor belt and she booked-in at the counter and was allocated her seat in the first class section of the plane. As they had an hour or two in hand, Paul suggested they drive over to the lovely water gardens adjacent to the airport, where they could have some private time together. They parked under a beautiful willow tree, with a cascading waterfall's tinkling sound for company. Paul put his arm around Rowin's shoulders, expecting her to respond to him, but instead, she seemed to be very far away in her thoughts. He was very disappointed and rather perturbed. She apologized for her seeming disinterest saying: "Paul, I'm sorry, I seem to have so much on my mind. I'm finding it really difficult to concentrate. In all honesty, I don't know whether I am doing the right thing. Please, try to understand. I can see you are very annoyed with me and I certainly don't blame you. Let's try and make these last moments special and peace filled. I need to leave Cape Town on a positive and happy note." Rowin gently removed Paul's arm and lay back against the headrest of the car seat and momentarily closed her eyes. Paul sighed deeply, feeling as though Rowin was lost to him already.

Rowin took his hand and kissed it: "Paul, you've not said anything. Are you having doubts about us? You must surely know how much I care about you? I will be returning you know. Don't go all melancholy on me now …"

Her new love, thought Rowin to herself – Paul Nicholas Blakeney – wildlife artist, author of great repute, whom she'd met five months previously at the invitation of his Publisher, prior to the almost completion of his fourteenth book on the wildlife of the Kalahari Desert. He had done all the drawings and writing for the book and Rowin had been duly commissioned by the Publisher, to add some of her incredibly beautiful photographic shots of the Bushmen (San) Tribe. She was of a minority breed, who had learnt their 'click' language and she was very fluent, and able to converse easily with these fascinating little Africans with their tight 'peppercorn' hair and their muscular little bodies. Rowin and Paul Blakeney, along with a party of twelve other people had toured up to the Kalahari, which Rowin knew like the back of her hand and had met with the tribal peoples. It had been an illuminating and fantastic experience for everyone and Rowin and Paul had an instant rapport with each other. They in essence 'spoke the same language' in more ways than one.

After their three weeks in the bushveld, they knew instinctively there was something vibrant and wild between them. Rowin had let her guard down. It had been a long dry seventeen year 'drought' for her and she had been aroused by this most fascinating and intriguing man.

Paul Blakeney, now sixty-five years old, widowed for fourteen years, had two sons and a daughter, all grown, married and with children of their own. He had four grandchildren whom he loved dearly. He was a born taleteller and a wonderful granddad.

Paul was of average height, with hazel eyes, which crinkled wickedly at their corners when he chuckled or smiled. His hair, now thinning somewhat, was still curly, but greyed and curled into wisps, touching his shoulders. He was a little portly, but had aged well and was still handsomely attractive. His presence was charismatically dynamic and commanded attention from all who met him. He had amazing patience, a quick mind and equally quick wit and humour. Conversations with him were inevitably interesting and stimulating.

His laughter was the attribute Rowin loved most of all about him, for it was never far away and coupled with the deep lilt of his English-Irish accent, fascinated her.

Paul was a most wonderful companion, at times he was deep and introspective and seemed to be an "old soul" from somewhere long ago.

Their relationship was born almost instantly on the day they met. For them, everything moved swiftly on lightning wings into a deep romantic liaison when they returned to Cape Town. Even at their mature age when they were together, they tingled with anticipation. Their meetings left them quivering with pulsating excitement. They were like two teenagers. Both were utter and complete romantics...

Never had they done so much laughing. Both felt they were tempting fate in their eagerness to be together. When apart, their telephones were a hot-line. Paul got on extremely well with her family. Rowin was warmly accepted by his. They found her a fascinating combination of natural grace, sincere warmth and never found her dull or boring or controlling. Paul fully appreciated Rowin's need to be herself and nicknamed her his "Free Sprite." He too, demanded his own space, for he was extremely independent and at times very stubborn – like an immovable rock, digging in his heels and refusing to be cajoled by anyone. He would not be dictated to by anyone either, but he had, on occasion, allowed Rowin to beguile and charm him into utter passiveness when he became like a tame, softly purring cheetah.

Always considerate toward her, he told her often how much she meant to him and how much he both respected and admired her. He admitted to himself – he was lonely...

In Paul's mind, she was the most wonderful thing that had happened to him in a very long time. He had been a solitary man for too many years. Rowin had shattered the image he and others had of him as a permanent loner, unready and very unwilling to form any sort of romantic attachment with the opposite sex. Many women had been after him as soon as he was widowed. He managed very successfully to elude their tenacious clutches. Rowin took him by surprise and likewise, he had done the same thing to her.

He had seen her at her worst and at her best out in the bush of the

Kalahari Desert and the almost animal magnetism she exuded swept over him in waves. His aloofness and patience when tracking the wild animals he sought to sketch and paint and his acceptance by the San Bushmen captivated her. Even with the presence of the other members of the small safari, Paul and Rowin seemed to be in a world of their own creation. It was an unforgettable safari for everyone. Africa was at her passionate best, from the blood red evening sunsets and golden dawns, viewing the wild rhino and watching a lion kill, tracking a female, elusive leopard and discovering her small, new cubs, to the evenings at sundowner time around the fires, drinking ice cold beer, waiting for the boerewors and venison to roast on the spit for their supper. The night sounds were fascinating, monkeys chattering, the roar of lion, the call of a jackal and the cries of hyena, all added to the soporific effect Africa had upon everyone. The African nights out in the wild bush were ebony black, with only the stars to light the way and the storm lanterns hanging on the few trees around the camp. The days were extremely hot and dust seemed to get into every pore of one's body. The nights were chilly and the warmth from the fires comforting. Many were the tales told around the campfire. There was much laughter and a deep respect for this amazing land and its fascinating peoples and animals. There was such a timelessness to everything. Manyana was another day. Nothing hurried here, as the days slowly moved to the rhythm of Africa and her beating drums. Their three black African trackers had brought their drums with them and each night, they beat out a pulsating, throbbing cacophony of sound, together with the twanging of the mbira. Rowin could never keep still when the music started and she would get up and move to the undulating emotions the tempo invoked. She danced like a true African and usually managed to persuade the other members of the safari to follow suit, teaching them the movements from a time immemorial, for music and dancing were an intregal part of African life. There was something primeval and fascinating about bodies moving in hypnotic fashion to the strident music of Africa on an inky black night...

:~

Rowin had quite nervously and rather cautiously informed Paul of the letter from her former husband. She had given him the letter and asked him to read it. From the letter, Paul realized Christian was dying. There was very little time left for him. Paul's heart almost sank when he knew what Rowin was about to do ...

:~

Paul understood why Rowin needed to fly to Australia. He was, in all honesty, not happy about her impending departure. He knew too, if he voiced his objections to her going or attempted to prevent her doing what she had to do, he could possibly lose his "Free Sprite." He trusted her implicitly and he would miss her desperately. She had become "his woman" in every sense of those words. He thought of her as his talisman. He had not yet told her how much he loved her and would tell her when she returned.

Rowin was not sure how long she would be away in far off Australia and she begged Paul to be patient and to wait for her to return to him. (She too, knew she was in love and she too would tell him when she got back) ...

:~

Departure day had dawned – a brilliant African day. Rowin hastily penned a short note in the Zulu language to Paul (she had been teaching him Zulu).

> Indoda umngane NgokukaPaulu:
> Wuza lapha. Usuku lokugcina... Isikhathi sesishayilo,
> manje, seku fanele ngihambe. Lalela kashle – ngicela

ungilinde, thembisa.
Size sibonanefuthi, lindela.
Thande Intombi
Fleur-Rowin
phinde khohlwa XXXXXXXXXX
Translation:
Paul – beloved Man-Friend
Come here (the last day…) It is late and I must go
now. Listen carefully – please wait for me, promise.
Until we meet again.
Love (your 'girl' and friend)
Fleur-Rowin
P.S. Never Forget… XXXXXXXXXX

∾

As he hugged Rowin at the airport, she pressed her note into his hand. They kissed lingeringly and very tenderly. All too soon, she was swallowed up in the crowd going through Customs and Security. As she walked through the barrier gates, she turned to wave to Paul and her family who had come to see her off on her flight.

Rowin was crying silently as she looked at them. She brushed the tears from her cheeks and smiled her brilliant smile, which seemed like a ray of sunshine to those she left behind and then she was gone…

∾

… As Rowin made herself comfortable in her roomy seat on board the South African Airways Boeing 767, she felt somewhat isolated and alone amongst the many passengers boarding. Fastening her seatbelt, she temporarily tipped her chair back, knowing all too soon the flight attendant would announce: "All seats must be in an upright position, etc…" Rowin needed to make herself relax. She closed her eyes behind her Armani sunglasses and ignored what was going on around her. Flying was not her favourite thing to do. She was dreading this long, tedious flight to Australia. After finally completing her lengthy letter to Paul, she had felt better, having had the need to share with him where she was at this present time in her life. Goodbyes were something she did not relish… Both her children – Sebastian and his pretty and vivacious French wife, Joseé and their children, four year old Christopher and two year old Georgiana; and Raine-Fleur and her husband, Andrew and their three children, twins Justin and Malachi and sweetly adorable three year old poppet – Anna-Fleur, were all there to bid her adieu with hugs, kisses and a few tears, even though they too would be flying out together two and a half days later.

Rowin wished now, she had not insisted flying out ahead of them, but she had not seen Christian Eastwood in seventeen long years. There had also been absolutely no contact whatsoever between them during that time. All legal matters, including their divorce had been through their attorneys. Their children had visited their father on several occasions during the intervening years, but he had not attended their weddings.

Rowin was filled with trepidation and the thought of her initial encounter with Christian. Her head began to throb, with a dull ache behind her eyes.

The palms of her hands broke into cold clamminess. She felt shaky and nauseous. Mentally counting to a hundred, she forced herself into calmness as she meditated.

The Boeing took off smoothly, gliding effortlessly into the air. She opened her eyes to capture the magnificent vista beneath the plane – Cape Town – with its surrounding mountain peaks and glittering aqua jewel-like oceans. The sun was just setting and the view was almost ethereal and awesomely breathtaking in its purest splendour…

Rowin thought of the man she had left behind in Cape Town. He had indicated to her he fully understood why she had to go on this sojourn, but did he really? Doubts flooded her mind and she was glad she had pressed her hasty note into his hand as he hugged her to him so tightly and kissed her deeply. He would find her letter when he returned to his maisonette…

∴

Well, there was nothing she could do now. She was on the flight and what would be would be…

She managed to eat the delicious dinner which had been served an hour after take-off. At least, flying first-class had its perks. The crayfish cocktail was superb, followed by a rare filet mignon a-la-chasseur. The English trifle dessert was delightfully decadent (Paul would have enjoyed the latter, as trifle was his favourite). As the flight attendant cleared away her tray, Rowin ordered a Kir-Royale cocktail, before settling down to try and sleep. As she sipped her drink, memories of her life flooded her thoughts and she swallowed and willed the sudden lump in her throat to go away… She would have given anything to have Paul sitting beside her. She glanced at her fellow passenger and with a start, realised she knew him. She hesitantly called out his name quite softly: "Temba?"

The man glanced up from the Cape Times newspaper he had been reading (he had been asleep when dinner was served, with his safari hat over his face). Rowin had not even looked his way when he had sat down in the seat next to her, so lost was she in thought.

He frowned and then a huge grin broke over his face: "Fleur-Rowin, is it really you?" The two had been friends from childhood, had been home-schooled together and over the years, they had worked together on so many diversified schemes, mostly involving the fight against apartheid. The last time there had been any contact between them, was on the day her divorce from Christian became final.

"Temba, what are you doing on this flight? This is just incredible." His deep African voice answered: "I'm on my way to Alice Springs to take up a research position at the Hospital there. One of the research doctors has had to drop out of the extended program due to illness and won't be returning. Apparently, very tragically, he has cancer and is dying. My wife and our teenage children will be flying out next month to join me."

Rowin looked at Temba: "Temba, the research doctor you are replacing is Christian. He has only weeks to live. Our own children and grandchildren arrive two days after I get to Alice Springs. I have not had any contact with Christian in seventeen years, but he wrote me a very heart-rending letter, pleading with me and begging me to come to him. I could not turn down his request, as I feel such a sense of obligation towards him, even after all this time. I am of course, wondering whether I am doing the right thing, but here I am. Oh Temba, I am so glad you are on this flight. I cannot believe you of all people are replacing Christian and that you are actually sitting next to me. Is this a coincidence, fate playing tricks? I am totally flabbergasted."

Temba took Rowin's hand in his and squeezed it gently. "Rowin, you've always had such a good generous heart. Yes, I think you are doing the right thing. Perhaps you and Christian will reconcile your differences and you never know, miracles do happen. Perhaps fate has decreed you are meant to be together, even now, when Christian is so gravely ill. Pray Rowin, pray, for guidance to do what is right. Listen to your heart. You always used to do this when we were kids."

Rowin looked into Temba's eyes, then looked down at her clenched hands: "Temba, there is someone else in my life now, whom I truly love and care about. I am not going to Christian as a last ditch effort to try and recapture the magic we once had. I need closure on the past and only Christian can do that for both of us. Time is running out."

Rowin carried a deep secret within her heart. This was a secret which had haunted and troubled her for seventeen long years. A dark thing which only three people knew of…

… Christian's affair with another woman, so many years previously, had destroyed his marriage and relationship with Rowin.

∼

Rowin and Temba continued to talk quietly long into the night. Finally, both dozed off into fitful, dreamfilled slumber to the endless droning of the aeroplane engines. The seemingly unending hours dragged on and on… Eventually the flight would land in Perth and then on to Alice Springs…

∼

… Rowin's last thoughts as she drifted off, were of the afternoon she had sent Christian away and she shivered, feeling great trepidation at the anticipated reunion with him: her once-upon-a-time-husband, whom she knew deep down – she still loved…

∼

Paul had driven home feeling very empty and lonely with Rowin gone for heaven only knew how long. He walked inside and was greeted by his ever faithful black tom-cat, Rufus. At least his beloved old cat alleviated his loneliness somewhat. It was now twilight as he looked out across the Atlantic Ocean, with Robben Island in the distance, place where Nelson Mandela, South Africa's first black President had been imprisoned – PRISONER NUMBER "46664" ... He thought of Rowin and their discussion on humanity and her words said with such definite clarity: "Paul, the human voice is so different from all other sounds, even a whisper can be heard and then the sound moves – almost silent – but not still in its dream of hope, strength and laughter. And their voices were finally heard and their whisper became a roar for those who fought so bravely for freedom. It is in my Africa where I remember them. You see, I can never forget to remember, for those who paid the price and are gone, still whisper to me and all I have left are the memories and the thought that corruption and greed can ruin all that which was hard won, scares and so appals me. Man's need to possess creates his greed and he becomes inhumane. Man's unhumanity to man is what will destroy the very fibre of democracy, if we turn our eyes away and our ears become deaf. War and killing will ensue. There is no glory in war and killing, only sadness and tragedy. I will return to my Africa, for she is deep within me. I think you understand fully where my passion must lie and know Africa will always call to me and claim me ..." He thought of their wild, passionate times together and he longed to feel her body close to his. He closed the sundeck door, calling to Rufus and the man and his cat walked through to the bedroom and it was then Paul saw the large white envelope with his name upon it, written in Rowin's script ...

He opened the envelope carefully, smelling her heady "Safari" perfume and felt her warmth and her presence as he read each word she had written upon the pages and drew comfort from them.

His telephone began to ring insistently. He picked up the receiver and the voice at the other end asked: "Is that Paul Blakeney? You don't know me, but I know Rowin Eugene very well. I am Nobukwe Nyandele. Rowin and I grew up together in Arniston. She asked me to meet with you whilst she's away in Australia. Can we meet tomorrow for lunch at the Tulbagh on the Foreshore?" Paul, taken aback by the call, muttered: "Love to meet up with any friend of Rowin's, but not tomorrow. I have a prior all-day appointment with my Publisher. How about next Friday instead around 11:00 am at MacKintosh's Coffee Bar on Shortmarket Street?" Nobukwe agreed to this plan: "Yes, sounds great. I look forward to meeting you." Paul inquired: "How will I recognize you?" and Nobukwe replied: "I shall be wearing a red French beret with a purple ostrich feather in it." (Although the same age as Rowin, Nobukwe was inclined to flamboyancy).

∴∾

Nobukwe had been at the Airport and noticed Rowin as she went through Customs (noticed too, the fond farewell between her and Paul). Nobukwe was Security Director at the Airport and made several enquiries into Rowin's travel plans. She decided to hatch a devastating plan against her friend, whom she had not seen in a very long time...

∴∾

Paul replaced the telephone receiver, mulling over the call... Picking up Rowin's letters, he went to shower, noticing Rowin's nightgown under his pillow...

Paul called to Rufus, as he walked through to the bathroom. His cat always loved to sit on the bathmat whilst he showered. Rufus came bounding along, rubbed against his master's leg companionably, purring. "Well old friend, only the two of us tonight, 'til Rowin returns. Dear old

Rufus – there's a huge empty space in my heart right now. Think you and I will drive out to Arniston tomorrow and meet up with William. We always enjoy each others company. The old man is remarkable for his age." Rufus' green eyes watched Paul intently, as though understanding each word.

Paul had not wanted to meet up with Nobukwe. (He had made the pretence of seeing his Publisher his excuse). Though refreshed after the shower, Paul could not rid himself of a strange uneasiness he felt. He could not ascertain what was disturbing him. He put his feelings down to missing Rowin…

Climbing into bed, he allowed Rufus to jump up next to him. (This was normally a strict no-no, but tonight he appreciated the closeness of his cat).

He re-read Rowin's letters, feeling her nearness. He dozed into a fitful sleep, her nightgown clutched against his chest, her letters on the pillow next to him. The strong southeasterly wind was blowing, rattling the windows…

Cynthia Elizabeth Sully

My dear Paul:

Before I leave you, I need you to know something which to me, is important. I want you to know where I am on my journey – hence my letter to you today to clarify matters. I have to be a free spirit always, for I must fly free to reach my own destiny. You know I am an inherent dreamer and a hopeless romantic…

This is the autumnal-journey part of my life (although I know Old Man Winter beckons ominously to me, I choose to ignore him completely).

I am no longer a beautiful young girl on the brink of intoxicating womanhood, waiting to explore a brave new world, with all her hopes and dreams intact, her body slender, firm and vibrant, her bud like a furled, delicate pink rose – not yet opened, merely waiting for the petals to reveal the inner sanctum of her naiveté, her soul pure and unblemished. Now, there are age lines midst the happy laughter ones and her brow is slightly furrowed. Her breasts are full and large enough to fill an honest man's hands and are still finely blue-veined, white as a dove, but softer now – their firmness long gone with the childbearing and nurturing of her babies. Her hips are wide and her belly rounded and rubinesque, like that of a sculptured alabaster statue from some bygone era, her navel deeply indented.

The woman you see before you, with her smile quite brilliant reaching to the outer corners of her grey-blue eyes – dark lashes long and lustrous – and brows deeply arched and somewhat questioning, is me – the person you have come to know so well over these last months.

Her eyes twinkle mischievously, as some wicked thought crosses her mind, especially when it involves dark black cherries and melted, molten chocolate. Her laughter is a little deep-throated and warbles up from somewhere deep inside of her. Her hair is still thick and full-bodied (though she does help nature along with the colour it was when she was young). This woman's body has seen the ravages of time and time has not always been kind to her. She

60

carries though, her many battle-scars bravely – perhaps a little shyly – should someone perhaps see them.

Her once lovely hands, small, have become gnarled and in the cold of winter, her fingers ache, but those hands still caress gently when requested to do so. Passion still surges joyously within her. She appears to be amazingly, seemingly stuck in thought patterns of her late thirties (probably because those years were good to her). She cares not what anyone thinks of her, for she is very much her own person. She asks only to be accepted for whom she is and prays each night there is still love to be found somewhere waiting to be discovered and to be explored and shared freely. She is what she is. She walks proudly, shoulders back and head held high. She acknowledges her Maker and owes each day to Him, for He allows her unwavering abiding faith never to fail her. She will tolerate much, but never make the mistake of pushing her to her limits, for you will lose her abruptly. She will accept you as you are and does not wish to change you. She asks only, that you do not try to change her into something or someone you demand. She is not perfect and asks that you see her for whom she truly is: her own person without apologies or excuses for herself or her past.

Paul, dear man, I am what I am. I am happy with whom I have become… there is a deep abiding peace within me and I live and laugh for the sheer joy and magic of the day, for it is so precious each day we are given. (Life is a gift to be honoured and revered fiercely).

Oh Paul, I do have walls around me still and there are barriers to protect my fragility. I am not afraid to reach out to touch you both emotionally and physically. I love to hold and to be held, especially when it rains or when the weather turn icy cold and chills the marrow of ones bones. To quietly hold and to be held, within a deep embrace, with not a single word spoken – thought patterns mingling together in uniting of the spirit.

I love all of the seasons, for each one is so very different, with my favourites winter and spring. The autumn saddens me for I hate the ending *of things beautiful...*

The wild seas and oceans are my lifelong companions and the blood of my beloved Africa surges in waves through my veins, for I come from an untamed, tempestuous and passionate land. I have walked her soft, white sandy beaches in all of her moods and weathers. I have felt her water spray upon my naked body – salty and tangy – as her sands course between my toes. I carry the passion and heat of this Africa so deep within me and she will call to me always, for she laid claim to me a long, long time ago. She was my first love and first love is never forgotten.

Paul, I share all of this with you, today, for I have given my heart to you to protect and to nurture.

Hold this fragile thing gently, for it is my most precious gift to you. I do not give this gift to you lightly...

Know I love you freely, as freely as I know how. Know too, I love you fiercely and passionately.

With deep love and affection – I am your free-spirit

Fleur-Rowin

P.S.   *I miss you already. I've left this letter for you to find when you get in from the Airport. I had intended to tell you of my love for you when I get back, but you know me – always the impetuous Rowin – I had to tell you now... I hope this does not scare you off...*

P.P.S.   *There is another envelope for you to open. Please do not open this for TWO weeks from now. The envelope contains a poem which I composed before I left. You are my friend and I am your companion.*

The seas and shells and beaches and winds are what I relate best

to, so I share my innermost soul's secrets with you ...
The second envelope is under the statue of "Pan" in your dining
room ...

Paul awoke at 6:30 am. The noise against his bedroom window had now become a loud banging as the tree branches were whipped by the southeasterly wind, which had become gale force in intensity. The garden furniture had blown over and the sun umbrella turned inside-out. Usually, the Bantry Bay side of the Cape Peninsula was very protected from the wind, but not this day. The sky was clear and the day already warm. The waves in the bay were white-tipped, as seahorses pranced, wild wind creating their movements.

He climbed out of bed to close the windows, for the curtains were whipping about. (Rufus complained at being disturbed as he had been curled up behind Paul's knees).

Paul walked to the kitchen and filled Rufus' bowl with his customary food, before pouring himself a glass of grapefruit juice. He filled the coffee-maker with water and fresh coffee and set this going to percolate.

He went back to the bedroom climbed back into the comfort of his bed and again, read Rowin's letters. He would write to her from Arniston. He had a great need to be around Rowin's possessions at her home and would use her room. (William was using one of the guest bedrooms). He would take Rufus with him, as he intended to stay a few days.

Paul was somewhat startled to realize how much he missed Rowin. He felt hollow and empty, visualizing how far away she was. Thoughts flitted through his mind and he contemplated flying out to be with her. He argued back and forth in his mind, finally concluding: he had to leave her alone to sort out her affairs with her former husband. His presence would not help and only serve to complicate matters more for her. This did not make him feel any happier…

∾

Paul rang William around 8:00 am and the old man was delighted he was coming out for a few days. As Paul set off, with Rufus in the cattravelcage, picking up Cornish pasties and chocolate éclairs (William's favourites), from the bakery in Clifton, he took the route over the back of Lion's Head toward Cape Town. Once through the bustling early morning traffic of the City, he headed in the direction of Somerset West and over Sir Lowry's Pass. Always a beautiful drive to Arniston, today Paul felt restless and still the odd feeling of trepidation which he could not shake off, persisted. Feeling very irritable, he turned on the radio.

∼

It had been a fortnight with no word from Rowin. No one had heard from her. Her two children and their families had flown out to Australia. (Paul and Mia had driven them to the Airport).

Paul had not had his coffee meeting with Nobukwe. He had postponed this, having come down with a nasty cold, which he had only just shaken off. He would meet with her the next day at the same venue on Shortmarket Street.

He had arrived back at his apartment after an interesting few days spent with William. Now, two weeks later, he opened the second envelope Rowin had left for him to find.

Reading the words of her poem, he felt very moved by her intense words. (He would attempt to call her later, though his previous attempts had proven fruitless). Paul cherished the lovely poetry Rowin had written. She had a wonderful way with words, managing to convey her innermost thoughts when she wrote.

Tomorrow's meeting would be interesting. He wondered what Nobukwe was all about…

∴

NAUTILUS AND SEA URCHIN ...

Thanda indoda ...
Paul – written for you ...

Forget not the echoes of memories
  Held captive in moments of summer
As desert sands blow timelessly
  A fine gossamer veil of pure whiteness
Encapsulating each thought's form
  Seas and dunes undulating rhythm of movement
Gently touch the shores over footprints left
  Now, washed away forever in secant line of tide
New footprints wait patiently and silently
  To leave their indentations in time
Sea wind touches the skin which feels
  Yet cannot see deep indigo night sky
Knows only its companion is safe
  Thousands of miles away
Awaiting a lover's quiet exploring
  On home's eventual return
When the only journey left
  Is one of standing still in joy's embrace
Vibrancy of closeness felt silently
  Sprays cool salty water in mist
Upon body aching for warm fingers touch
  Once, they were alone and strangers
Now, silently she bid's him in her thoughts
  "Take this hand I offer you
  Walk with me Eden's paradise
  So beautiful I weep

Be not afraid…"
Heat of day's now sleeping sun
Warms her naked abandonment
As she bends low to find perfect pebble
Shells collected midst treasures of seaweed
Found along pristine, lonely shores
Africa's passionate vibrancy of wildness
Unspoiled reaches out to caress the pain inside
As tears fall through wet lashes
Healing the ache of solitude
And wash ghosts of old away forevermore
Hope and laughter companions
In silver moonlight and stars
Of Southern Cross and planets of Sirius and Jupiter
Lay on wet sand to feel an Ocean's surge
Of healing balm with ebb and flow
Of waves at midnight
Cold and shocking and freeing
Freeing, freeing, freeing
Rare Nautilus hears the voice of Sea Urchin
And they become one in body, mind and spirit
Yet remain separate entities
Each unique in their own right of passage
Their own wondrous creation's unique honesty
Africa's spellbinding intensity
Has allowed her daughter to go to another land
Knowing her love remains for all time into eternity
Sea Urchin must return to Nautilus
Simunye – ulwandle – we are as one sea…

my loving thoughts always

CHAPTER TWO

CHILD

… whose full name is Fleur Rowin Elizabeth Eugene the initials spelling out: F R E E. Will she ever be really free? Free to seek her dreams and to find peace midst the turmoil?

The mid-April day was chilly and rainy. The cold west wind blew in gusts and heavy clouds scudded across the skies of the Cape Peninsula. The ocean water was a dark greeny-pewter grey and huge waves crashed onto the white sandy beaches in relentless battering of the elements.

… the little girl – Fleur-Rowin – sat quietly, lost within her childlike thoughts on the worn, shabby, yet still elegantly grand, highbacked tapestry sofa. She was five years old, small for her age, though she made up for this with her extremely high-spirited nature, her volatile moods and her spunkiness and always had to have the last word in any situation. She had large grey-blue eyes, like the ocean on a stormy day; and these were long lashed and almost too large for her round little face with its cheeky up-turned nose and its dusting of tiny freckles. (Sun kisses her beloved father called them). Her ears were like two perfect tiny shells. Her straight, dark brown hair was thick and bouncy and hung just below her ear lobes, in a neat 'bob' cut, with a long fringe across her forehead. Rowin's bubbly and exuberant nature was unusually subdued.

Young Rowin, together with her father William and her stepmother, Felicity, were living temporarily with Felicity's parents – Henry (Pa) and Elsie Eaton, at their home in Saint James, a seaside suburb of Cape Town overlooking the majestic Indian Ocean. The young family's accommodations were at the side of the Eatons' somewhat grandiose home – a semi-private flat, comprising of two small bedrooms, small sitting-room and a shower bathroom. The three of them shared all of their meals with the older Eatons in the great dining room of the main house.

Henry Eaton was extremely fond of his only daughter and delighted to have her and her husband to stay, but he could not abide young Rowin and was always consistently mean and quite nasty toward her.

Rowin and her step-grandmother – Elsie – were very close and she doted upon the little girl, more so because her own daughter, Felicity, had no patience with Rowin and would punish her mercilessly when

William was not around. (Felicity and her father, Henry, were of a like-minded temperament).

Rowin stared unblinking at the fireplace in the small sitting-room of the flat. Two antique brass candlesticks, large and over-sized, were placed at one end of the mantle. These were family heirlooms brought over from County Cork in Ireland, in 1893. They held creamy-white halfburned pillar candles, their melted wax touching the brass overhang at the tops of the holders. At the opposite end of the mantle, stood a beautiful mosaic plate, its tiny half-inch tiles a myriad of shiny colours – beige, terracotta, grey, cream, blue and sage. The latter two colours were so reminiscent of the weathered old pieces of glass found washed up on the beaches of the Cape. The plate stood on a highly polished brass stand. Both plate and stand had been presented to Rowin on the occasion of her christening by her godmother – Lynetta Worth – who lived near Brighton in England. Resplendent between candleholders and plate, a large, wide black-framed photograph hung on the wall. The photograph, beautiful in its intensity of colours, was of two large seagulls perched on an ornate, weathered railing – the waters of the Atlantic Ocean the backdrop. One gull had a grey-white speckled head, the other a pure white head. Their golden beaks had small bright red markings on the lower sides – almost as though – someone had added a daub of lipstick to each one just for the fun of it. The gulls appeared to be almost in the room, and looking right at one with their beady black eyes, also slightly red-rimmed. They looked ready to peck at any food morsel greedily.

Rowin had forgotten how many times she had pretended to be the lady-gull with the white head. In her vivid imagination, she pictured herself flying as a gull just above the ocean water of the cold Atlantic. She would be diving down and then swooping upwards in a perfect curved arc, heading miles and miles across to where the Atlantic met with the Indian Ocean at Cape Agulhas. Oh, she was a laughing, carefree gull, abandoned in her wildness, floating high on a windpocket in the silvery moonlight which bathed the waters of the mighty ocean in sheerest gossamer moonbeams. The quiet whisper of the night's breeze her only companion in her solitude. There would be twinkling stars resting in the magnificent Southern Cross constellation, peeping and winking at her and she would reach out and touch them with her wings and she would think of her real mother, the mother she never knew...

Rowin, used to her own company most of the time, was old beyond her tender years and was somewhat of a lonely child, who adored the sea and soft white sands of the Cape Peninsula. The gulls, terns and sandpipers seemed to beckon to her and she thought of them as her playmates when her many cousins were not around. She loved collecting shells and small pieces of sand-polished, coloured broken glass along the beaches and had quite an extensive collection, together with dried starfish and sea urchins (anemones).

She continued her daydreaming, sitting quietly, most unusual for Rowin and her eyes filled momentarily with unshed tears. She blinked these back and swallowed hard, for Rowin would never allow herself to ever cry. (Indeed, she could hardly remember how to do so). To weep was something almost alien to her nature. Her breathing was barely audible or perceivable. There was simply the slow, timorous, rhythmic rise and fall of her tiny ribcage, visible through the thin white muslin of her longsleeved frock. The frock had a high waist tied with a wide pink satin ribbon sash. The bodice of the frock was exquisitely smocked with tiny pink rosebuds, which also adorned the neckline with its neat satin Peter Pan collar. Tiny mother-of-pearl buttons fastened the frock at the front.

∵

Rowin was awaiting punishment. She knew she was about to receive a severe beating (yet again), from her stepmother. Rowin knew this time she did deserve to be punished for she had been very naughty.

Rowin had discovered chocolates. These had belonged to her step-grandfather – Henry Eaton. They were expensive and imported from Belgium and where liqueur-filled. Rowin had been searching for her sketchbook and coloured pencils when she opened the sideboard drawer and found the beautiful box – red and gold with its tasselated ribbon ties. Curiosity got the better of her and she lifted the box out of the drawer, sketchbook and pencils completely forgotten. She lifted the lid and tissue paper and black cardboard and resplendent in black paper cups were delectable delights, the like of which she had never seen before. Twenty of them… Rowin could not resist the mesmerizing temptation before her and promptly ate fourteen of the chocolates, one after the other in great haste. Liqueur ran down her chin and chocolate smudged her nose and she, Rowin, was in seventh heaven.

Dark, rich, creamy with intoxicating centres – chocolates – oh, so very delectable, tasting like the nectar from the gods. It had been worth stealing them, more so to upset the miserable old man than anything else. To do him out of his pleasure was tantamount to Rowin's actions, for he was a mean, miserly old codger, who never shared anything with anyone. She thought of him an a ogre, put on this earth to torment her whenever he had the inclination to do so. He would still derive some pleasure though, as he watched her beaten on her bare bottom in front of him by Felicity. Rowin's punishment (for her), would taste all the "sweeter" this time, even though she felt a little nauseous from her indulgence. She felt a little wicked, guilty and scared… Rowin refused to let a single teardrop run down her plump young cheeks. She mentally willed herself to be braver than the bravest knight from days of old in the book she was reading. She was an avid young reader and could read before she turned five. When reading, she would pretend to be the heroine or princess in all the favourite fairy tales she paged through. Suddenly, with a start,

Rowin began to think of her well being and self-preservation. She began to rub her bottom through her cotton knickers really hard, until not only her hands but her bottom was stinging-red. She had learned to do this, after overhearing a conversation from the kitchen between the two young, coloured serving-maids, when they were about to be chastised by their own mother. It certainly helped when your bum was stinging-red so those awful beatings were not quite so horribly, atrociously painful.

Rowin always knew when she was about to be chastised in cruel, painful fashion. The old hallway and long passageway floorboards of wide-planked yellow-wood would creak loudly, as heavy tread footsteps came menacingly along their surface, moving all too swiftly over the Persian rugs, headed in her direction. She would cringe initially, take an enormous deep breath and steel herself for the onslaught of her punishment. Rowin would detach herself mentally and force her mind to drift off into her own private world, where her gulls would play and fly and where no one and nothing could reach her or penetrate her inner sanctum of safety. Her eyes became almost vacant as she stared at nothing, awaiting the customary onslaught of the beating. Her secret place was far from the hell of being made to feel nauseating fear, made to feel so totally worthless and inadequate. Hard as Felicity tried, she could never break Rowin's pride or her spirit. It was a true battle of wills: that of a little girl and the adult placed in charge of her life. When Felicity would finally turn away angrily, Rowin would face the fireplace, as Felicity instructed her to do and be forced to stand on one leg for another ten minutes and then be sent to her room. As Rowin stared at the fireplace, her eyes would move upwards and she would look at the gulls, stick her tongue out at Felicity, who had never once caught her doing this, and sigh deeply. Rowin would mutter under her breath: "Witch, witch, witch." And she would not cry …

It seemed like an eternity she had been sitting. The heavy footsteps began coming towards her… Rowin almost gasped momentarily and began to shake, before her self-control took over…

The welcome sound of an automobile's engine and horn tooting outside in the long, sweeping driveway, distracted her and also, the 'ominous' footsteps.

Old Pa stood up and went to the large carved oak door, just as Felicity got there as well. Rowin breathed sighs of relief and smiled to herself gleefully. She had temporarily won a reprieve. Still, she did not dare move, but instead allowed her eyes to drop down to her shiny black patent leather shoes, fastened around her neat little ankles with narrow straps and tiny, satin-covered black buttons. Her shoes and her frock were sources of great pride and joy to her. They gave her much pleasure, for she adored pretty things. Her clothes and shoes had been given to her by her Aunt Joanna, who was her father William's eldest sister, (her beloved father was the eldest of five children: two brothers and three sisters). William was much-loved by everyone. Encircling her ankles were petite white 'frills' edging her crocheted cotton socks, another gift from Aunt Joanna. (Joanna had no children of her own). Rowin's shoes were her favourite possession and she looked after them most carefully. There was not a single mark or scratch upon their shiny mirrored surfaces. Every Sunday night, without fail, she painstakingly cleaned those shoes with petroleum jelly. Her father had patiently shown her how to do this. The shoes were lined with the softest suede-kid imaginable – in a creamy-buff colour, reminiscent of melted milk chocolate. Aunt Joanna had bought the shoes for Rowin, in Paris, France, when she and her husband Peter had contemplated moving to Malta, as he was an advisor to the British Royal Navy.

The front door swung open and Aunt Joanna, Aunt Beth and Aunt Annabel, rushed in, in their usual noisy, cheerful manner. Hugs ensued all round. The aunts were always so much fun and Rowin was their favourite niece. She ran to each one of them in turn and had kisses planted affectionately upon her cheeks. Aunt Beth announced in her forthright way: "Come along Felicity and Rowin, time to head off to see William," and promptly placed Rowin's tartan hat on her head and helped her into her coat and off to the car the small girl and four women went. (A quick wave to old Pa).

The automobile sped along through the early morning traffic of the small seaside village of Saint James. They stopped for tea and scones in Constantia. And then onto the Military Hospital in Wynberg, where William lay gravely ill.

∻

Rowin was reminded of another car journey a year and a half previously. This trip had been to the wedding of her father to Felicity, whom he had married in a grand ceremony, when Felicity was just twenty-one years old. Rowin had worn the same outfit. It still fitted her, though a little snugly now, but she had not grown very much at all. Oh, how she longed to grow tall like her cousins. Her 'three' grandmothers were always telling her she 'needed to fill out.'

Thinking back to the wedding, made her blush scarlet. Right in the middle of the ceremony, she had broken away from Aunt Annabel (Aunt Joanna and Aunt Beth had been Felicity's matron-of-honour and bridesmaid), and rushed down the long, red carpeted aisle, bedecked beautifully with red roses and baby's breath and organza ribbons, up to the altar rail where her father stood with Felicity.

Rowin announced in a very audible, though tremulous voice: "Daddy-love I need to go and pee right now. It's really urgent." There were murmurs and gasps, and chuckles and an astounded look upon the pompous officiating parson's face, as Daddy-love turned to look at Rowin, who was by now tugging on the tails of his morning suit. He had a look of utter desperation on his face. He looked at his 'almost bride,' and very politely excused himself, leaving her standing at the altar. He took Rowin by the hand and led his little girl through a side door next to the altar and headed for the W.C. (water closet).

He was rescued by the parson's bustling, larger-than-life wife, who took over attending to Rowin and he returned to the disrupted ceremony. The nuptials continued, midst much amusement, clicking of tongues and shaking of heads and with the parson muttering: "Bloody child..."

The bride was furious. Rowin was barred from attending the rest of the ceremony. After the register was signed and witnessed and the choir sang 'O Perfect Love' – the newlyweds walked down the aisle to Mendelsohn's Wedding March played by the organist and church bells pealed. Felicity did not wait to greet anyone, instead, she went in search of little Rowin. The bride was so very angry, for Rowin, to her mind, had deliberately upstaged the bride on HER day. Felicity grabbed Rowin by her hair when she caught up with her, turned her upside-down and soundly walloped her backside, for her misdemeanour of 'her call of nature.' This beating was to be the start to years and years of punishments and beatings. Rowin was absolutely shocked by Felicity's actions, for she had never been spanked like this in her entire young life. She looked at Felicity and said: "I want my Daddy-love, you're just a mean, horrible person." Rowin was duly slapped across her face by Felicity. A mean, stinging, backhanded blow like a whiplash, which left a red welt on Rowin's cheeks and brought tears to her eyes. Rowin did not shed those tears. She refused to do so, but her lower lip trembled. From that day forth, Felicity was never able to make Rowin cry. Felicity screamed: "Your father is NOT your Daddy-love anymore, for he's mine now. You, Rowin, are an utter nuisance. You should never have been born. You are as black as sin. You are to call your father: papa or sir from now on."

Rowin's father walked into the room and saw his new wife and young daughter glaring at each other. He quietly said to Rowin: "Girly-love, Felicity is your new mummy now and I am giving you over into her care. Be my good little poppet, say your prayers each and every night whilst we are away and when we return, you are to obey your new mummy at all times without fail. Remember, I do love you, but mummy has to come first now."

Rowin was devastated. She looked at Daddy-love with such a look of bewilderment. She – Rowin – had been ousted from her previously secure position as Daddy-love's only little girl. How could her father have done this to her? She wondered to herself whether she would ever again hold that very special place in her father's heart...

As she gazed into her father's deep blue eyes, she whispered to him: "I SHALL always call you my Daddy-love and NOT papa or sir and I will love you forever. I won't love Felicity, you can't make me. She's a horrid old witch, witch, witch, so there." Felicity had already left the room, before Rowin's rebellious tirade. Daddy-love said "Please Rowin, you must learn to love Felicity for my sake, for it will make life a lot easier for both you and I. She is my new wife and you have to accept her as your mother, please." He lifted his daughter into his arms, hugged her tenderly and they both sighed deeply. Rowin shook her head and the two of them went to join Felicity and greet their waiting guests...

∿

The day had been a long one for Rowin, used to a long afternoon nap which she hadn't had and she was tired. First the church nuptials and then the magnificent wedding reception, made a long day. Over two-hundred family members and guests had attended and the day was deemed the society event of the year. Rowin longed for her bed at her Grandpa Noah Huddlestone's house in Mowbray. To sink into the mattress and pull the down filled quilt up to her chin, hug her teddy bear to her would be bliss indeed.

Suddenly, there was a flurry of movement, much cheering and noise, as her father and Felicity got ready to leave for their honeymoon. (They had planned to drive up the Garden Route of the picturesque Western Cape, and stay at Plettenberg Bay). Champagne corks popped, the bride's blue garter was thrown by William and Felicity tossed her calla lilies and rose bouquet high. Midst much laughter and a shower of rose petals and confetti, the seemingly happy wedded couple were gone.

Daddy-love had forgotten, in the excitement, to bid his daughter 'farewell.'

For Rowin, the sudden realization, for the first time in her life: 'goodbyes are lonely.' She sped after the departing Jaguar sedan, crying out: 'I WILL always call you my Daddy-love. You belong to me. Come back, please. I need you, you, you. Come back and hold me close now.' Of course, Daddy-love did not hear her and only the wind carried her words… To Rowin, it seemed her entire little world had come to an abrupt tragic end. As she stood in the middle of the long, curved driveway, it began to rain – a soft fine drizzle at first – more like a sea mist – and the westerly wind began to pick up and blow the leaves and tree branches. Instead of crying, Rowin howled and wailed her despair, like a lost, frightened lion-cub, abandoned in the veld. She jumped up and down frantically, hysterically. Mud splattered her socks, shoes and frock. She rocked herself to and fro, gazing up at the fast darkening sky. Thunder began to rumble in the distance, and lightning flashed across the horizon. She saw one bright star, which seemed to shine down upon her. The star was the Evening Star. Soon it too, was obliterated by heavy, scudding clouds, which also covered the moon. There was an eery blackness all around Rowin. She felt cold, desolate and unwanted. Did anyone even care what happened to her, she thought to herself?

She knelt down in the middle of the driveway and her head drooped onto her chest in sad resignation. Now the rain came down in torrents and rivulets of water ran down the tip of her nose, like the tears she had not shed earlier. Within minutes she was drenched to the skin, looking a picture of utter misery and dejection. Rowin did not move. She wished the cold rain would melt her into a puddle of nothingness...

∴

... Rowin felt a warm hand placed upon her shoulder. She looked up with a woebegone little face at the grey-haired lady who belonged to that hand. "Girly-love, I'm your Granny Elsie. Come Rowin, I'm here to take you home to my house for tonight and tomorrow at lunch time, your Granddad Huddlestone will collect you. May I be your friend Rowin? I would truly like to be." So much warmth and compassion was reflected on the older lady's countenance, which had become careworn with the passing of the years. Rowin held out her tiny hand to Granny Elsie. She stood up and buried her woebegone young face in the soft folds of Granny Elsie's royal-blue silk skirt and in a trembling, wobbly voice: "Granny Elsie, I feel so sad. Please hold me tight like my Daddy-love does and don't you ever let me go. I'm so cold."

Elsie hugged the bedraggled child close to her, oblivious to the rainwater which stained her silk outfit. She held her large umbrella over both of them. Rowin was shivering uncontrollably, as hand in hand the pair walked back inside to the warmth of the great hall, where the guests were still mingling, talking, laughing, drinking and dancing, not at all in a hurry to leave. The wedding celebration and festivities would last until day break. The Cape Coloured Band hired for the occasion were strumming on the guitars and banjos. The tune being rendered was "Suikerbossie." Their lead singer sang the Afrikaans words: "Suikerbos ek wil jou hê. Wat sal jou mama daarvan sê..." His fingers tickled the ivories of the old upright piano and both of his feet banged the piano pedals up and down in staccato fashion. The coloureds could always be relied upon to throw themselves into the rhythm of the melodies and tunes they so expertly played to their captive audiences, infusing everyone with gaiety, mirth and merriment. The Coloureds, like the Africans, had the sensual passion of Africa in their blood and left nothing to the imagination when it came to the gyrating movements of their bodies in time to the beat of the music.

Elsie, still holding onto Rowin's hand, went in search of her husband – Pa – and catching up with him at the bar, with a glass of Scotch in hand announced: "Henry, I think it is time we all went home now. It looks as though you've had far too much champagne and whisky already. I'll get someone to find our chauffeur to drive us back to Saint James." Old Pa glared at his wife with such a look of annoyance and in a very alcohol-slurred voice: "Elsie, m'dear, I'm not leaving. I'm celebrating my only daughter's wedding nuptials, so don't try and dictate to me. Go home and take the bloody brat with you, she and you are both irking me" and with that he turned on his heel and lurched across the room unsteadily. His wife sighed…

Elsie, together with Rowin, collected her velvet evening purse and silverfox fur wrap with its stuffed head and tasselated tails. The fox's glass eyes glittered wickedly in the soft candlelight. Elsie glanced at Pa, now attempting to dance with one of the younger women guests, shook her head and asked one of the coloured waiters to find her chauffeur to bring the ancient Rolls Royce around to the front of the hall.

As the chauffeur drove Elsie and Rowin back to Saint James from Arniston, Rowin fell asleep almost instantly. Elsie had removed Rowin's wet clothing and had wrapped her in a green and blue plaid cashmere rug, always kept in the boot of the car. The rug was soft and comforting and Rowin snuggled up next to Elsie, feeling warm and safe. She had a new 'old' friend and an amazing relationship was forged that night between the older lady and the little girl. Elsie was to become Rowin's mentor in the years to come. How very different Elsie was from her daughter Felicity.

∵

The torrential rain poured down, seemingly to wash away all which was ugly, distorted and sad.

∵

Rowin's new life with her father and 'new' mother was about to begin. She would miss living at Granddad Huddlestone's house in Mowbray, for he had been so very kind to her over the years she and her father had spent under his roof, with dear Hildy (her nanny) her friend also. Rowin's maternal grandmother had once again appeared on the scene. Rowin had an instant mistrust of Mary (Shale) Huddlestone, who would be moving back into the Mowbray house, after William and Felicity returned from their honeymoon.

Grandma Mary had attempted to befriend Rowin, but Rowin refused to even acknowledge her presence and would not even address her as 'grandma.' No amount of cajoling or punishment could make Rowin got to Mary. Rowin, usually a friendly little girl avoided any form of contact with Mary. In Rowin's mind, this woman was someone she did not like and would never trust…

∵

… abruptly, Rowin's thoughts returned to the journey she, Felicity and her aunts were making. She had no idea how very ill her beloved father was. His battle wounds from the Second World War had suddenly flared and William had immediately been hospitalized…

… Rowin sat on the empty bed in the four-bed hospital ward at the Wynberg Military Hospital. The ambulance had brought her father William from the smaller hospital in Simonstown, as there were three new specialists at the Military one. Her step-mother, Felicity had talked with the doctors for over an hour, with her aunt Joanna listening in to the Specialists' advice. Her father had developed gangrene in two of his toes on his right foot, caused by shrapnel still imbedded in the foot. There was also blood poisoning to contend with and William's system was not responding to the medications and drugs prescribed. Dr. Ramsay felt his leg needed to be amputated at the knee. Dr Freman felt they could save the leg by doing a vein transplant and only removing the two gangrenous toes. Dr van Zyl, who was her aunt Annabel's brother-in-law sided with Dr Freman. William and Felicity would have to decide and sign all the medical forms for the operation, whichever was decided. The procedures were scheduled for the following morning at 7:00 am. No time left for indecision.

Felicity, always the ditherer was useless in any emergency situations. She always procrastinated, Annabel would have to help her brother to make, hopefully, the right decision along with Joanna and Beth.

William was wheeled in and gently lifted onto his bed and a cage placed over his legs. Rowin looked terrified when she saw how pale and weak her father was. William motioned for her to come to him: "Rowin, you've grown at least two inches while I've been away. Come, hold Daddy's hand and wave your magic wand and make me better."

Rowin climbed off the bed she had been sitting on. With aunt Beth's help, she went over to her father and saying in a very quiet and worried little voice: "Daddy-love, I've brought my turquoise ring for your to wear on your pinky finger. It belonged to my mummy, remember? Lydia, my new nanny, says it comes from Hluhluwe in Zululand, where her family lives and that this stone has magical powers. You must wear it all the time." William took the ring from young Rowin and looked at it remembering…

He thought back to when he had given the ring to her mother – Elizabeth Huddlestone.

They had just begun to court and whilst window shopping one Saturday morning, she had spied the lovely ring in the window of an antique jewellery store.

The couple had met at the Church they attended (Cape Town Harrington Street Church of England). They both came from Christian backgrounds and were very strong in their faith. They had joined the Church Badminton Club and were excellent competitive players. They played a hard game.

∴

After only six weeks, William and Elizabeth knew they were in love. William asked her father, Noah Huddlestone, for his daughter's hand in marriage and they were wed a month later. Old Noah adored his child and he knew her happiness was very important to him and readily gave his blessing.

William bought Elizabeth a small, four diamond ring, but she had expressed the desire for the antique turquoise ring they had seen. William bought this for her as well. He went down on one knee and formally proposed to her, saying: "Elizabeth, I love you with my heart and with my life. The turquoise ring is for your December birthday, as this is your birthstone and the diamond ring is to celebrate our engagement. Will you marry me as soon as possible?"

William produced a small black velvet box from his jacket pocket, which contained both rings. Elizabeth was so moved by his sincerity and accepted his proposal. William placed both rings on her fingers: one on her ring finger of her left hand and the other on the index finger of her right hand. She wore those rings until the day she died. (The rings were later presented to Rowin on her fourth birthday. She too had a December birthday).

The marriage between William and Elizabeth took place in May of 1940.

William was a Captain in the South African Armed Forces – an aircraft-reconnaissance gunner with the AK-AK Division of the Army. He served and fought for his country in the Desert Campaign and had seen fighting in Ethiopia-Abyssinia and Egypt. Their marriage was so rushed, as he was waiting to be called up to fight in the Italian campaign. This was delayed and he returned to the Sudan and Egypt. He rejoined his contingent just four days after they were married. Elizabeth was devastated when he left and inconsolable. He was away from her from May 1940 until February 1943, when he returned on a one month furlough, due to his war injuries. For one entire month, they were so deliriously happy and Fleur-Rowin was conceived during this magical time. She arrived the day her father came back again, on December 14th of 1943. The birth of their daughter amazed and thrilled them both and Christmas that year of 1943 was very special indeed. They were living with the Huddlestones' and had a small flat at the back of their house on Rouwkoop Avenue in Mowbray. All too soon, William had to leave to rejoin his fighting men and their farewells were both poignant and sad. At least Elizabeth had their baby to keep her mind off William's departure. On a beautiful summer morning in January, just at daybreak, William took his leave of his two girls and family.

… Army orders, effective immediately. William's contingent were due to ship out from Durban, bound for the Red Sea and fighting on the European front.

The day William was due to sail, his father-in-law – Noah Huddlestone – wired an urgent telegram to him. Elizabeth was gravely ill and not expected to live.

∴

Elizabeth was at home with baby Rowin, when she began to feel nauseatingly ill. The right side of her abdomen began to ache. The pain became worse and worse. Within the hour she was doubled over and gasping. Unable to walk, she lay on the floor, baby Rowin next to her. This was where her mother, Mary, found her. Elizabeth was unconscious, the baby yelling to be fed. Mary tried to rouse her daughter and realized something was very wrong. She ran across the street to the corner store and asked the grocer to call for an ambulance urgently, as there was no telephone at the Huddlestone house.

The ambulance arrived minutes later and with the shrill sound of the klaxon ringing, Elizabeth was attended to by the two medical orderlies. They told Mary to get over to the hospital as soon as possible. This was a very serious situation – and to contact her husband.

Elizabeth was rushed to the Wynberg Military Hospital, an interminable journey. Her prognosis was very grave indeed, for she had lapsed from unconsciousness into a coma in the ambulance.

Before her mother had found her, Elizabeth had tried to write a note: 'Help me someone, please. William I need you, please come to me … I'm in terrible pain … baby Rowin is …'

Noah arrived home minutes after the ambulance had driven away. He found an extremely distraught Mary and a wailing baby Rowin. He also found his daughter's note. After Mary had relayed the series of events leading up to the note, he contacted William's Commanding Officer. The army were very sympathetic and arranged for William to have immediate compassionate leave.

Next door neighbours drove Noah and Mary and baby Rowin to the hospital, where they waited for news. Elizabeth was barely clinging to life. Noah felt there might be a glimmer of hope, if William could get back in time and by some miracle, Elizabeth might respond to her husband's presence.

The next hours were critical. There was no change in Elizabeth's condition. Her parents waited for news. Noah went to the hospital chapel and prayed. He found little comfort in the words the military chaplain offered him.

Meanwhile, William was on his way back from Durban to Cape Town. There were no Military transport planes or vehicles headed to his destination and having no money for the train fare, he began to hitchhike back. A three-day journey at the best of times, this was war-time and petrol was rationed. It took him close to four days to reach home. He stopped only for drinks of water along the way. There was little to no extra food to be had with the rationing in place, but one of his army buddies had given him a dozen Ouma rusks and another soul had given him a large piece of dried biltong. He was desperate to reach Elizabeth in time.

∴

Elizabeth was barely clinging to life. The doctors and specialist attending to her, had discovered two blood clots in her system and severe peritonitis had set in after her appendix had burst. They had operated immediately on her, but here was little they could do for this once vital young woman …

On his arrival at the hospital, dishevelled, dirty and utterly weary, William was shown into the Intensive Care hospital ward. (The lady who had directed him to the ward, was a young receptionist by the name of Felicity Eaton. She and the other two receptionists sensing how distraught the young soldier was, offered to fetch him a cup of tea and gave him a hot, wet facecloth and towel to wash his grimy face and hands with. He thanked them, but was impatient to see his wife. The hot, sweet tea seemed to revive him a little).

When William finally saw Elizabeth, he was shocked at her appearance. She was deathly grey, her cheeks and eyes sunken. She was wearing an oxygen mask and there were intravenous tubes everywhere. Her father was by her bedside. He hugged William and then left the room. William took both of Elizabeth's hands in his and he wept. Through his tears of exhaustion and emotion, he prayed for a miracle. He loved this young woman – his wife – so much. He felt her hands stir in his. She drifted out of the coma – a miracle. She was staring at William – her beloved husband – with tears in her eyes. She motioned to William to remove the oxygen mask. He did so. She was trying to speak to him. She was desperately weak and her words were at first, whispered inaudibly. With a supreme effort, she fought to speak coherently: "Willy, my Willy, I knew you would come. I love you so much. Our love is forever. Willy, I think I am dying, but I'm not afraid. I love our little Rowin. Promise me you will take care of her. She's all I have left to give you ..." William tried to choke back his tears. He kissed her tenderly, as she closed her eyes. He sobbed as though his heart would break and lay his head upon her breast.

Elizabeth's breathing had become shallow. William placed her oxygen mask back on her face, just as her parents came into the hospital ward, followed by the nurse and two of the doctors. The doctors asked everyone to leave. William refused to go, as did her parents. Elizabeth opened her eyes one more time and struggled to get the oxygen mask off. The nurse removed this for her. Elizabeth looked into her husband's eyes and quietly and softly said: "Willy, I love you and I love Rowin and dad and mum, I love you too. Look after our baby" ... and then she was gone with a quiet little sigh and a beautiful smile on her pain-ravaged face. She had been such a lovely, joy filled young person. She was only twenty-three years old ...

William was to remember her always, as that young woman, for she would never grow to be old and grey, but always and eternally a youthful spirit ...

William was devastated when Elizabeth's life ended. Her father and mother heard her final words. This was the worst day of their lives. Grief-stricken, the Huddlestones' held their daughter's hands for the last time. They left the hospital room, allowing their son-in-law to have his final minutes with his wife. Their neighbour brought baby Rowin in to be with her father. Together father and daughter would say their farewells.

William gazed down at Rowin, who was fast asleep. He began to cry quietly. The baby opened her eyes and looked at her father's tear-stained face and she let out a heart rending wail, as if she knew her mummy had gone from this war torn world.

William's words to his young dead wife were very moving and private, said from his heart, both from himself and their daughter…

Theirs had been a timeless love. A love very tender, very warm and very true. A first-time love for both of them and first love is never forgotten and never ends, even with the passing away of a life. Their time together had been too short. All too swiftly happiness had been snatched away from this young couple. Not only soldiers died during wartime, but those they loved as well.

William had not wanted to leave Elizabeth's side, but Noah had silently walked into the room and gently drew father and daughter away. Mary and their neighbours – Marcus and Emily Rushton – were in the 'Grieving Room' waiting for them. As they walked along the corridor, their footsteps echoing hollowly, at the Nurses' Station, someone had turned on a small radio and the lilting tune playing softly, was an old wartime favourite, sung by Very Lynn: 'We'll Meet Again – don't know where, don't know when…'

It was a sombre, silent and sad drive back to the house in Mowbray, where Elizabeth had lived all of her life, both with her parents and with her husband and young baby.

The sun was just setting as they walked into the house. The maid – Hildy Biko – had lit a comforting fire in the large living room and there was coffee and tea for them. When told the news, she sobbed uncontrollably, for she was devoted to baby Rowin and Elizabeth.

Hildy took the baby and said she would find a wet-nurse for her. Rowin had not taken well to the cow's milk she had been fed over the past few days, when Elizabeth could not feed her baby.

It was Noah who ran a hot bath for William. He found comfort in doing small things to alleviate his own devastating grief. Mary excused herself and announced she needed to get out and have some fresh air – her way of dealing with her own grief. She did not come home that night and Noah asked no questions of her the next morning when she appeared.

∴

On a cold, wet, gloomy morning in April of 1944, Elizabeth was laid to rest. So many family and friends gathered to say their farewells to this once vibrant and lovely young woman.

Noah Huddlestone paid all the funeral costs for his daughter, as William, like most soldiers, was underpaid and had little to no money. William, a proud man, felt so badly, having to ask his father-in-law to help him out financially, and he promised to pay back all borrowed moneys to Noah (and this he did later for he was a man of honour and a man of his word. In time, many years later, William would make his fortune and he would remember Noah's kindness and generosity and made sure he would lack for nothing as he grew older).

∴

Elizabeth's favourite flowers – tiny, sweetly perfumed English violets and tiny pink rosebuds – were placed upon her casket. Her best friend from childhood, Tessa Johnson, had picked them from her beautiful garden in Rondebosch. (Tessa had been matron-of-honour at her friend's wedding).

William read the eulogy with a voice which shook with emotion. He had wanted to do this and all those who attended Elizabeth's funeral were so moved by his words.

Only granted two weeks emergency compassionate leave, the grief stricken husband/soldier returned to his duties. He flew to Durban, leaving Rowin in the care of her maternal grandparents. His own parents had wanted him to leave Rowin with them. Later – he would rue the decision he had made…

∴∼

William, now trained as an aircraft gunner, was due to fight over Italy. The military fighter plane he was scheduled to fly in, left before he could get back to his troopship in Durban. The plane was shot down over the Mediterranean. Had he been on that plane, he would have lost his life and Rowin would have been orphaned. Through the circumstance of fate, he was again, recalled to Cape Town…

∴∼

Elizabeth's mother, had decided rearing a small baby was not for her. Whilst her husband – Noah – was away in De Aar, she made the momentous decision to have Rowin adopted. (Her daughter's best friends, Tessa and Frederick Johnson, were unable to conceive a child of their own. They were only too delighted to adopt Rowin and rear her as their own daughter).

Mary set the wheels in motion for the adoption by forging both William's and Noah's signatures on the adoption documents. Adoptions were arranged through the Postmaster-General in Cape Town during wartime. With all the necessary legalities finalized and in place, Rowin was handed over to the Johnsons on April 25th, 1944, at 9:00 am on a cold, rainy morning. Her maternal grandmother was malevolently delighted to "get rid of the baby" and as soon as this was done, went off to meet with her secret boyfriend, a liaison, which had been going on behind Noah's back for eighteen months.

∴∼

Noah, a most kind hearted gentleman, arrived home after a three week absence, on May 16th, 1944. He had been away on business for the South African Railways, training new recruits, as train drivers. The house on Rouwkoop Avenue was deserted, not even Hildy, the maid was in evidence. The house seemed to have a neglected, empty feel to it, as though no one had lived in it for weeks.

Later that evening, Mary arrived home, with a suitcase in hand and greeted her husband very coldly. Noah was rather puzzled and somewhat bewildered by her attitude toward him and inquired: "Mary, is something wrong? Where is little Rowin? Why are you so aloof and cold? This is not much of a homecoming my dear." Mary answered: "Noah, I've been away for a few weeks too and Rowin no longer lives here. I've given her up for adoption and all the papers and signatures are in place and there's absolutely nothing you can do about it."

Noah gasped in disbelief and took Mary by her shoulders: "What have you done this time, Mary? What have you done with my granddaughter? Was William a part of this awful thing? I cannot for a single moment believe that he would give up his child. He loved her with all of his heart, just as he loved our own daughter. Where is my little Rowin? And where have you been whilst I was away training the new recruits?"

Mary had such a look of contempt and loathing on her face as she replied: "I never wanted a baby in this house Noah, both you and William knew that, but my wishes didn't even come into the equation. I have a life to lead socially and refuse to be tied down by a child. Sorry, but that's the way it is and no, William knows nothing of this. I forged his signature on the legal adoption papers and it is too late now, to do anything about it. Also, I might as well confess everything. I have been having an affair with someone you do not know, for the past few months. Eighteen months to be precise, right under your nose. You are always away on so-called business and I simply got tired of waiting around for you to wake-up to the fact I want a fun life more than I want you or a baby. I don't want a divorce and I shall continue to live here in this house, but I will lead an entirely separate life from you and that's the way it's going to be." Noah was stunned. Mary stormed out of the house without a backward glance.

Noah was shaking from head to toe. He poured himself a double Scotch whisky and as he tried to sip the fiery alcohol, his teeth chattered against the crystal glass. He sat down in his old, brown leather armchair and put the tumbler on the table next to him. He put his head in his hands and tears welled up in his eyes. He and Mary had been unhappy for quite some time but he had never suspected her of infidelity… There had been too many losses recently…

It must have been hours later when he finally arose. He went to Mary's closet, got down two large suitcases and her hatbox and proceeded to remove all of her clothes, hats, underwear and personal items. A methodical man always, he folded everything carefully. He walked along the passage to the old box-storeroom, found five large cartons and continued to pack the rest of Mary's belongings into these. He dragged everything to the front porch and waited for Mary to return, which she did hours later.

In a tired, sad voice Noah announced: "Mary, I have arranged for a taxi to remove all of your things tonight and you, along with them. We no longer have a marriage, that is obvious. I will never forgive you and if you want a divorce, I shall not oppose it, but you will have to pay for it. This house is in my name and you are not on the title and we are not married in community of property, so my dear, there it is. Take it or leave it, I have nothing more to say to you, except this: go to your lover. I really do not care what you do, but I will find Rowin and I will contact William to let him know what you have done behind my back and his back. You are a despicable bloody woman and I want nothing to do with you from now on. You will leave my house immediately."

Mary still refused to tell Noah where Rowin was and she stood at the front gate, waiting for the taxi to arrive. The driver loaded all her boxes and suitcases into his vehicle. She climbed into the back seat, pausing for a moment to look back at Noah outlined in silhouette at the front door. The night was icy cold ...

∴

Noah was on the point of collapse and spent the remainder of the night in his armchair, falling asleep in sheer emotional exhaustion sometime just before dawn.

He awoke to the sound of the doorbell at around 8:00 am. He sat up, feeling chilled and numbed, walked to the door, thinking Mary had returned. Instead, the person at the door was the maid – Hildy – with a worried look upon her round face. It was obvious to Hildy that Noah had been weeping and she said in her always, kindly voice: "Master Noah, you look very ill. What can Hildy do to help master? There have been terrible things going on while master was away. The missus gave Rowin away and the Postmaster was here to sign important papers. The missus said it was all top-secret and master didn't want little baby Rowin anymore and neither did her daddy, as he would probably die in the war fighting in Italy anyway. Is this true master? You know master, Hildy really loved our little Rowin like a mother, 'cause baby's mother is gone to be with the angels. Why did no one want our beautiful baby master? It is a terrible thing not to love a child, 'specially when her mommy is dead too."

It was cold standing on the doorstep as Hildy's words tumbled out. She was so distraught and sobbing by the time she was finished.

Noah took her by the arm and gently led her to the old, large, cosy kitchen. He filled the kettle, placing it on the hob to make a pot of tea.

Hildy sat down on the old riempie stool, still crying. Old Noah handed her a clean white handkerchief from his vest pocket and she blew her nose loudly. Noah looked at Hildy questioningly: "Hildy, I am so very glad to see you. Yes, our Rowin is gone. Do you know where she is? I must find her and contact my son-in-law immediately. I have sent the missus packing and she would not tell me what has happened to Rowin, other than she has been adopted by someone." Hildy answered: "Master, I know all about the goings-on in your house. The missus has a boyfriend and after you left, he stayed here for a few nights in the missus' bed and then the Cape Town Postmaster came and there were a lot of papers signed and then master's daughter's best friends arrived and signed something and took Rowin with them. They leave Cape Town next week for Australia and Rowin will be going with them."

Noah's face was incredulous and pained as he made the pot of tea. Hildy also told Noah, she had been sacked by Mary, and she had not been paid her wages for March and April. Noah said he would rectify the non-payment and immediately got his cheque book out and wrote Hildy a cheque, adding another ten pounds to the wages owing, for he was a generous man and Hildy was like part of the family. He re-instated her and said he most certainly would need her once again to look after the house and in a very sure voice, announced: "I will get Rowin back, one way or another. I will contact the Postmaster-General and get him to apply to the army to have William sent back to Cape Town post-haste. I am sure, in the circumstances he will be granted compassionate leave once again."

At 9:00 am, Noah walked over to the corner store and asked to use the telephone. This was urgently important business… He placed his desperate call to the Postmaster-General, explaining what had happened, how Mary, his wife, had forged both his signature and that of Rowin's father. He then caught the train through from Mowbray to Cape Town and in person arrived at the main post office and was ushered into the sombre office of the Postmaster-General. The army Group-Captain was also present and the forged adoption papers were rescinded, a call placed to the Johnsons to bring baby Rowin into Cape Town immediately and hand her over to her grandfather. William was contacted as well – his ship had not yet sailed for the Red Sea, and he was flown back from Durban to Cape Town that very morning and granted extended compassionate leave. The Johnsons had not known of Mary's cruel deception and aghast at what had occurred, but very unwilling to give Rowin up and return her to her father and grandfather. They felt she belonged with them. The police were contacted, along with the military police and arrived at the Johnson home and informed them they were there to collect baby Rowin. They complied with the injunction and so sadly, said farewell to the child they thought would be theirs forever.

Later that evening – William Eugene once again arrived in Cape Town, having been flown into the military base airport at Ysterplaat. He was driven by jeep to his father-in-law's home to be greeted by Noah, Hildy and baby Rowin. He put his arms around the old man and sighed deeply … He had lost his young wife and had come so very close to losing their baby daughter. Hildy was holding the baby and handed her gently to her father. Rowin opened her eyes, for she had been fast asleep and gazed up at her father with a very serious expression on her face and then it was as though a rainbow had appeared out of nowhere and she smiled a huge smile, knowing somehow she was safe in the arms of the man who loved her with all of his heart. He would raise her up to stand on mountains and she would walk the sandy beaches of Africa and swim in the oceans. She would grow up into the lovely young woman she was destined to become. William would dream dreams for her and teach her all he knew about loyalty, kindness, strength, hope and there would be laughter once again in all of their lives. He would also teach her about integrity and that one's conscience towards one's fellow man should be tantamount to one's beliefs in oneself.

William looked into Rowin's eyes and it was as though he could see her very soul. William whispered to her: "Little Rowin, everything that I am, I give to you now. It's more than enough that you are my girl. I will hush you to sleep. I will hold your hand. I will be the rock for you to lean upon when you search for solid ground. I will teach you to dream your dreams and be there to wipe your tears. I will give you everything I can for I truly loved your mother and you are part of that love. When you gaze up at the stars – look for the Southern Cross constellation, for those stars belong to your mother and she will always look down on you. Oh Rowin, how I miss your mother, but you are here and granddad, Hildy and I will raise you in the way you deserve to be raised. That is my promise to you."

Slowly William walked to the nursery. Rowin's crib and all of her baby things were gone. Granddad emptied a large drawer, pulled out from the bottom of the closet in his room and a makeshift crib was made for Rowin to sleep in. Hildy had managed to hide Rowin's teddybear and the primrose, hand-crocheted woollen coverlet, her mother – Elizabeth's hands – had so painstakingly made, whilst she awaited the birth of her child. Her christening mug – silver – engraved with her name and a miniature silver bracelet had also been put aside safely by Hildy and were given to William after he put his baby to bed. It was such a bitter-sweet night.

When Rowin had been fed and tucked up and was fast asleep, both William and Noah walked outside and breathed in the cool night air. They searched the Cape night skies for the Southern Cross stars and with tears steaming down their cheeks, these two men gave thanks for the safe return of both William and Rowin. Life would go on ... Real men are never afraid to cry ... They would find the strength needed in this time of war. The war would end one day and there would be laughter and there would always be hope. The wind whispered softly. They would get through this first night together and with the dawning of a new day an innocent child would bring them much joy. With the loving help of their maid, Hildy, between the three of them, they would raise Rowin. They would be there for her first years and then time and tide changed everything.

∿

William would no longer be able to serve as a fighting soldier. After his first week back in Cape Town, he applied for a position as a Medical Orderly at Wynberg Military Hospital, working the night shifts, five nights a week. This allowed him special time with Rowin during the day. She was an extremely good baby and slept throughout most nights, without awakening until 8:00 am each morning.

Her maternal grandmother – Mary Huddlestone disappeared with her lover to Southern Rhodesia. It was nearly two years before she contacted her husband Noah. Mary never did apply for a divorce, but she came back into their lives when Rowin turned four years old.

∿

A year after William began working at the hospital, he ran into Felicity Eaton – the receptionist who had given him a cup of tea, the night his wife had died…

∿

… William looked at Rowin holding out her mother's turquoise ring to him. He slipped it onto his pinkie finger. Aunt Beth had lifted Rowin up to kiss her father. He was so very tired and the effort for him talking with Rowin earlier had exhausted his last reserves of strength.

Felicity and Joanna walked into his hospital room, together with the three specialists. They told William about the decision to operate on his leg the following morning at 7:00 am.

William was adamant and refused to allow them to amputate his leg, unless everything possible had been done to save his limb whilst he was on the operating table. The specialists agreed to his request.

He looked at Rowin once more: "Rowin-love, I'll be here for you and Felicity one way or another. I made a promise many years ago to your first mother, I would always take care of you and I will. I have never broken a promise yet and I do not intend to do so now."

The ward-sister arrived and ushered everyone out. William needed to rest. Rowin held tightly onto her Aunt Joanna's hand and as she reached the door, she broke away and ran back to her beloved father, took his hand in hers and said: "My Daddy-love, I'll be waiting for you and the stars of the Southern Cross will be looking out for you, 'cause they're mommy's stars. Bye for now, love you, …" William quietly smiled at her and motioned for his wife, Felicity to come back to him.

Rowin ran to her aunts, leaving Felicity to tell William her news: she was going to have a baby in the spring. William's eyes lit up with pleasure at the news. He was thrilled, just as Felicity was. Rowin would have a little companion and life would be good. There would be laughter.

~

After Felicity left, William felt extremely weak. The ward sister came in to see him and give him an injection to make him sleep. He hated the sensation of the morphine as it flowed through his body, leaving him lightheaded and nauseous, but it did ease the terrible pains in his leg and hip and he soon dozed off into a fitful, restless sleep.

At 5:00 am, he was once again awake and given the customary enema, uncomfortable in the best of circumstances and made doubly worse with his war injuries. Never a man to complain, William groaned and prayed for the strength he would need to endure whatever lay ahead for him on the operating table.

His mind wandered to thoughts of the property he had so recently purchased out in Arniston, for he had decided he would move away from Cape Town and go into farming. This was a pre-step to buying more land in the future, for his great-uncle Michael had written to him, indicating he wanted to leave Ireland and settle in the Western Cape region of South Africa, needing to fulfil his lifelong dream of going into viticulture. He had written to William's brother and sisters as well. Time would indicate what the future would bring...

The medical orderly arrived to give William his pre-operative medication and then he was wheeled to the operating room. Sudden fear lurched at the pit of his stomach and his last thoughts were of little Rowin placing the turquoise ring into his hand...

∶∾

William awoke several hours later groggy and in great pain, with a nurse bending over him, adjusting his oxygen mask and inquiring whether he wanted a sedative and a sip of water or a teaspoon of crushed ice. All he could do was murmur: "Did they take my leg?" she patted his shoulder and told him the doctor and specialists would be in to see him shortly. She administered the sedative injection and William sank into a restless sleep...

CHAPTER THREE

REVENGE OF THE REBEL

... the final straw broke the young camel's back, wreaking havoc along its way and an irascible man learns a lesson ...

These were exciting times, five families, pulling up roots, to move from Cape Town to the south western Cape coastal area between Arniston and Struisbaai – not far from the confluence of two mighty oceans.

∼

Rowin's father – William – and his four siblings, his younger brother Richard, and sisters, Joanna, Beth and Annabel, had inherited a sizeable legacy from a great-uncle in County Cork, Ireland, where their family had originated from.

Their uncle – Michael O'Neill Eugene had never married, having lost the love of his life to his best friend instead. Michael had made many trips out to South Africa and had fallen in love with the beauty of the spectacularly scenic Western Cape region. He had also gotten to know his great nephews and nieces really well, staying with each one in turn, after they had married and had children of their own. He doted, in particular on William and Joanna and when he had died, left the major portion of his legacy to them, but in no small way, neglected not to include the other three.

Michael O'Neill Eugene had always been interested in viticulture and the winegrowing of the Cape region had fascinated him and he and William had many long conversations, discussing the probability of purchasing a wine Estate should a lucrative and viable property become available. William had been keen to make an offer for a partial share in the "Belle-France Estate," when a portion of the land being farmed for canola had been up for auction and he had successfully bid on this, with the money being supplied by his former father-in-law, Noah Huddlestone. William and his second wife, Felicity, had married in Arniston at the small Anglican Church, bordering on the "Belle-France Estates and had held their wedding reception at the Estate manor house great hall, thus the area held special meaning and memories for William.

Before Michael had died, he had written to all five of his nephews and nieces, informing them of his intentions, to move permanently to South Africa, in order to pursue his life-long dream of owning his own winery and lands, He wanted them all to go into a consortium and share the profits and farm the lands in the surrounding area as well. Unfortunately, he had, in the midst of his planning, died in a boating accident, but had written his Last Will and Testament naming his five relatives.

The 'five' had decided, after weeks and weeks of discussions, to honour their late uncle's last wishes and to wait for the opportune moment to purchase a vineyard. The opportunity presented itself sooner than they had anticipated...

The owners of the "Belle-France Estates," wanted to relocate to their ancestral homeland of France and the huge Estate was up 'For Sale.' For the Eugene family, it was as though, fate was on their side. After much haranguing and working out all of the massive legalities, they now owned part and parcel, all of the Estate lands, manor house, five other smaller Cape Dutch style houses and fishermen's cottages and farm cottages on the lands. They had also purchased the wineries, including the bottling plants and large oaken vat halls as well. There was enough money left over to do major renovations on most of the outdated buildings.

Theirs was a chance of a lifetime, to work together not only as a large family, but to establish their knowledge and reputation as fair-minded landowners, who had their workers' well being in mind.

William's brother, Richard and his wife Patrice, had met at University and both had trained in viticulture. Beth, their sister, had met her husband Ari Ben Jordan, whilst holidaying in Cyprus and both had lived on a kibbutz in Israel, where their children had been born, so were well-versed in agricultural and farm aspects of life. (They had returned to South Africa).

Annabel would be a 'silent' partner, along with her husband Robin vay Zyl, as he was very involved in South African politics. Robin was one of the 'New Breed' of young politicians, who had rather radical ideas for the times, even though they were members of the extremely stoic National Party, who were in power ruling South Africa. The Party's dominant rule would last for many years. Robin and his family were often away in either Pretoria or returning to Cape Town for the summer sitting of Parliament.

The owners of "Belle-France" had agreed to remain for six months, in order to train the new owners, for there was much to learn in order to facilitate a smooth transition of ownership and continued running of the lucrative property.

Joanna and her husband, Peter Robinson had returned to Cape Town, after a short stint in Malta and Peter had decided to resign as Military Advisor and Attache to the British Government and was looking for something different as a career and felt this would be a wonderful opportunity and fill the gap which was missing for him and his wife, unable to have children …

Joanna was thrilled, for she was extremely close to all of her siblings, but William most especially. William had fully recovered from the major surgery on his leg. The specialists had saved his leg, but he had lost two of his toes and now walked with a pronounced limp. William, always the soldier, was a stoic fighter and his determination and positive outlook had been instrumental in his rapid recovery. There had been some serious moments, when the blood poisoning presented some complications, but he had pulled through with the knowledge he had a lot to live for. As he lay in his hospital ward, his thoughts often turned to his first love – Elizabeth – and although he had remarried, he felt that Elizabeth was watching over him and wore her turquoise ring, which their daughter Rowin had given him the day before his surgery.

Years later, he still wore the turquoise ring, much to Felicity's annoyance…

:~

There was much which annoyed Felicity. Though she loved William dearly, she resented his daughter. Without realizing, William often mentioned his first wife's name during conversation and Felicity reacted by becoming petulant and took out her bad moods on poor Rowin, an innocent young victim caught often in the middle.

Felicity had been spoilt all of her life by her father and although her mother tried to balance this out by being quite strict with her, Felicity always got her own way. William was made to feel extremely guilty if he spent time with his daughter and to keep peace on the homefront gave into Felicity's demands. She was a very difficult person to please and there were times when William wondered why he had ever married her. In front of William, Felicity was always as sweet as pie toward Rowin, but behind her husband's back, she was often unkind and very spiteful and mean. Rowin learned to keep out of her step-mother's way, from an early age, but she would never get used to the almost daily beatings which she received. During Felicity's pregnancy, she suffered constantly from morning sickness and this went on well into her eighth month. Her mother – Elsie – took young Rowin under her wing and the daily beatings ceased for a while. (Rowin would be eternally grateful to her friend and step-grandmother for this…)

The lady and young child would spend hours and hours together, either on the beach at Saint James, Dalebrook or Fish Hoek or in the beautiful gardens at the Eatons' lovely home. Elsie also enjoyed spending time with her daughter's in-laws – James and Rosemary O'Neill Eugene. This gave Rowin the opportunity to get to know her other grandparents, whom she was very fond of. James doted upon his grand-daughter and she was the favourite of all of his and Rosemary's grandchildren. Rowin had a way of enchanting people with her spontaneous nature, complete honesty, coupled with an innate curiosity for everything mischievous or fun. Never one to beat around the bush, Rowin always got straight to the point 'in medias res' which on occasion got her into serious hot water. Her grandparents – Noah Huddlestone, James and Rosemary and step-grandmother Elsie, could never spend enough time with her and this made her feel very special and cherished. Felicity's constant haranguings and beatings never seemed quite as bad with the knowledge that her grandparents loved her. She knew too, that her beloved father cared for her but he was obliged to devote a great deal of attention to his second wife… He always, always made special time for Rowin though and when she was older and wanted to know more about her real mother, he would take her aside quietly and privately and tell her all he could remember about his first wife – his first love. Noah too, would talk to Rowin about Elizabeth and though her mother was not with them, she felt she was somewhere 'close' and had never really left her.

∴

No one had told Rowin that soon she would have a sibling, though she wondered why Felicity's stomach seemed to get larger and larger. She thought to herself, Felicity must have been eating too much… Felicity was going through a 'sewing frenzy' and one thing she did enjoy, was sewing beautiful outfits for Rowin. With each 'new outfit' – Rowin in her childlike way, hoped Felicity really did care about her and love her…

Rowin adored her sister from the day she arrived in her world. Felicity had a home-birth in the October of 1949. Rowin had been cautioned by her step-grandmother, Elsie Eaton, to sit quietly in the living room at the yellow-wood writing desk in the bay window and to watch for the doctor's arrival, for he was going to bring a wonderful gift for Rowin. Rowin and Elsie had become very close over the preceding months and Rowin had enchanted the older woman with her endearing ways and her spirited demeanour. Rowin was constantly up to one prank or another, along with her cousins. She was definitely, very much, the "leader of the pack," even though some of her cousins were older than she was.

Rowin was also the bane of old Pa's life. Pa had been particularly nasty to her on one occasion, pulling her hair and pinching her and giving her a sharp kick on her rear end. She had not done anything wrong. She happened to be in the wrong place at the wrong time and he was annoyed by her presence. They were living temporarily with the Eatons' until the renovations had been completed on the old Cape Dutch farmhouse, William, her father had purchased in Arniston. These would not be completed in time before the birth.

∴~

As Rowin sat patiently at the desk, she began to fidget. She was tired of colouring pictures in the book Elsie had given her and she had finished her bowl of porridge. She wondered where her step-mother, Felicity was, for she had not seen her all morning. She had not minded this, but Felicity was always the one who made her breakfast and she had been sewing her a lovely blue gingham dress which she said would be ready for her to wear on this particular day. Rowin was somewhat disappointed and gave a deep sigh. She so badly needed to have a pee, but Elsie had forbidden her to move and go down the long passage to the luxuriously appointed bathroom. Rowin had a plan. She would just nip across the hallway to her grandparents' bedroom and get the porcelain pee-pot from under her grandmother's bed and use it. She opened the living-room door and peeped out, looking in both directions, dived into the bedroom, wriggled underneath the bed and grabbed the pee-pot and dashed back to the sanctuary of the bay window of the living room and 'did' what she had to do. She was about to return the filled potty to the bedroom, when she heard the sound of her grandmother's footsteps.

Oh panic, what could she do to hide the evidence and the fact she had 'moved' from the room? Ah, she spied her stepmother's favourite potted plant in its large brass container, emptied the contents of the pee-pot into it, opened the sideboard cupboard door and placed the now empty pee-pot inside, with the Villeroy and Boch best china dinnerware and closed the cupboard door and stood looking out of the window. (It would be many months before the 'pot' was discovered). She watched, as the Doctor arrived with his bag and saw grandmother Elsie usher him into the hallway. Elsie popped her head around the living-room door, smiled at Rowin, who happened to look very guilty, and said: "Oh good girl, but by the look upon your face, I think you've been up to some sort of mischief. Stay where you are, I'll be back really soon." Rowin nodded her head and felt most thankful she had not been caught.

About forty-five minutes later, granny Elsie was back with a huge smile on her face and held her arms out to Rowin. As Rowin ran to her, wondering why Elsie looked so happy, Elsie announced: "Rowin, come with me right now. Let's go and see Felicity. Your mummy has something so wonderful to give you." Rowin asked: "Is it my new dress? Mummy promised me it would be ready for me to wear to Cain's birthday party this afternoon." Elsie took Rowin's hand and almost ran down the hallway to the semi-private apartment.

Elsie seemed to be in such a hurry, Rowin could barely keep up with her ... As they reached the bedroom door, Rowin heard the sound of a baby crying. There in Felicity's arms lay a red-faced, though beautiful baby, crying lustily, Rowin stared and Felicity smiled at Rowin and motioned her forward. Rowin was rooted to the spot with such a look of disbelief on her face and asked" "Where did that baby come from? Did the doctor bring it in his black bag?"

Elsie and Felicity chuckled and the doctor smiled, along with the midwife, whose arrival Rowin had not noticed earlier. Felicity, looking very tired said: "Rowin, this your new baby sister. Her name is Mia Tansy. Daddy will be very surprised when he gets home this afternoon from Arniston, to know he has two daughters, so you will have to learn to share him with your new sister from now on." Rowin looked at the baby and gently took her tiny hand and kissed it tenderly. The baby stopped crying and her fingers curled around Rowin's. Rowin's heart seemed to skip a beat as she looked at her new sister with awe.

"She's just like a little doll and I think I love her 'cause she's my sister. Can she come to Cain's birthday party with me this afternoon?"

Rowin bonded with her sister immediately. There was never a mean word between them as they grew up and they remained the best of sisters and friends throughout their lives.

Rowin was told to return to the living room, where old Pa had ensconced himself in his black leather wing-backed armchair. He was smoking one of his very smelly cigars and had a glass of Old Brown sherry in his hand. He looked at Rowin over his gold-rimmed spectacles, and asked her to fetch him a covered ashtray, which she did. She knew better than to disobey him… As she passed the receptacle to him, he lunged across at her, pulling her hair, pinching her arm, spun around and kicked her shin, laughing evilly as he did so. Usually she managed to move away from him extremely swiftly, but her mind had been on her new baby sister. She ran from the room, his malicious laughter ringing in her ears. Why, oh why, was this old man SO nasty and mean toward her? Perhaps it was because he was totally bald with a head like a polished dome and the sun had done something to his brain, she thought to herself. He always did the same things to her and either kicked her rear end or her shins. She was really angry this time though, for it spoiled the wonderful excitement of having a new sister. She vowed she would pay the old man back, one way or another. She and her boy cousins would have to have a secret pow-wow at the birthday party that afternoon…

Whilst waiting for her Aunt Joanna to collect her for Cain's party, she planned to teach old Pa a lesson he richly deserved for his crass unkindness. This would be something Pa would never forget.

Rowin was delighted that Felicity had actually finished her new dress the night before the birth of Mia Tansy. There were times when Felicity could really be nice to Rowin. (Perhaps the 'niceness' had something to do with 'pangs of guilt' for her constant chastisement of Rowin). Rowin entertained thoughts of forgiveness toward her step-mother, but in her heart of hearts, she acknowledged the fact that the screaming, shouting and beatings, ultimately would continue ad infinitum…

∴∽

This was such a delightful October day. Springtime in the southern hemisphere. The first crocus flowers and snowdrops were already in bloom in Granny Elsie's garden. Nature's tantalizing mementoes were promises for the future as the season moved toward summer. African summers were hot and intense.

As the car sped along the coastal road between Saint James and Kalk Bay, waves broke with a soft swish along the huge rocks below them, for it was low tide. Time seemed like the wingéd shadow to Rowin and Aunt Joanna, chattering away like two magpies and then they stopped for a few moments to watch the gulls and terns wheeling and diving for fish. They lapsed into companionable silence.

Rowin felt particularly pretty in her blue gingham dress with its high, empire waistline and large white sailor collar. Her new white leather slip-on pumps and long, white knee-high socks complimented and completed her outfit. Her hair was tied back in a ponytail, gathered together with a blue gingham ribbon.

Rowin loved the sea in all of its vastness and she was often caught daydreaming imagining she was viewing life through a seashell. Her favourite seashells were the sea urchins and the beautiful nautilus and she had a sizeable collection of these intricate treasures.

∴

… the birthday celebrations were over and a most marvellous time was had by all.

Rowin had managed to get her cousins, Cain, Patrick and Jonathon into a secret huddle to discuss how they could hatch a plan to pay her step-grandfather back. Plans were afoot. The three of them were coming over at the weekend for Sunday lunch together with their parents and siblings and they planned to go tadpole fishing and frog hunting.

∴

On a Sunday morning, Pa always took a long and very leisurely bath. No one was allowed use of the bathroom when 'King Pa' was in residence. He always liked to have the bathroom window open, for he inevitably smoked his cigar in the bath tub, whilst reading the Sunday newspaper. The children, led by mischievous young Rowin, would tip a large jar filled with tadpoles through the window into the bath tub. They would wait to see the outcome under the bathroom window…

∴

Everyone had arrived at Elsie and Henry's home and Pa – as usual – was having his Sunday soak in the bath tub. (He never deviated from his set routine). The hatched plan was put into action, with Rowin standing on Cain's shoulders, whilst Patrick and Jonathon held onto his legs to keep him steady. Pa was leaning forward in the tub with his back to the window. Rowin very carefully leaned right inside the window and silently emptied the contents of the glass jar into the water, undetected by Pa. Very carefully the boys helped her down and the waiting began…

… For what seemed like an eternity, nothing happened and then all hell let loose. Old Pa shrieked at the top of his lungs: "Bloody hell, what's going on? Help! Elsie! I think I have some terrible disease."

At that point he leaped out of the bath, flung open the bathroom door and ran down the passageway toward the living room where everyone was assembled ready to meet William and Felicity and their new baby daughter. Half of the family came flying when they heard Pa's shrieks and screams for 'help' obviously not realizing what had happened. There was old Pa in all the glory of his birthday suit – entirely naked – not even a towel in sight. Pa was mortified. Everyone was stunned and flabbergasted and then they laughed and laughed, especially when the 'disease' was discovered to be about a hundred tadpoles in the bathwater. Rowin and her boy cousins had of course disappeared around the back of the large greenhouse and were writhing around killing themselves with helpless giggles and laughter. No one suspected them and the naughty prank they had pulled. Everyone said the tadpoles must have come through the cold water tap …

Rowin was not yet finished with teaching Pa a lesson. She had coerced her cousins into collecting about two dozen small frogs as well. Whilst everyone was calming an irate Pa down, the four children had finally stopped laughing and were about to descend upon Pa's and Granny Elsie's bedroom WITH the frogs. Whilst Patrick and Jonathon kept watch, Rowin and Cain retrieved Pa's pee-pot from under his bed and very carefully tipped the brown paper bag of frogs into its interior replacing the pee-pot lid as they did so. They pushed the pee-pot back into its original place and crept away quietly.

During the night, when Pa awoke from his slumbers and lifted his nightshirt to use the pee-pot just as he did each and every night, he got the fright of his life. As soon as the lid of the pot was lifted, frogs jumped out in all directions, and of course, Pa 'missed' the pee-pot entirely as he urinated all over the floor. Granny Elsie did not know just who croaked the most: Pa or the frogs. All pandemonium broke loose, as the servants came flying, William and Felicity were woken up, as well as the baby and the perpetrator of the dastardly crime – Rowin Eugene. Oh my, how everyone laughed, except old Pa. It took hours to catch all of those frogs. Everyone knew it had to be Rowin who had played the prank. She did not say her cousins had been party to the plan, but instead took the full blame for her actions. Her boy cousins were in awe of their heroine. Oh my, was she severely punished. Besides a severe whipping with a bamboo cane, which left welts on her tender young back, her favourite toys were given away, her teddybear from babyhood, which old Hildy had saved, was burned. Her lovely new dress and new white shoes were given to one of her girl cousins and she had only bread and water for five days. The only time she was allowed out of her room, was to use the bathroom and she had to have cold water baths for a month. Pa was ready to kill her. He was so upset and angry, he booked himself onto a cruise liner and sailed from Cape Town to Durban staying away for a full month. By the time he returned, William, Felicity, Rowin and baby Mia had moved to the newly renovated home in Arniston.

Pa Henry James Eaton never spoke to Rowin ever again, right up until the day he died. Granny Elsie still had time for her though and became Rowin's confidanté as she grew into womanhood. She secretly took Rowin aside and they laughed together over Rowin's pranks. Granny Elsie had enough of Pa's tyrannical ways and wished that she had had Rowin's gutsiness to stand up and fight back against the injustices meted out to her. When no one was looking, she made sure Rowin had some tasty morsel to eat, other than the bread and water Felicity insisted was part of her punishment. Rowin felt that her punishment had not been very fair and she was still very rebellious inside and was bound and determined to 'do' one more thing against Pa before they left to live in

Arniston. She hated the way Pa treated her dear Granny Elsie and she so wished she was coming with them. And she was heartbroken and devastated over the loss of her teddy bear ...

∴

On the morning Rowin left with her family, she went outside to the rain barrel under the eaves at the side of the house with her little watering can, turned the tap on the barrel open and filled her container half-full. She quietly walked inside to the living room, got down Pa's decanter of Old Brown sherry, which was almost a third empty, and poured the brown rainwater into it, filling it to the top. She replaced the cut-glass stopper and put the decanter back into place. Old Brown sherry? Old brown rainwater? She hoped Pa would have terrible stomach-ache when he drank the concoction ... she'd also added a couple of dead dung beetles, a grasshopper and some dead flies ...

∴

... and then life changed for the better. They loved the house in Arniston. Rowin could run wild along the sandy beaches. She and her cousins no longer had to go to school, as two tutors were engaged to teach them their lessons each day, along with the children belonging to the servants who worked in the Great House and in the vineyards. All were tutored and schooled and learned exactly the same lessons and when it came time to write the National school exams, all of the children, both black and white passed with excellent marks. There was no "apartheid regimé" in Rowin's household and the incredible loyalty between the whites, blacks and coloureds, lasted a lifetime, though this had to be secret and literally, "kept under very tight wraps" for fear of reprisals and recriminations in a society which precluded any friendships between mixed races. Whites had to live a separate existence from blacks. Blacks had to live a separate existence from whites. Apartheid's laws were harsh and insensitive, but they were the law of the land and law of the strict ruling Nationalist government in power. As Rowin and Mia grew up, they would both rebel openly at times against what they considered to be unfair and unjust...

CHAPTER FOUR

CHILDHOOD LOST FOREVER

... a young girl grows up one night. She asks herself a question most seriously: "Do I really want to grow up in this world of pain where people I love die? I am so frightened ..."

Rowin had just turned twelve years old and her half-sister was seven. The two of them were great friends and totally inseparable. Felicity was very envious and quite jealous of the closeness between the two sisters. She was very possessive with her own daughter and did everything she possibly could to shatter the close bond between the two girls. She also spoiled Mia at every opportunity. This had little effect upon the child, for she was naturally sweet-natured and adorable. She had golden curls and her mother's large, beautiful green eyes. Mia was tall for her age, compared to her sister, who was tiny and short, and still full of mischievous antics and always getting into trouble of some sort or another.

Felicity would spank and beat Rowin almost every day for even the slightest misdemeanour and little Mia would beg her not to lash out at her older sister. She would always cry the tears Rowin refused to shed and comfort her sister and tell her she loved her and she was the best sister in the world. Mia's tears were entirely wasted upon her mother and the awful punishments would continue, day in and day out.

… Rowin had decided to go to bed early. She had a dreadful headache after eating too many chocolates. (Chocolates were her weakness – she simply could never get enough of them – and inevitably paid dearly for her indulgences). She had attempted to read from a new novel by the South African authoress, Shilon Cloeté, but after only two pages, had turned off her bedside lamp and fallen asleep instantly. She had awoken about an hour later after hearing a muffled thump and a short scream. Half awake, she wasn't sure whether she had been dreaming or had only imagined the noises. Suddenly she was very wide awake and began remembering all manner of things from the past and the present. She lay with her hands under the back of her head. She thought of her favourite person – her beloved father – who was presently away with Felicity. She missed her father so much, but when it came to her step-mother, she was more than a little relieved when she was not around, for it meant a wonderful reprieve and a welcome break from the usual daily punishments meted out to her by Felicity. She remembered her father's last words to her and her little sister: "I love you two girls so much – be good, say your prayers each night and say and do nice things."

As Rowin attempted to settle down once again, after getting up for a drink of water, she felt restless. The night was unseasonably warm and very humid. She pulled the window curtains open and opened the sash window at the top, hoping cool air would blow into her room. The night was inky dark, as she clambered back into her four poster bed. She felt edgy. She closed her eyes and yawned and again thought of her father and Felicity. She wondered if they were having a good time on their cruise to the Seychelles. Felicity had been very depressed over the past weeks. She had suffered a miscarriage, losing a baby boy during the fifth month of her unplanned pregnancy. A total hysterectomy had unfortunately followed this tragedy. William felt time away, fresh scenery and just the two of them together might help his wife cope with her emotions, for she seemed headed towards a nervous breakdown. Always compassionate and considerate, he felt deeply the loss Felicity had gone through. He felt devastated himself, for he would loved to have had a son. His two girls – Rowin and Mia though – meant the world to him…

∾

Rowin fell asleep, cooler now, as a rumbling storm approached. Rain on a dark night fell from heavy skies. There were no bright twinkling stars and the moon was hidden somewhere behind the storm clouds.

∾

Rowin had awoken to the sounds of screaming. The shrieks were a terrified cacophony of anguish. She sat up, frightened and terrified. She silently clambered out of her bed, thrusting her feet into her soft, blue slippers and sped across the room to her closed bedroom door, opened it and went into her half-sister's bedroom, Mia was also awake and sitting up. She had turned her bedside lamp on and her room was bathed in soft pink light. She looked at Rowin and whispered: "Rowin, what's going on? What's all that screaming about?" Rowin's reply: "Mia Tansy, I don't know. Perhaps we should go and find out." Both girls crept out of Mia's bedroom, proceeding cautiously towards the noise, which was coming from the kitchen. They were both shaking and trembling nervously. Rowin held up a finger to her lips, motioning Mia to remain silent. Where was everyone? The house was in total darkness. Usually the hall lights were left on. Those screams were bloodcurdlingly terrible. What was happening? The two girls, hearts pounding, stopped for a moment.

… as Rowin and Mia cautiously inched their way along the dark passage from the sleeping quarters of the house, they reached the great hall and crept through to the large living room, continuing onwards into the dining room. The horrendous screams continued, muffled now. As the two girls tiptoed silently along, Rowin had collected one of the large brass candlesticks off the yellow-wood mantlepiece in the living room. She had absolutely no idea what she intended to do with the object. Somehow, it made her feel a little more secure. They reached the kitchen door. Rowin looked at Mia holding onto her nightgown tightly. Rowin turned the door handle silently and then quietly, cautiously opened the door. The scene made her gasp in sheer terror …

There was blood everywhere. Rowin pushed Mia back into the dining room immediately and whispered to her to run as fast as she could to the stables and hide.

⁓

No one had seen her enter the room as she silently hid behind the kitchen door, by now, too petrified to move. She was shaking, her teeth bit into her lower lip, as she whimpered.

Two uniformed policemen had tied one of the maids – her friend, Nonqaba (also called Janet) – to the kitchen table. She was naked and bleeding profusely. She had been savagely raped by both men. Suddenly, Nonqaba who was groaning piteously, began to scream and scream, almost insanely. The smaller of the two policemen drew his loaded revolver, held this to Nonqaba's head and shot her at point blank range. Her body contorted, heaved one more time and lay very still. Rowin sprang into action like a person depraved, leaping across the kitchen, she hit the policeman who had shot her friend, across the back of his head with the candlestick, knocking him unconscious with the force of the adrenalin-pumping blow. The other policeman, at first stunned, drew his truncheon and lurched toward Rowin, who stood rooted to the spot, unable to move momentarily. She saw him coming for her and attempted to move out of his way, but slipped on the blood pooling on the floor from Nonqaba's body. His truncheon connected with Rowin's forehead and cheek with a loud cracking sound, knocking her to the floor. She tried to crawl under the table and he hit her again, This time on her lower back. She kicked at him futilely as he pulled her from beneath the table and kicked her viciously. Rowin lay groaning in agonizing pain on the kitchen floor. The policeman ripped at her bloodstained nightgown, tearing this from her, when suddenly the outside kitchen door opened and a young black youth stood upon the threshold. It was Temba, who moved like a lightning bolt toward the policeman, who had now drawn his revolver, aiming this at Temba. Temba ducked as the shot went wild. He tackled the policeman who fell to the floor. His head hit the marble tiles with a huge thud, splitting his skull. He was stone cold dead. Temba fell across the body of the dead man. The room had rapidly filled with people. First to arrive was Aunt Joanna, followed by her husband, Peter, horrified at the bloody scene before them. Temba was struggling to get up. Joanna rushed to Rowin and Peter dashed to the pantry door, shocked to see two naked girls holding onto each other – both bleeding – both raped. The bludgeoned, unconscious policeman was tied with rope, trussed like a chicken. He came to, finding Peter shaking him by his scalp and dousing him with water. He spat in Peter's face, yelled: "Julle mense is kaffir-boeties. Ons sal julle doodskiet…"

The girls were all carried to the living room and wrapped in blankets. Rowin, shivering on the sofa, eyes huge in her face, the ugly red welt across her bruised forehead and cheek now swollen, began to push and kick, flailing her arms and then became still. She could not speak. She could not even cry. She was in shock. Suddenly, she pulled away from Joanna, leaped up from the sofa and screamed: "Mia, Mia, Mia…" She tore through the room, blood covering her feet as she slipped and slithered across the kitchen floor, out through the kitchen door, she ran towards the stables. She was oblivious to her nakedness…

Mia was hiding in one of the horse stalls, crying her heart out. As she saw her sister coming toward her, she ran to her with outstretched arms, sobbing. The two girls collapsed onto the stable floor and it was then that Rowin fainted…

~

In those horrendous moments, Rowin's childhood had been shattered by what she had witnessed. She was only twelve years old. Thank God she had the presence of mind to send her little sister running to safety.

It was during those awful minutes, Rowin's "cause" for justice against the oppressed was forged and born. Overnight, she grew up with such painful abruptness.

When William and Felicity arrived home, it was to a very changed and sombre household. They had been informed of the shocking events by radio telephone on board ship and were devastated.

Three innocent, beautiful young black girls had been brutally violated, beaten, raped. One had lost her life – viciously murdered by a brute, a so-called 'officer of the law.' Mia was safe, thanks to her sister's quick thinking, but Rowin had come close to being raped and possibly also losing her life. All the girls had been home-schooled together, done part of their growing-up together, had become good friends together. Nothing would ever be the same … The night had been mind-shattering, ugly and horrendous …

Now the beginning of the real apartheid regimé was rearing its ugly head in all of its disgusting horror right on the Eugene families doorstep …

~

The two young police constables had heard Rowin and Mia's parents were away and had decided to seize the opportunity to have, as one of them was heard to say: "… time to have some fun with those black bastards the Eugenes' call friends." Unbeknownst to them, Joanna, Peter and the girls were at "Belle-France."

~

… a new, bright sunny day had dawned after the long rough night experienced by those at "Belle-France." Tragedy had hit home hard to everyone.

The police – still at the homestead – continued their questioning and investigation. The bodies had been taken to the local morgue and the two raped girls – Nobukwe and Thokozile had been rushed by ambulance to the Hospital in Caledon. The atmosphere was one of desolate grief, people whispering in hushed voices.

Fleur-Rowin was awake, staring unseeing, her face bruised and swollen, her cheekbone hairline-fractured. She was so very still. She had slept fitfully, tossing and turning, her restless sleep filled with shuddering nightmares. She was in so much pain – mental/physical. Old Hildy, visiting from Mowbray, had sat in the rocking chair alongside Rowin's bed. She had finally slept once Rowin had dozed off. Hildy's hands were neatly folded in her lap, with a tartan rug over her knees. Throughout the night she had held or stroked Rowin's hands. Many times she had cradled Rowin as an infant in that chair, gently cuddling her to sleep, singing in her melodious African voice the zulu songs from her own childhood. Rowin made a sudden animal sound, screaming out in sheer terror for her father and Mia. Hildy awake immediately, moved to Rowin's side, trying to calm her.

Joanna came flying into the room. Rowin sat up rocking to-and-fro. The family doctor arrived. He had administered a strong sedative earlier, to calm Rowin, allowing her to sleep. He gently took Rowin by her shoulders, assuring her William and Felicity would be home the following day and injected another sedative into her arm. Rowin lay back on her pillows, lapsing into sleep almost immediately.

Horrendous nightmares would haunt all three girls – Nobukwe, Thokozile and Rowin throughout their lives, for deep, searing scars had been left upon each one's soul, when childhood had abruptly ceased for them on that terrible night…

∴

Nonqaba's sad funeral was held twelve days later. All of Rowin's family attended, along with Nonqaba, Nobukwe and Thokoziles'. The keening and ululating of the African women was heart wrenching and mournful, achingly sorrowful. Hildy Biko's voice could be heard as she sang the traditional African song "Tula Baba" – Hush Baby – No Tears. This was a traditional song, sung to the African children at bedtime – a lilting, sad lullaby. (Many of the children in African villages grew up without their fathers who left the tribal lands to work in the cities or the mines, enabling them to send money home to their families. The song was sung to comfort and console the children, and the words would tell them their fathers would return one day, but so many of those fathers did not come back. Life was so very hard when you were a black person in South Africa).

"… *hush my child, my little child, keep quiet my little one. Daddy will be home in the morning. There is a star which will shine, and it will guide him home.*"

As Hildy sang, holding Rowin's hand and that of young Nobukwe, Thokozile placed seashells from Rowin's special collection on Nonqaba's small coffin as she was placed in warm Mother Earth, her grave freshly dug. There was such a pall of deep, deep silence over all those assembled. The women's wailing and keening had ceased and only the comforting cooing of the lilac-breasted turtle doves could be head above the strident noise of the cicadas buzzing.

Earth covered the coffin and the shells and it was then that the African drums began to beat. The beating ceased only when the sun set on the day of Nonqaba's funeral…

∴∿

… from the end of the earth will I cry unto thee, when my heart is overwhelmed lead me to the rock that is higher than I. For thou hast been a shelter for me, and a strong tower from the enemy …
PSALM 61:2 and 3 – THE HOLY BIBLE

∴∿

As the sun rose after a long night of weeping, the drums once again began to beat, mourning a young black girl, who had not yet had a chance to live out her life to its ultimate destiny of old age. Never would she run along a beach, splashing through the salty waves. No one would ever hear her lilting African voice as she sang, going about her day. Her lovely smile had been frozen in time. Her young body violated, torn, bruised and bloodied. She would never know the joy of first love. There would be no young man, asking for her hand in marriage and paying the 'lobola' bride price to her father. She would never bare children and leave a legacy of new life. She was dead. She was dead. She was dead. Her precious lifeless body had been placed in the ground and would turn to dust. Her soul would live on. Her indomitable spirit would rise and shine brilliantly and one day, her death would not have been in vain. One day, the hatred between races would end. There would be laughter. There would be joy. There was "hope" for a brighter tomorrow, when man's inhumanity to man would cease…

∾

…Nonqaba, Nonqaba, the drums beat out your name. Your name is whispered on the wind. Nonqaba you will not be forgotten. Rest peacefully young maiden. Nonqaba, Nonqaba, we loved you so much. Death seems so final for those left behind for they cannot bring you back to life, only remember you into eternity.

For six days, the drums beat relentlessly and there was a strange emptiness and hollowness to life. For six days unseasonable, wild storms lashed the coastline from Cape Agulhas to Cape Saint Blaize but nowhere else beyond either of these coastal points. There was thunder. There was lightning. There was rain. Everyone felt tense and uneasy. No one wanted to venture outside, preferring instead to remain indoors. There were power failures and candles were lit, along with oil lamps during the hours of darkness, lending an eeriness to everything. And the wind howled…

Abruptly, after the six days, a brilliant sun broke through the pall and the gloom. The wind ceased its howling along with the beating drums and around the fresh grave which was Nonqaba's, tiny wild flowers had sprung up overnight; it seemed, paying homage to a young maiden... Sitting next to the grave was a young white lamb. Nonqaba had befriended this little creature and the lamb used to follow her everywhere when she was outdoors. Every time the lamb was led away from the grave, she kept on returning, until one day – she disappeared... The Africans say to this day, if you quietly sit near Nonqaba's grave, you will hear her voice singing on the breeze and you will hear too, a little lamb bleating for her mistress to return... and at sunset there is an amazing sense of serenity and peacefulness which will touch your heart.

... but for now, the nights seem too long and too dark and there appear to be no answers to the questions asked. The pain of loss too great to comprehend. In this beautiful, beautiful land of South Africa, how can there be such hideousness, such cruelty?

> *...air of night's darkness*
> *heavy with moisture*
> *day's night now cooled*
> *with the deluge of rain's tears*
> *on her pillow she sobbed*
> *all bloodied dust washed away*
> *leaves a clean ribbon of long road*
> *on the long walk to freedom*
> *for her tribe...*

:~

Justice was to be meted out to the policeman perpetrator. He was duly arrested, detained and then arraigned.

Weeks later, after his 'defence' had been prepared by skilled lawyers, he appeared in court to be charged. The courtroom was packed each day of his short trial. There was no jury, only a presiding High Court Judge.

After the Judge deliberated briefly, the policeman was found "not guilty of any crime for he was only doing his duty."

The young policeman's father was a well-known politician, very high up in government circles and brother of the Minister of Justice, who bought off the presiding Judge for a huge monetary price. There were gasps from those in the courtroom, followed by a huge uproar, when the spectators went into a frenzied raging storming of the room. Shots were fired right in the courtroom by the armed police escort and two black women were killed in the debacle. Outside, all hell erupted, with bottles being hurled at those in authority, as well as stones and anything else that could be thrown. Cars were upturned on the streets and set afire. The courtroom windows and doors were smashed. Reinforcements were hastily summoned – both police and army in an attempt to subdue the angry crowds. The riots continued late into the night. The angry protesters refused to back down and a State of Emergency was declared. It was a mob gone mad.

William and Richard Eugene, together with Ari Ben Jordan and Peter Robinson, had attended the court hearings and were there when the verdict was handed down. Robin van Zyl had been cautioned that if he attended, he would be arrested. William, Richard, Ari and Peter managed to slip out of a side door, before the angry crowds had reacted.

The policeman was ushered safely out of the courtroom and it was arranged that he would leave the troubled area immediately. He would be transferred to another district, hundreds of miles away. This guilty man did not even receive a rap on the knuckles.

As he climbed into his car outside of his house, which was well guarded at 9:00 pm that night, his driver suggested to him to lay down on the floor of the vehicle in case there were any incidents. He complied, not even glancing at the person driving the vehicle. Three hours beyond Cape Town, where the fiasco of a trial had taken place, the car drew to a halt. The driver got out and opened the back door to allow his passenger to climb into the front passenger seat. He also opened the boot of the car and out climbed someone else. The driver casually walked away into the night and a gun was pointed at the head of the policeman by the former occupant of the boot. The revolver had a silencer attached to the barrel. A single shot was fired.

Out of the darkness, loomed four people – all masked – all gloved. A sack was pulled over the policeman's head and he was strung up onto the stout branch of an acacia tree where the car was parked.

His body was discovered the following morning by a passing patrol car. His genitals had been severed and placed into the pockets of his trousers. Justice had been served in a most brutal fashion.

Robin van Zyl vowed that he would see to it, that those involved in the farce of a trial, would pay for their corruptness. He was angry and disgusted … (He had no involvement in the killing of the policeman– others had decided his fate)…

∿

The Judge who had presided at the trial, was found dead the following week. He had shot himself in the head. The police reports stated his death had been a suicide. Had the Judge committed suicide? Or had someone meted out his punishment? There was no suicide note, nor note of explanation. The Judge's fingerprints were not on the gun used. There were, in fact, no fingerprints in evidence on the weapon…

Security for all government officials and judiciary were tightened up. New security laws were immediately enacted and a state of tension reigned everywhere. Outdoor meetings for blacks were curtailed and a government ban was enforced. The apartheid regimé would swing like the pendulum of a clock, with a timebomb attached to it, waiting to explode…

… slowly and sombrely, "soi-disant" – life pretended to return to some semblance of normality at "Belle-France." Everyone had been tremendously affected by the brutal murder of the young African girl – Nonqaba. Being a black person in South Africa, was indeed hard, even at "Belle-France" where there was equality among all races. There was still the government instituted/instigated sense of division between those who were black and those who were white or those who were coloured or east Indian…

… apartheid, apartheid, rearing its ugly head. Two main cornerstones of apartheid had arrived with the passing of two laws. One – the "Population and Registration Act," second – the "Group Areas Act." The Government were now authorized officially, to classify **ALL** South Africans according to race. Tests to decide Black from Coloured, Coloured from White, resulted in many tragic instances, where members of the **SAME** family were 'classified' differently. It all depended on whether one child had a darker or lighter skintone. Totally absurd distinctions were made as to the size or thickness of a person's lips, or the amount of 'curl' or frizziness of their hair. People began to rebel, some used skin lightening creams, had their hair straightened and white sympathizers had their hair 'permed' into tight frizzy curls.

The Group Areas Act forced the ultimate indignity for the formation of residential apartheid. Each racial group *could* own land, occupy homes or premises **ONLY** in its **OWN** separate, designated-by-government area. The Group areas act forced the removal of peoples who had resided in areas for decades. When African or Coloured dominated villages, towns, communities were designated as "white" areas, blacks/coloureds were forced out violently and relocated elsewhere when nearby white landowners refused to have blacks or coloureds living near them or wanted their land. (Later, 'new' Bantustans would be created exclusively for the African population).

There were riots. There were protests, There were peaceful marches organized, which inevitably became violent when the Africans were shot at, with many innocent casualties ... Africa's blood would flow like a river in the months and years to come ...

The Eugene families all continued to resist this apartheid evil. Many of the family clan worked 'underground' in helping boycott what they knew to be so wrong. Many went in fear and they awaited reprisals from various government quarters. South Africa became a police state overnight.

People did not sleep peacefully ...

… the sun was blinding. The tangy smell of the salty sea, flowing under the mysterious cliffs at Arniston, sounding like ghostly music, coupled with the wind, as four young girls, Rowin, Mia Tansy, Nobukwe and Thokozile walked together. The endless miles of beaches between Arniston and Struisbaai, captured their footprints in the white sands, as all four attempted to find a degree of comfort in the crashing waves, white-crested seahorses jockeying for position, seemingly vying for attention… The girls usually walked or paddled in the water in silence, sometimes holding hands, sometimes with tears cascading down their cheeks for they ached for so much which was lost for evermore…

～

Rowin began to withdraw into herself as the weeks moved timelessly into months. On those days when she was alone on the beach in her solitude, she would run into the cool waters of the ocean, wishing with all of her heart those salty waters would cleanse her from the endless nightmare of that fateful night. Only the patience of her father and Hildy's constant vigil would comfort and eventually draw Rowin out of her maelstrom of sadness, misery and abject pain. Little Mia would often hold her hand when they slept fitfully and she cried many tears for her beloved, older sister. The two sisters shared a room for many months, too terrified to sleep alone…

～

… childhood was lost forever never to be recaptured, but womanhood would beckon to Rowin. There would be tinkling laughter again and hope would return anew for a brighter tomorrow for all of them…

CHAPTER FIVE

WOMANHOOD BECKONS
AND HOPE BECOMES REALITY

*... the long, hot days of an endless summer made for
a restlessness, a seeking for more fulfilment than the
oceans and white, sandy beaches offered. Her rebellious
nature demanded so much more ...*

Almost midnight. The headlights form the large land rover shone through the branches of the oak trees lining the driveway which led to the Eugene homestead. Rosemary and James O'Neill Eugene had collected along the way at Gordon's Bay, Noah Huddlestone and Elsie Eaton.

The O'Neill Eugene's lived way up on the slopes of Table Mountain, at Oranjezicht (a suburb of Cape Town). They had become great friends with Noah Huddlestone and Elsie Eaton.

Elsie's husband – Henry – had died in a riding accident two years previously. Noah's estranged wife – Mary – continued to live in the old house on Rouwkoop Avenue in Mowbray. (He had allowed her to move back, after her extra-marital affair had come to an end, but the two lived entirely separate lives). (After a few years living under the same roof as Mary, old Noah decided to move to Gordon's Bay and he and Elsie, struck up a romantic courtship and she eventually moved in with him, after selling her large home in Saint James).

Noah and Elsie were two of Fleur-Rowin's favourite people and though people 'talked' about the two setting up house together at Gordon's Bay – they were blissfully happy and their joy spilled over onto all who encountered them. They were so totally devoted to each other and a more delightfully romantic pair you would seldom find.

Noah had offered to divorce Mary, in order to 'make an honest woman' of Elsie, but she wouldn't hear of it, for she was way ahead of her time and quite content to let things be as they were. It would take at least two to four years for a divorce to be made final and the elderly pair felt time was of the essence for them. (It suited Mary Huddlestone too, she then would never have to make a commitment to the various men she was constantly involved with).

The four grandparents had decided to surprise young Rowin for it was her birthday the following day. The four would stay on until after New Year and join in all the festivities and celebrations of the Yuletide season. They were always welcomed warmly by the various family members and the 'clan' had grown over the years and there were many occasions for celebrating and always something going on to entertain any guests who might deign to arrive announced or unannounced.

William and Felicity were waiting up for their guests to arrive. It was a heatfilled, balmy night. Not even the hint of a breeze rustled the leaves on the vines and huge old oak trees. The only sound to disturb the quietness, was the constant noise of the cicadas and the laughter and shouts of the coloureds and Africans, who had small cottages along the north border of the farmstead. Delicious fresh boerewors cooking on their small open fires, tantalized one's tastebuds, for the workers and servants were partying late. It was December 13/1959 and all those who laboriously worked for the 'clan' received early Christmas "boxes" (rewards for their labours over the preceding months). There were toys for the children, staple foods for the adults, as well as a personal gift for each one and a monetary bonus. All was well, but the bitter winds of change had long been blowing.

∴∽

Tonight there was laughter and hope for a brighter future tomorrow, for all those fortunate to be under the care and protection and love of the Eugene, Robinson, Ben Jordan and van Zyl families.

∴∽

… A brilliant sun was rising along the distant mountains. The summer day promised to be yet another glorious one and the heat would intensify to over one hundred degrees Fahrenheit before noon.

∴∽

Homebaked fresh bread, together with the fragrant aroma of roasted

Kenyan coffee wafted through the air. Elsie had kissed Noah's cheek (he was reading the morning newspaper), and slipped a pale-blue terrycloth robe over her pyjamas. Wanting to be the first one to wish Rowin for her birthday, she tiptoed to her bedroom and quietly tapped on the door before opening it. Rowin did not stir – still fast asleep – her tousled hair spread over the white pillow, just the curl of a smile on her lips, her long dark lashes caressing her cheeks and a hand tucked beneath her chin. Elsie gazed down at the beautiful young girl. She looked so fragile, innocent and tender hearted. (Her peace filled countenance belied her impish naughtiness and stubbornness and loyalty). Many thoughts crossed Elsie's mind for she loved Rowin dearly. She said a silent prayer, asking that guardian angels surround and protect this very precious young girl and that the nightmares which still plagued Rowin would haunt her no more. Somehow, most of Elsie's prayers were usually answered, for her faith was great in her Abba-Father ...

~

Rowin stirred and stretched, yawned and opened her eyes, sensing there was someone in her room. Sleepily her face broke into a huge smile when she saw whom her visitor was. She sat up and held out her arms to Elsie and the pair hugged. Elsie looked at Rowin: "Rowin, I wanted to be the first one to wish you on your birthday and I succeeded. Oh, how wonderful it is to be sixteen. My, it takes me back to when I lived in England, so long, long ago. Well, my dearest girl, may this year be the most wonderful of year's for you." Elsie tiptoed out, leaving Rowin to her thoughts, after opening the curtains for her.

~

Rowin, as she lay in her bed, wondered what this next year ahead would bring. She had one year of home schooling left, before writing her senior certificate finals. Her cousins Jonathon, Jacob and the twins, Patrick and Noelle would be sitting their finals as well. All of them were tutored together, along with twelve of the coloured and African children, among them Nobukwe and Thokozile. Rowin and the two African girls had become inseparable since that fateful night years before, though Nobukwe was often withdrawn. They had often talked over plans and dreams for their futures. Rowin adored photography and had won several competitions on her wild life photographs. Her grandfather – James O'Neill Eugene – had encouraged her in her pursuits. He was himself, a brilliant photographer and also a world renowned safari guide. He often took Rowin along on his safari adventures and she, like him, had developed a loving respect for the wild animals of Africa. He had also taught her how to shoot both a rifle and a pistol and she was an expert shot and could outshoot all of her cousins.

William had spent hours with his two daughters, patiently teaching them how to paint in oils and watercolours. He also had a passion for classical music and he imbued this in his two girls, who adored Tchaikovsky, Mozart and Bach, though he himself preferred the more sombre Beethoven. Mia learned to play the piano very easily, but Rowin was too impatient and hated with a vengeance practising all the scales in order to master the technique of true classical piano playing.

William also taught the girls all he knew about viticulture. He had a dedication for creating wines of outstanding quality. The cool Atlantic and Indian ocean breezes, together with long hours of African sunshine, with sufficient rain and rolling, cooling mists, all contributed to the excellent quality of the grapes his vineyards produced, for the earth the vines grew in, proved to be excellent soil. His three sisters were all part of the success of the vineyards. Joanna and her husband Peter Robinson, still having no children of their own, called the 'vines' their offspring. Beth and Ari Ben Jordan were more than capably proficient in exporting the wines overseas. Their eldest son, Cain, had no interest in participating in the family viticulture interests and was a medical student at Cape Town University and he would later do a post-graduate course at Oxford, England, specializing in tropical medicines.

Richard, William's younger brother and his wife Patrice ran the retail and wholesale selling side of the winery, together with the small, intimate restaurant, with its beautiful ambience and décor, attached to their home at Struisbaai. The latter was a very popular venue and visitors, both local and from overseas, would drive miles and miles to experience the tasting of the wines, coupled with an amazing table of fare – all South African Cape cuisine. Bookings were made months in advance for seating at the restaurant which was named the African work "SIMUNYE."

The Eugene brothers – William and Richard – worked well as a team and with the Robinsons', the Ben Jordans' and Annable van Zyl (her husband Robin continuing in politics), made a formidable group, who were determined to continue to work toward the success of their venture. It had been an enormous undertaking.

∴

William knocked loudly on Rowin's door, together with Mia, they came in with a large tray.

Rowin absolutely loved to have breakfast served in bed and resplendent upon the tray, were hot scones, strawberry jam, clotted farm cream thick and golden, fresh baked bread with butter, crispy bacon rashers, grilled tomatoes, mushrooms and onions. Freshly squeezed orange juice, halves of passionfruit and a small pot of coffee. "Mmmmmm" : was the only comment Rowin could make, as her father and Mia wished her for her birthday. From behind her back, Mia produced a pale pink rose in a bud vase. The rose was called 'Fleur' and was one of the family favourites, picked that morning by Mia, especially for her sister. Mia did this each year on Rowin's day. William looked at the two girls chattering away. He noticed the sadness which still lingered in Rowin's eyes. Would she ever get over that dreadful night?

William had tried everything to encourage Rowin to move beyond the tragedy of losing her friend and the violation of the other girls. Noah had suggested that her old nanny from babyhood, Hildy Biko, come out from the Mowbray house to the homestead. Noah came out himself, to spend endless hours with his beloved granddaughter.

Hildy slept each night in Rowin's bedroom and little Mia had also been moved into her room, as she was terrified to be on her own. Hildy sang both girls to sleep, holding their hands tightly in her careworn black ones. The two girls were the children Hildy never had and she cared for them deeply. She also spent a great deal of time with her niece Nobukwe, comforting her as best she could. Some nights Rowin would ask that Nobukwe and Thokozile be allowed to sleep with them, for she feared for her two black friends. They seemed to have recovered somewhat, though Nobukwe would carry deep bitter anger and scars within her soul forever.

Felicity suffered from a nervous breakdown after the horror of that night and had been in a sanatorium for several months. This had been a respite in a way for Rowin, for the incessant beatings had ceased. When Felicity returned, she was a much calmer and kinder person to be around, but she was prone to angry outbursts at times, with no apparent reason.

Rowin learnt to simply keep out of her way. Granny Elsie stayed for long periods of time to keep an eye on Felicity and her girls. Rowin would talk to Elsie about everything and their relationship was one of absolute trust. There were no secrets between them. Between William, Noah, Elsie and Hildy, laughter began to be heard in the house, though it took many months for the spontaneity to return to this wonderful place, filled with love and sunshine…

:~

… William sighed. Today they would celebrate and give thanks for so much which was good and honest and true. When the 'clan' got together, nothing and no one could stop the happy moments from spilling over onto all who would be there. Being twelve years old had been tough on Rowin. Turning sixteen, her life would take on huge responsibilities from the choices she would make.

:~

The families made sure their workers, both in-home and in the fields, were well looked after. Everyone was part of the larger picture for the future and the loyalty, camaraderie and feeling of truly belonging, was incredible to witness. This continued to be 'kept under wraps' due to the harsh apartheid regimé in place. This made for extreme carefulness, when strangers were around. Everyone knew which side their bread was buttered and there was much at stake should loyalties be put to the test. There were always rumours abounding…

William and Richard had the same ideals: that all men are created equal, no one man better than another. This ideology of course, completely contradicted the government's National Party beliefs.

All of the children were taught from a very early age to respect others and one could only wish they indeed, lived in a perfect world. One could dream…

:~

Robin van Zyl was extremely instrumental in successfully protecting his wife's family members from the many questions asked by his political enemies in the stoic Nationalist Party government. He was a clever man, as well as having his Doctorate in South African and Roman-Dutch

Law. There were numerous occasions when he quietly, behind the scenes, managed to help many of the black leaders banned under the apartheid laws in South Africa, to escape the harsh injustices meted out in their attempts to seek freedom for their cause. He was a shrewd businessman and under the guise of the vineyards, moneys were smuggled out to aid the Africans who had fled their homeland when forced to flee for their very lives. He worked solidly, hand-in-glove with his brothers-in-law. There were many long nights when the midnight oil burned in secret, into the early hours of the dawn ...

∻

... Rowin had enjoyed her breakfast in bed and Mia had removed the tray returning this to the kitchen. Rowin, still in her striped cotton pyjamas, sat on the window seat in her bedroom – daydreaming. She stood up, stretching lazily and went to fetch a glass of lemonade. As she walked past her father's study, she overheard William talking to her Uncle Robin.

She had lingered, hoping to chat to her father about her birthday celebration – a braaivleis later that day. Unintentionally, Rowin had overheard her two African friends' names mentioned – Thokozile and Nobukwe. Some of the girls' close relatives who did not live at the "Belle-France" estate were to be moved to one of the new hated Bantustans, created by the Nationalist Government. The year was 1959 and eight separate, ethnic bantustans were now in place, a forerunner to the actual foundation for the 'grand apartheid scheme.' The passing by Parliament, of the Promotions of Bantu Self-Government Act was implemented. Around the same time, the Government introduced the very cleverly termed "Extension of University Education Act." This very effectively barred non-whites from "racially" open-universities. De Wet Nel – Minister of Bantu Administration and Development – informed

South Africans that every individual's welfare and every population group could best be served and developed within its own national community area. The races would, in all ways, including education, be entirely separate. He concluded, Africans could and would never be able to be integrated into a white community. Seventy percent of the population were black Africans and they were apportioned only 14% of the land in South Africa. The new policy now mandated, that even though two-thirds of Africans lived in so-called 'white neighbourhoods,' they could, by law, only have citizenship in their "own tribal homelands," Unfair? Unfair? Unfair? Absolutely. The Prime Minister was heard to remark: "The creation of the Bantustans would engender so much goodwill, they would never become breeding grounds for rebellion." Of course, 'twas quite the opposite, for the rural areas were in total chaos and utter turmoil and confusion. The ANC held its annual conference that December. In Durban, Natal Province, that city's extremely vocal and dynamic anti-pass demonstrations were taking place… All Africans now were forced to carry a Special Government issued Pass. (The Africans and their sympathizers termed this derogatorily: "dompas.") At *all* times, this pass had to be carried and shown to the authorities whenever it was demanded. The mood of the country was angry. No pass – no work – no money – no food…

William and Robin were extremely concerned for the safety of their workers at "Belle-France" and Robin would have his hands full in the days ahead to work miracles secretly, behind many Government officials backs, to pull many strings in high places to obtain passes for their people to remain in the area.

Rowin was shocked. Surely all people who were born South Africans had a right to live where they wanted to? Surely one could go to the university of one's choice, regardless of your skin colour?

∴

Rowin made up her mind to speak to her father at her first opportunity to catch him on his own. She had decided to fight for the rights of her friends. They were *all* South Africans. She knew a little about what was happening with this Nationalist government in power, but she wanted to know a great deal more. She was determined, on her sixteenth birthday, to fight for what she believed to be true, right and honourable. No one and nothing would deter her...

She had heard William say all the black pupils who were tutored with his daughter and her cousins, would not be allowed to write the senior national examinations. Rowin was shocked at this unfairness.

The black population were fighting for their very lives, their very existence. There were protests everywhere. Certain areas were inaccessible to the press and the government skilfully used this to their own advantage. Hundreds of innocent people vanished, disappeared, were jailed, banished, prosecuted, tortured, beaten, and murdered. The cruelty was abominable and much of it was cleverly concealed. One might term this as akin to nazi-ism at its very worst...

:~

Rowin would study and write her exams. She would attend Cape Town University if she obtained her Matric University Certificate and undercover, she would fight for the cause of freedom for all races in South Africa. Her father would be proud of her. She was only sixteen years old, but she had not forgotten that dreadful night when her young black friend had been raped and murdered and her other two friends Thokozile and Nobukwe had been so violated and raped in her own family home. Rowin was a feisty young woman who knew right from wrong and like the leopard, she would hunt in darkness and trap her prey in order to seek justice for the wrongs which were being committed in the name of the apartheid regimé of the Nationalist Party of South Africa...

She would celebrate this birthday with her sister, her cousins and her friends of all races and the rest of her family, but she had made a pact with herself. The Nationalist Party had made a pact with the devil. She had made hers with God...

All she had to do now, was to win over her father into allowing her to become involved in what he was already immersed in and which Felicity was not altogether happy about. Yes, the years into the future would be dangerous ones. Rowin would never falter in her beliefs and would always give of her best, sometimes to her detriment. She most certainly was no ostrich with its head buried in the sand, pretending not to see what it did not want to see.

Hope.

Strength.

Laughter.

One step to begin the journey of a million dreams under African skies. Woodsmoke on an open fire. Lion on a savannah plain. Drums beating to the pulsing of one's heart. Waves crashing where two oceans meet. Rowin was indeed a child of Africa...

∿

Rowin longed to hear the laughter of the tribe...

∿

... They had all passed with flying colours and were awarded their Senior Certificates. Matric university pass with honours and distinction for Rowin and her cousin Jonathon. Wonder of wonders, their young friends Thokozile and Nobukwe were allowed to write their examinations after all. The two African girls had done very well and their was much jubilation in the new year of 1961.

... Grandparents – James and Rosemary were taking Rowin on

holiday with them to Paris, France, as their congratulatory gift to honour her achievement. They had wanted to have Thokozile accompany them, but the South African government refused to issue a passport for her to travel overseas. The girls were terribly disappointed. The O'Neill Eugenes' then attempted to apply for a passport for Nobukwe and to the excitement of all, this had been granted. There had been no explanation as to why Thokozile's application had been denied. (Could it have been due to her father and mother having strong ties to the banned African National Congress?) Thokozile's application to study further at the university of Grahamstown had also been refused and she was devastated. So much unfairness. She was however, after much negotiating by William, through his brother-in-law – Robin – granted permission to work towards her degree in South African History by correspondence. This would have to be done through the University of Stellenbosch and had to be done in the Afrikaans language, which was NOT one of Thokozile's home languages – these were Zulu and English. She was fluent in Afrikaans but it was yet another added bone of contention to make life more difficult for a black person. Nobukwe would be allowed to study at Fort Hare University College, between Fort Beaufort and Alice in the Ciskei region. This was the only residential centre of higher education for blacks in South Africa. All over, in Southern, Central and Eastern Africa, this place was a "light" for young Africans wanting to study. So many young black people desperately wanted to further their education and were prevented from doing so, as no adequate provision had been made for them.

Nobukwe was grateful, yet angry at the same time and she smouldered inside. Though she was Rowin's friend, she was secretly extremely jealous of her and her accomplishments. She had deep-seated resentment, built up over time that she – Nobukwe – was the underdog and that Rowin had been given everything she wanted. Even her own black people loved and adored Rowin. Jealousy was a very nasty encumbrance in Nobukwe's life which distorted much for her.

Even on the "terrible night," Nobukwe's own Aunt Hildy, had first gone to Rowin to tend and comfort her, when her own niece had fared far worse. Nobukwe felt 'she' was family and her aunt had gone to the white girl, putting Rowin's needs ahead of those of her niece.

Nobukwe refused to accept Rowin's passion for standing-up for the plight of the African. How could she be genuine? Rowin's skin was white. She was irritated when Rowin called her and Thokozile, her other sisters. They were black girls, how could they ever be sisters when they were not related?

In a strange way – they WERE almost related… Nobukwe's real father was a white man – Henry James Eaton – Rowin's step-grandfather. Henry had coerced and tricked one of the servant girls in his home, namely Nobukwe's mother, Iris, to sleep with him several times. This was against the law in South Africa. For a white person to have sexual relations with a black person was tantamount to treason. Henry had also blatantly cheated on his wife, Elsie. Elsie never knew what had transpired and when Iris had left their employment when she was eight months pregnant with Nobukwe, only Henry, Iris and Hildy Biko knew of the tawdry affair. Elsie had asked no questions, but had felt very sorry for Iris, who was only eighteen and had given her a box of baby clothes. Baby Nobukwe was born in December 1943, just a week before Rowin's birth.

Iris was Hildy's youngest sister and it was she who arranged for her to move in with relatives in the Arniston district. Without asking any questions, they took the young pregnant girl under their wing. They knew Nobukwe's father must have been a white man for she had green eyes and a very light, coffee coloured skin. Fate had a strange way of allowing the paths of Rowin to cross with Nobukwe's years later, when Rowin's father and his family had bought the "Belle-France" property…

:~

Nobukwe had always been curious as to her parentage, but her mother remained tight-lipped, fearing that if the truth came out, she would be imprisoned for having slept with a white man. Henry Eaton had also threatened Iris that if she ever revealed the truth, there would be dire consequences for her. Life was full of complications in Nobukwe's world, but she was a very determined young woman and she would dig up the past somehow to find out her mother's secret. Every family, black or white or in-between hid skeletons in their closets... Henry Eaton had provided for his illegitimate daughter and every six months, cash had arrived in a brown envelope, delivered by courier to Iris. He had done this for years, for although he was known to be a mean, egotistical and self-seeking man, he did have a conscience. He never sought out Iris or his daughter, but every time he looked at his step-grandchild Rowin, she reminded him in some strange way, the he had a young daughter the same age and he took his anger out on Rowin at every opportunity when she was little.

:~

... Hildy had decided to spend a short vacation with her sister Iris, in Arniston. Iris had developed a nasty, persistent cough and Hildy felt she had not been looking after herself and she made an appointment with a specialist in Bredasdorp for her sister. The bus journey seemed never ending on this boiling hot summer day, as the two women set off together. Hildy was shocked when she saw her sister. Nobukwe had written to her aunt, fearing her mother was gravely ill. She had been right. Iris had developed tuberculosis and would have to be moved to the Infectious Diseases Hospital on Somerset Road in Cape Town immediately. Arrangements were made to transport her by ambulance that very day. Nobukwe and Hildy were also tested for tuberculosis and were 'clear.' It was all so very worrying for Nobukwe, left to close up her mother's small one-roomed cottage. She had been told her mother was in the final stages of the disease and would never return to Arniston. Nobukwe's mother was dying.

Rowin offered to help Nobukwe sort out Iris's tiny home. She was turned down flat by Nobukwe. Rowin was very taken aback at Nobukwe's surly attitude and put this down to her friend's distress over her mother's terminal illness.

Nobukwe decided in the circumstances not to go on vacation to France with Rowin and her grandparents. She wanted and needed to be within reach for her mother. Nobukwe was devastated at the terrible news and wanted desperately to find her father …

∴~

Baby clothes, a rattle, a glass perfume bottle … Nobukwe sat on the floor of her mother's home reading a letter from a box of old photographs and letters, receipts, cards and odds and ends. She had gone through everything belonging to Iris. She sat with tears running down her young cheeks. Her mother's funeral had been held two days prior to this day of heartbreak for her daughter. Her mother had so very few possessions and it had not taken Nobukwe long to sort and pack everything. Iris had only lasted two weeks at the Hospital and had died peacefully in her sleep. Her body had been cremated due to the tuberculosis and her ashes brought back to Arniston by her daughter and Hildy Biko.

The funeral service was attended by only a handful of family. Nobukwe refused to allow anyone from "Belle-France" to attend and this had puzzled Rowin but she asked no questions. Hildy could not understand her niece's decision either and questioned the girl at length, for the Eugenes' had all been so good to her family. Hildy received no answers to her request for an explanation.

∽

… Nobukwe's young body rocked back and forth as she wept for her mother. She was sick at heart for she had discovered that Henry James Eaton was her father – a white man – Rowin's step-grandfather, father of Felicity … Rowin's stepmother was young Nobukwe's half-sister. Her mind could hardly comprehend the news. She would never meet her father, for he had died in a riding accident. Her mother had accepted money from this man for years. Nobukwe had always wondered why her mother never went to work or why she always seemed so very sad and distant. Nobukwe's distress turned to violent rage and anger. She began to throw all of her mother's possessions around the room, smashing and breaking whatever she could lay her hands on and then she crumpled into a heap on the stone floor, sobbing and repeatedly banging her head against her mother's chair. All she could do was scream out her rage and pain against what she had suffered as a child of twelve and what her mother must have suffered as well… All at the hand's of white men. "Bastards, bastards," she lamented. "Isigwebo, isigwebo, bulala, bulala. Ngedukile. Ngedukile. Kuphuke ingilazi…" (Judgement, judgement, kill, kill. I have lost my way. The glass is broken…)

Nobukwe was hysterical, beside herself, as she wailed her anguish and this is how Hildy Biko found her…

∽

Hildy held the young girl and cried with her. She had known of Iris' heartbreak and how Henry had used her for his own pleasure and lust. What could she say to this girl, her niece?

"Nobukwe, dry your tears. You must continue to keep your mother's secret for her. Nothing can be gained by telling the world. Your mother carried her shame to her grave and you must do the same, please in the name of your dead mother, Nobukwe do this ..."

Nobukwe pulled away from her aunt and said angrily: "I will never forgive those who have violated my family. I will seek my revenge. Wait and see what I will do. I look at Rowin, who says she is my sister and my friend and I hate her. She has everything and we, we black people, what do we have? The crumbs off the white man's table and then they use us. They pretend to help us and say we are all equal, but we are not. We are black and the colour of our skin dictates what our lives will be, not whom we are as people, or how brilliant or clever we are, or how kind or beautiful we may be. The whites want what is rightfully ours. I don't care whether they are born here – they are the interlopers Auntie Hildy."

Hildy took Nobukwe's hands in hers and looked deeply into her niece's green eyes: "Nobukwe, Nobukwe, there are many, many good white people who are helping us. One day, this terrible scourge of apartheid will be over. Rowin is a good person and sincere in all she does and she cares about you and Thokozile. Don't turn against her and her family. They are the ones who are helping us at great peril to themselves. Not all white people hate us blacks and not all blacks hate the whites. You must learn compassion in this great land of South Africa. The scales will balance everything one day. Our race are a patient people. All will happen in God's good time, not ours. Pray to Him for guidance and our answers as to what you must do in life. He will grant you peace and a better understanding of why certain things happen. The black person's load is heavy but we are a proud people. We must and will hold our heads up high. You must believe this or you will become bitter and there will be no peace, no happiness for you my child. I know of what I speak. Why do you not change your mind and go with Rowin to Paris? This is a wonderful chance for you to make things right with Rowin, for she has done you no wrong and she does not deserve your anger and hatred ..."

"Auntie – stop! *I* am my mother's shame. *I* am Africa's shame. *I* am the bastard child of a black woman and a white man. Someone WILL pay for what has been done to this Biko family. Yes, someone will be held accountable... I wish to be pure AFRICAN and I can never be that. I am tainted, soiled..."

Hildy shook her head and wrung her hands. She trembled from head to toe, witness to the terrible pain her niece suffered. Nobukwe refused to be comforted and then she said to her aunt: "Yes, I will go to France! I will use every opportunity to get as much out of these whites as I can. Rowin can be my friend and I will pretend to be hers. She's so caught up in all her fine ideals and causes, she'll never suspect for a moment, how I truly feel about her, her family, and the goddamn Afrikaners and their Nationalist government and this filthy apartheid regime. Don't worry Auntie, I'll be fine, but my day will come to avenge all the wrongs we have suffered, endured and lived with. There will be retribution and my revenge will be so sweet."

∴

April in Paris was a beautiful experience. Rowin and Nobukwe did everything together, laughing and enjoying every moment of the two weeks they were away. On the surface it seemed a lasting friendship would endure everything to come... which way would the worm turn and which way would the pendulum swing?

CHAPTER SIX

FIGHTING FOR JUSTICE AND FREEDOM

... when we hear the laughter and the sadness of the Tribes leaves our land forever, we will know our fight is won. Oh let there be laughter soon, let us not lose hope and dear God give us all the strength we need ...

… under punishing, overwhelming heat of Africa's Kalahari Desert, the still blazing mid-afternoon sun poured a coppery sheen over the arid, reddish sands and scrubland vegetation.

Tiny ants crawled along the sand, searching for a cooler spot to build yet another anthill. Three large vultures circled, looking for the pickings from any carcass, discarded by the lions which had prowled the area earlier, after feasting off their zebra kill. The lion pride lay in the shade of a huge baobab which looked like an upturned tree with its roots sticking in the air. The tree was about a quarter of a mile away from the small lake and waterholes, where the other animals were drinking or sleeping alongside the banks where it was cooler and vegetation lush. Flamingo, in a curtain of flapping pink wings and long dangling legs – an enormous flock – scattered suddenly into the still air, leaving the waters of the small lake and mudpools. Their feeding had been disturbed by a herd of elephant with their calves (about forty-three in total). As the pink flock took to the hazy-blue skies en-masse, the first bull-elephants arrived, followed by the cows and little ones. It was all a most fantastic sight, absolutely magnificent and a wild-life photographer's dream…

Rowin had her long range telephoto camera with her, along with her father's old hunting rifle (she never shot anything but photographs and she was firm in her belief nothing should be killed for mere sport or avaricious greed and pleasure. She loathed animal trophy hunters with a passion. She was a trained markswoman and a crack shot and if necessary, in an emergency, certainly knew how to handle a weapon). No one ever trifled with her when it came to the business of shooting, for she could outshoot all of her cousins and her half-sister.

As Rowin watched the African tableau unfolding before her, photographing the scenes of the wild, she quietly nudged her companion, for her ears had picked up the sound of a small approaching aircraft. Her companion – a tall, rugged Australian from Alice Springs, nodded to her, he too had heard the small plane, a Cessna with false identification. Their long, tedious wait was almost over …

The waterholes and small lake were brimful at last. The long, seven year drought years had finally ended. It had taken a debilitating toll on both wildlife and vegetation. Water now flowed in abundance. The zebra, springbok, wildebeest and antelope were not disturbed by the loudly trumpeting pachyderms, though the noise they made was booming. All animals shared the waterholes, even the lion, cheetah and leopard, for without the precious commodity – water – the very existence and survival of the animals, large and small, would be threatened. Each animal knew its boundaries.

∻

The herd of elephant had trekked a long distance to reach the water. They could smell water from miles away, as camels do. They were thirst crazed, after eating amarula berries along the way. The berries were always such a temptation to these hugely magnificent creatures. They would rarely resist the pink coloured tiny fruit. Usually, when their greed got the better of them, they paid quite dearly for their indulgences, for after resting and sleeping, something the berries caused them to do, when they awoke they had excruciating headaches.

The trumpeting-roaring sounds of the elephant sounded sadly and painfully pathetic, for they had agonizing "hangovers," especially with the size of their huge heads. They rolled around on the ground groaning, rubbed their heads against any tree or rock boulder to alleviate the acute suffering. They seldom learned a lesson from their folly … Those delicious amarula berries were far too tempting.

As they plodded into the refreshing water – even though it was tepid from the heat of the sun – all would drink thirstily and deeply and the little ones needed no nudging into the pools by their elders. The little babies and youngsters frolicked happily like small children, pouring water and mud over their backs and each other. They used their young trunks in delirious abandonment, submerging themselves playfully. Their initial exhaustion completely forgotten. This was what bliss was all about if you were an elephant. Originally, there had been over three thousand of these magnificent pachyderms in the area. The herds had been decimated, initially by the Germans a hundred years ago and then by the South African hunters during the war of independence in the early nineteen hundreds, before South Africa became Unionized. There were approximately fifty to sixty elephant remaining, but the herd had grown to about six hundred over the intervening years. These elephants had become much 'leaner' than their predecessors and other African species, but they had far larger feet and could move faster and more swiftly. They also had long memories and they remembered what the human species had done to them. Subsequently, they were nervously aggressive, if they felt they were threatened. They were very watchful of their young and extremely protective, herding together should any emergency arise.

The elephants were often referred to as desert elephants, but they were more "desert adapted" and all tribal peoples respected them.

Rowin and her companion were down wind of them, in comparative safety and had no intention of disturbing the herd, for a marauding elephant was not to be trifled with. A screen of thick thornbush camouflaged them, as they sat in a small furrow between a kopje and eroded rocks and huge boulders. The boulders appeared to be almost arranged into an amphitheatre for viewing the tableau of Africa's wild creatures.

∶∾

A welcome whispering breeze disturbed the quiet stillness of the afternoon. Rowin felt restless as Christian Eastwood removed his suede-skin safari hat and mopped his brow, for the heat was intense (almost

114°F). He drank deeply from his water bottle, slung over one shoulder. Christian was a doctor, specializing in tropical medicines with a particular interest in malaria and in any newly appearing tropical diseases. He was also "a man on a mission" – sympathetic to the cause against apartheid. He personally, along with Rowin, supported CAAN (Congress Against Apartheid Now). (Caan/Cágn translated into the word "bushmen" – name of the bushmen peoples who live in the Kalahari Desert region, Namibia and Botswana. "San" was another word used for these small, compactly built bushmen). Christian was also a close friend of Rowin's cousin, Cain Ben Jordan and the two men had studied a post-graduate course together, on tropical medicine and diseases at Oxford University in England. They had also worked on a kibbutz in Israel for a year.

The two young men had become firm friends over the two-year course and their time on the kibbutz had been both illuminating and challenging. The latter had taught them much about bush-warfare and desert conditions. Cain had introduced Christian to Rowin and also to the ongoing fight against apartheid's cruel and merciless regimé, which many white people (along with the black population of South Africa), abhorred. The fight against apartheid had to be carried on underground, for the repercussions if caught, were imprisonment, torture and possibly the death sentence. People lived in fear, but the black population continued to hold their heads up proudly, though in forced subservience to an untenable regimé. Their spirit would not be broken by the yoke of oppression they were forced to wear.

The Nationalist government's ruling party had introduced apartheid in full-force when the nation voted in a Referendum to become independent from the British Commonwealth. The Union of South Africa, created in 1910, was now to be known as the Republic of South Africa, thanks mainly, to the extremely clever scheming machinations of Dr Hendrik Verwoerd and his Nationalist Party, consisting of mainly verkrampte Afrikaners. (No blacks were allowed to vote. They did not have the right to do so). There were far-reaching consequences with this apartheid regimé.

Rowin's uncle Robin was a member of the Nationalist Party, but he was one of the minority parliamentarians to be secretly AGAINST the apartheid system. He had to be extremely careful though, with what he said and what he did, or he would be ousted from his very powerful government position as Minister of Finance. Robin van Zyl was a clever and brilliant politician. He had his ways and means of aiding and abetting and helping; undercover, the black people who were so sorely oppressed. At times he was suspect but nothing could ever be proven against him, although one of his political enemies demanded Robin be placed under house arrest and resign his position. His enemies vowed they would see him hanged.

The Ninety Day Detention Act was implemented on May 1/1963 by a Nationalist government who enacted legislation designed to destroy in no small way, that which they deemed to be illegal organizations – namely those of a political or military or communist nature. There were at the time, extremely irresponsible acts of terrorism being committed by the organization POQO (poqo: Xhosa word for independent). (This group were not connected to the ANC). This Ninety Day Detention Law, the General Law Amendment Act; waived the right of habeas corpus and empowered ANY police officer to detain ANY person WITHOUT a warrant on grounds of SUSPICION of a political crime. Robin van Zyl's position in government became extremely dangerous for him. Nothing had to be proven against anyone. One could be detained/arrested under this guise. No legal trial was necessary, one could not have access to a lawyer. There was no protection against self-incrimination. No charges needed to by layed. The Ninety Day Detention declared Police Chief – John Vorster – could be extended until 'this side of eternity.'

With this unjust, brutal law, lives and livelihoods could be disrupted and South Africa was transformed overnight into a police state – a totally harsh, unbending dictatorship. Democracy? This did not exist. Nazism? This certainly…

Sanctions against South Africa would begin by other nations in the intervening years. South Africans, who were not Nationalist supporters were afraid to voice any political opinions or any opinions whatsoever against/about the stringent apartheid regimé for fear of recrimination. As Rowin admitted confidentially: "Pretend to be an ostrich and bury your head in the sand or like the three monkeys; hear no evil, see no evil, do no evil, instead quietly and secretly work for what is fair and just and right, if this is what you believe in. If you have a sincere conscience do not support this evil."

With the new laws and amendments in place, South Africa's police became so much harsher and more viciously savage in dealing with prisoners, especially political prisoners. They were treated abominably and routinely beaten, with reports of torture by electric shock, suffocation, sleep deprivation, hot/cold water torture and other bestial acts.

One LONE vote was cast in Parliament AGAINST the Ninety Day Detention Act, and this was by liberal Progressive Party representative – the brave – Helen Suzman.

~

In October of the previous year – 1962 – the African National Congress, held its first annual conference since 1959. The Organization was deemed illegal and banned in the Republic of South Africa. They met openly, in Lobatse, in Bechuanaland (Botswana). Also meeting at that time, though secretly, was CAAN… This group was supported by white South Africans wishing to work with the black underground organizations to rid their country of the dreaded apartheid regimé. (Whites who sympathized with the ANC, could not become members of this organization, banned like others). All of this information, Rowin and Cain had quietly shared with Christian Eastwood, around a campfire, six months previously, at her small beach cottage in Arniston.

They imparted more information as time went by. Christian had indicated he wanted to become a part of their fight for freedom.

Legal penalties increased and were ordered for anyone having membership in illegal organizations. The sentences could range from five years to the death penalty for as the Nationalist government termed it: "furthering the cause and aims" of communism or other banned organizations.

Many political prisoners were RE-detained with no charges laid and sent back to prison. All that was needed was the mere suspicion of something untoward politically against the government in power.

Rowin also shared much with Christian about the way of life and how it HAD to be lived in South Africa. Friend could turn against friend, neighbour against neighbour, especially if there were old unresolved grudges.

A white person could not be friends with a black person and vice-versa. You could not entertain a person in your home, if that person's skin colour was not "white" and yours was.

All blacks had to carry 'special passes' if they wanted to work in white areas, for there were separate areas for all races to live in.

Segregation. Segregation. Segregation ALL the way. Busses, trains, taxis, schools, universities, clinics. Separate entrances for whites and blacks in buildings, hospitals, parks, beaches. Job reservation for whites. Even in God's house: churches – the blacks had to sit at the back and some churches would not even allow black people to attend. Was there a separate entrance to heaven too? Would a white person become contaminated by associating with a black person?

Aha, but the blacks WERE in the homes of the white people. They were servants: the maids and the gardeners, the chauffeurs, the childrens' nannies (even wet nurses in some cases for feeding infants). But still not good enough to associate with whites? The blacks in menial service were grossly underpaid by the majority of white employers. They still had to pay the same prices for everything. Bread cost the same, as did milk and everything else, including medicines and bus fare. When people bled they bled the same colour of blood whatever their colour of skin might be. Those 'verkramptes' refused to hear any of this.

The Sabotage Act of June 1962 was also implemented. This allowed for the even more stringent House Arrests and bannings not subject to challenge through the Court Systems, restricting the liberties of citizens of the country to those in the most extreme of fascist dictatorships. Sabotage now carried a minimum penalty, without parole, of five years with a maximum penalty of DEATH by hanging. The actual wording of the Act was so broad, activities such as illegal possession of a weapon (and that meant any weapon of any description, even a pen-knife), or trespassing, COULD constitute an act of sabotage. No statement made by a banned person could be broadcast or reproduced in any way whatsoever. It became a criminal offence, punishable by up to two years in prison, to have in one's possession a 'banned publication' (even the innocent children's book "Black Beauty" was banned. If you had a copy, it was confiscated).

Rowin admitted to Christian she had a copy tucked away. The book amongst other items, was well hidden in a secret alcove at her Arniston cottage. There was a section of the wall inside her living room walk-in fireplace, where four bricks could be removed, a small lever turned, which looked like a flue-opener, to reveal a metal panel when pushed a certain way would move to the left, similar in fashion to a pocket-door, revealing a small room and tunnel. The tunnel led down to the cliffs near the beach and had been used on several occasions to get wanted "subversives" away from the police search parties.

~

… the hum of the plane was above them, now clearly visible, flying fairly low over the flattened plateau to their east. A flashing coded message was seen by Christian and Rowin and they flashed back their reply it was safe to come in for landing. There were no hidden patrols or disguised area wardens.

The couple left the protected screen of thorn bushes. Near another large baobab tree: loaded the cameras, supplies and rifles into a jeep and drove to where the plane had now landed. Rowin hardly waited for the jeep to come to a standstill before she agilely leaped over the low passenger side-door and ran toward the four young black men, their ages between twenty-two and thirty, as they deplaned.

Her tan veldskoene kicked up fine dust as she flew 'on wings' across the desert sands. Her powerful range binoculars swinging around her slender neck, in tandem with the lion tooth she wore on a leather thong. (The tooth was her good-luck talisman. Her paternal grandfather – James O'Neill Eugene had presented the talisman to Rowin at her christening. A bushman (cagn) tracker he knew from his old safari days had taken a liking to James and insisted he wear the tooth around his neck for good luck. The tooth had been a much prized possession, but when Rowin's mother had died when she was an infant, granddad James wanted her to have something African to 'change her luck.' He felt his little grandchild had suffered enough of a loss from too early an age. Having more than a "touch of the Blarney" and being very much a man of Africa, granddad James was very superstitious by nature. The lion tooth had been worn around his neck when he fought during the First World War in the trenches of France).

In typical spontaneous enthusiasm, Rowin flung her arms around each black man in turn. All four were very special to her. They had grown up with Rowin and her half-sister and all had been home schooled together.

The young mens' parents were all workers on the Estate, either in the homestead or on the lands and vineyards. The young men were like the brothers she and her sister never had.

Whatever the ruling Nationalist government had decreed, they all felt they were blood-relatives such was the closeness and bond Rowin's family had with their workers' families. Black or white, they were loyal to each other. All had the same excellent education and were well-versed in all academic subjects and fluent in four languages: English, Afrikaans (which were mandatory in all schools), Xhosa and Zulu.

The four men – Sithole, Umzimwe, Ukhozi and Temba – greeted Rowin and Christian warmly. For the men, it was good to be back home in Africa. They had been abroad in Sweden for over two long years, waiting and longing to return. South Africa's terra-firma felt good…

Each man had been given a designated area in four different black locations (townships): Mitchell's Plain, Nyanga, Langa and Kya-lishu. Each would live among trusted black families, sympathizers to their just cause of dismantling the apartheid regimé. The men would secretly train their people for an eventual uprising and revolt against the cruel, stifling inhumane government.

∴∿

Rowin and Christian had been working for some time through the underground networking system, along with other sympathetic whites, using their professions as a cover and guise: Rowin's as a wild life photographer and part-time safari guide and Christian's as a specialist in tropical medicine. (Rowin's initial involvement began from her first days at the University of Cape Town, when, as a rookie student, she joined a group of anti-apartheid sympathizers).

Thus far, their secret scheming and planning and disruption, together with the banned CAAN had worked successfully. This group, was the sixth group of trained black sympathizers and members Rowin and Christian brought back into South Africa. Many had fled the country when the unfair laws were put into legislation.

This time though, was far more personal for Rowin and her determination they not get caught was uppermost in her mind. They walked toward the jeep, clambered on board, returning to where the second jeep lay camouflaged under the baobab tree. Rowin realizing time was of the utmost importance, hastened everyone to get moving as quickly as possible. They cleared the area for any signs of themselves, to allay suspicion should a warden be on patrol and prepared for the long trek back to the Arniston region.

The plane had already turned around and taken off, dipping its wings in farewell. The Cessna was but a dot on the hazy horizon.

The plan was for them to split up in case they had been spotted or were stopped. At least, hopefully, one if not both vehicles and their passengers would reach their circuitous destinations.

Christian and Rowin were not new to this situation. They were well acquainted with the dangers and perils involved and the treachery from some of the so-called trusted contacts. They would travel under the cover of darkness most of the time. Umzimwe, Temba would go with Rowin in the first jeep and Sithole, and Ukhozi were to depart with Christian. There would be an hour wait between the departure of the vehicles. They would not be travelling together and were each taking slightly different routes down to Upington.

Christian's plan was to take the longer, safer route back via Cape Town and onto Port Beaufort. Rowin would by-pass the Western Cape area and head directly there…

As Rowin departed, she waved Christian goodbye, blowing him a kiss as well. Time to leave the hideout near the Kalahari-Gemsbok National Park border, close to Botswana, (formerly Bechuanaland). This had been an excellent place for the Cessna to make its drop-off target. There were many safari companies who flew visitors from overseas into this section. The Cessna would not seem out of place in all the air traffic coming and going.

Rowin worked her way down through Upington as the shadows lengthened and travelled right through the night. They passed Clanwilliam, Citrusdal, across the Middleberg Pass, with a short stop to refuel and eat at the small dorp of Bokfontein. Through the Gydo Pass, onto Ceres, Mitchell's Pass and Worcester, Robertson, Bonnievale and Swellendam. Finally to Port Beaufort at San Sebastian Bay near Cape Infanta. The four men would link up with the next underground members.

$\sim$

The journey took close to two and a half days. Both Rowin and Christian drove for as long as their stamina lasted. Precautionary measures had been implemented to ensure their safety and that of their precious passengers. It was incredibly dangerous for all involved. The tension could by felt by everyone. Rowin was exhausted and found herself longing for Christian's companionship. Her two passengers were weary beyond measure and slept for most of the journey, bumpy as this was, for jeep travelling was uncomfortable at the best of times.

The wait had been lengthy for Rowin and Christian at the meeting point. The intense African heat was debilitating. Even Christian, who was more than used to the Australian outback, conceded this trip at the height of summer was almost too much even for his amazing stamina.

Christian had grown fond of Rowin over months of working closely with her. Their relationship had not progressed beyond supporting the fight against apartheid, they had though, become close friends and confidantés. Whilst the endless wait for the plane and even in the intense heat Africa offered with little respite, had not prevented a 'stirring in

Christian's loins' for the lovely young woman he seemed to be spending more and more time with. They had sat shoulder to shoulder, hidden from sight in the bush. Christian was about to put his arms around Rowin and kiss her, wanting to test her reaction, when the sound of the Cessna had disrupted his amorous advances. Would she have responded to him?

Africa had something which made men behave irrationally. The pulsing, throbbing, vibrant, unspoiled and untamed beauty of the continent had a soporific and mesmerizing effect upon ones sensibilities. There was a wildness to everything, where one desperately wanted and needed to unleash pent up emotions and feelings.

They had watched a bull and a sow elephant mating near the waterholes, heard the beasts trumpeting, and then nudging each other almost tenderly when their animal copulation was done. It was a very moving and fascinating experience which they had observed together. An act – so natural – in the preservation of the species, yet it touched one's heart deeply. He noticed her neck and cheeks were blushing.

Thus far, Christian Eastwood had eluded the many young women who had attempted to ensnare him and claim him as their ultimate prize. Women were always drawn to him. He did not even need to seek out their company. He had a natural charm and charisma about him. He was also highly intelligent and well-spoken. He seemed vibrantly alive and he threw himself into anything he was passionate about or believed in. He was a brilliant doctor, wonderful son and a sincere friend.

He was very similar characterwise to Rowin's own father.

Women sought him out and when he walked into a room, all eyes turned in his direction. He was never boring, always attentive and caring, both to his patients and acquaintances.

Christian's parents were both from Bath, in the county of Somerset, England – also medical doctors. They had emigrated to Australia when Christian and his older sibling by eighteen months – Barabara – were nine and eleven. His parents were involved with the Flying Doctor Association, hence the eventual move, first to Cairns, Queensland and on to Alice Springs.

His accent was one of his most charming characteristics, a mixture of upper-crust British, with a defined Aussie twang to it. He was already beginning to pick up a little of a South African lilt as well, which made for rather interesting comments when people wondered where he was from. He was tall and both rugged and muscular, with dark curling hair, an aquiline nose and deep-blue eyes. He was quite the hirsute male.

… As Christian continued the journey down the last leg of the trek, he knew he would meet up with Rowin once again. They had pre-planned this meeting before departing the Botswana border. He found himself looking forward to this encounter eagerly.

The two of them would have five weeks of summer to spend in each other's company if they chose to do this. They were more than ready for this long overdue break from all things dangerous. He would again be renting the beautifully renovated cottage, which Rowin's family owned. The cottage was adjacent to Rowin's own one.

… Christian's first encounter with Rowin had been unintentional. He had arrived a day earlier than expected from a conference in Vancouver, Canada. He strolled down to the beach in the early morning, after the sea mist had disappeared. He spread his bright beach towel on the soft white sand and was reading from a medical journal – The Lancet – when a sea nymph, notably, Rowin had come dashing out of her back door, stark naked (the only suit she wore was her birthday one), and headed into the sea water. She had not seen Christian, a mere stone's throw away leaning against a sheltering rock.

The day was already becoming warm and promised to be sultry and humid. By noon hour, the sun would be beating down relentlessly. All so typical of an African summer day along the coast.

Rowin's spirited dash into the ocean had left the normally well-composed Christian: stunned. What a little sea nymph she was as she swam through the breaking, foaming surf, laughing delightedly to herself as she did so. She was so unabashedly free in her spontaneous joyfulness. She took Christian's breath away. Seawater glistened like crystal jewels on her deep-tanned body and the tendrils of her wet hair clung to her face and neck like fronds of delicate seaweed. She basked in the sunshine, a wild free spirit…

Rowin loved her nakedness and was never self-conscious of her beautifully formed vibrant young body. Her breasts were full and firm and her nipples brown from the sun. Each nipple extended at least half an inch and were hard and taut from the coolness of the refreshing sea water. (She would suckle her babies well when she gave birth to them).

Her belly was flat and her navel deeply indented, her hips were wide and flaring, perfect for childbearing. Rowin reminded Christian of a young klipspringer buck. She was not excessively tall, only five feet two inches, compared to his rangy six foot frame.

She had an energy about her which was pure and natural with no pretences to something she was not. One could feel her nervous energy and sense her inner, as yet, untouched sexuality.

In his mind, Christian thought of her as deliciously-delectably-delightful.

She had certainly 'turned him on sensually' as he felt the sudden rise of his manhood, contained safely by his Speedo swimming trunks. (He could not rid himself all day, of his half-erection. Like the Bushmen of the Kalahari, this appeared to be of a permanent nature. Three ice cold showers in the late afternoon finally alleviated his problem. He had not wanted to satisfy his desires himself).

:~

Their formal introduction came the next day, with an invitation from Rowin's cousin, Cain Ben Jordan – to a braaivleis at his parents' home at Struisbaai.

This was a large family gathering event, commonplace as the "clan" loved getting together and socializing. Invitations to these were much sought after and the hospitality and bonhomie was what everyone loved most about this family. The wine estate settings, both at Arniston and Struisbaai were breathtaking in their vista. The ancient Dutch gabled homes with their stark two foot wide white walls, kept the interiors of the homes cool to the heat from outside. All the many windows had large seating alcoves and in the winter, it had been Rowin's delight to sit and read in one of them, following the wintry sun as it moved around. The sash windows were open today, to catch whatever small breeze might waft across the grounds. Particularly beautiful in these homesteads, were the eighteen inch wide planked floors, in both emboya and yellow-wood, burnished over the centuries to glowing hues. All members of the family were in evidence today. Her father and stepmother were the last to arrive. William took an instant liking to Christian when they were introduced. Rowin and Christian too, had an instant rapport.

The lunchtime braaivleis lasted until after midnight. No one was in any great hurry to end the delightful day under the oak trees.

This evening was warm and balmy and time moved effortlessly towards the bewitching hour. The southern hemisphere stars twinkled in the evening heavens and the moon was full and golden. The evening sunset in its brilliance, had been hypnotically magnificent and all seemed well with the world, bathed in gold, copper and amber. Wine from the family vineyards flowed freely, as did the brandy, port and sherry. The braaied beef and boerwors delicious, accompanied by vetkoek, coal-baked local potatoes and varying salads. The aroma of home baked bread from the great kitchen ovens of the manor, tickled the senses and made one's mouth water, the churned butter melting into the crust and fine textured loaves. Dessert followed much later – traditional koeksisters and malva pudding and brandytart.

This was a noisy, jolly, happy gathering of the family clan and their friends at Cheetah Point House. Christian took his leave of the family just after midnight. Many of the family members would stay overnight, preferring not to take the long drive back to Cape Town, Gordon's Bay and Somerset West.

Christian was tired out but relaxed, with a contented aura of happiness surrounding him, as he climbed into the comfortable double-bed, back at the cottage at Arniston.

… Next morning, he whistled to himself as he showered and thought of Rowin Eugene. She had filled his dreams during the night and disturbed his sleep, making for a restless night.

∿

… The arduous drive continued with his two companions, Sithole and Ukhozi. Christian realized with a huge jolt and gut-wrenching sensation in his belly, he had fallen for a little, wild SouthAfrican maiden, named Rowin Eugene. "Oh my, is this what they talk about when they say: you'll know it when you fall in love …"

Once again he felt a familiar stirring in his loins. He fought the feeling. He almost desperately and urgently longed to hold Rowin in his arms. He wanted to possess her and to be possessed in turn by her. He wanted to make love to her slowly, deliciously, taking all night, then tenderly, until their passion grew with untamed wildness and exploded in climax. He wanted to suck her nipples, pulling them deeply into his mouth. He badly wanted to unleash all that was pent up within himself and her.

Christian recognized he had not merely fallen for Rowin's sexuality or her body, but the entire package which was Rowin. Her brightness, kindness, generosity, intelligence, her respect for others, sincerity and graciousness, her wonderful liveliness, and her passion for what she truly believed in, had beguiled him and left him in no doubt, he wanted to spend the rest of his life with this tantalizing, intriguing person. Her feistiness and wit intoxicated and amused him. There was nothing about her, he did not like.

He made the decision: he Christian wanted more of her and he would set out to have more.

… He muttered under his breath and struggled to concentrate on driving the jeep. Sithole enquired: "Chris man, what are you muttering about? Are you alright?" Chris replied: "Sithole, I think a certain woman has bewitched me with some sort of African spell." Sithole knew whom Christian was talking about: "Chris, be very careful if you make a move on Rowin. She has a very tender and innocent heart. Don't break her heart or you will have all of us to answer to." Christian nodded. Ukhozi chuckled and interjected: "Rowin is not to be trifled with. She's a deep one and should you push her to her limits and hurt her, she will turn from you and flee. You will never win her trust back and she will never return to you." Christian, hands clenched on the steering wheel of the jeep, nodded his head at the two black men and pondered upon their wise words. He would remember this conversation many, many times over the intervening years. He announced in a very serious voice: "Sithole and Ukhozi I am going to marry Rowin Eugene in September." Christian was ready to lay down his life for this wild, untamed little woman … He was eager to be with and to explore every inch of her persona …

Christian's need was great. Would Rowin assuage the aching in his heart and longing in his mind? Africa's emotional intensity had created feelings within Christian, which he had never experienced before and which he knew not how to deal with. His calm and rational thinking had deserted him. He would do anything and everything necessary to ensure Rowin would become his wife, be his partner in life forever, bare his children and always be his companion and friend.

Christian, not giving to praying often, said a prayer that day to the Almighty, with such earnestness, it shook him to the core. He refused to entertain the possibility she – Rowin – might turn him down. (He would be devastated if she did). Christian had fallen hook, line and sinker for a lovely little South African "**intombi**"... This love was love in all its purest simplicity, sensuality and tenderness. In the heat of the day, he shivered momentarily at the sincerity of his feelings...

CHAPTER SEVEN

CAPE AGULHAS WEDDING

... love is the very greatest gift of all for love is patient, love is kind, love does not worry, does not boast, love never fails and I will give to you faith, hope and love and the greatest of these is love ...

The September morning's early dew had evaporated quickly, knowing somehow, the urgency of the day required warming sunshine to prompt it into action. There was much to be done before earth's orb reached its zenith at noon.

This glorious late-winter-into-early-spring day was a wedding day. True to his vow, Christian Mark Eastwood was to wed Fleur-Rowin Elizabeth Eugene, the woman he had tumbled into love with. At precisely 1:00 pm on the wildly beautiful beach at Cape Agulhas, confluence place of two mighty oceans, the couple would pledge their love to one another.

The romantic setting, was fitting somehow, for in its unspoiled simplicity of the elements, love would unite as the oceans melded.

∴

Agulhas was where Christian had proposed marriage to Rowin (first asking her father for Rowin's hand). That late July winter's day, had been a wild and stormy one as the pair walked along the beach together, bundled up in fleecy hooded parkas. Holding hands, they paused to collect shells and broken tumbled coloured pieces of seaglass washed up on shore. They loved to walk in the rain on a stormy day. The waves were hugely gigantic and powerful, the sea a deep pewter-green. The wind whipped the tops of the waves and blew the spray horizontally whilst the foghorn at the Agulhas lighthouse boomed out, like a huge groaning hippopotamus in labour. Christian and Rowin leaned against the stone pillars marking where the oceans collided, attempting to find shelter as the storm had reached galeforce intensity. Rowin's scarf whipped across her face as she attempted to twist around her neck its fluttering, tasselated tendrils. Christian laughed as he caught the ends of her scarf, drawing her close to him. He bent down to kiss her rain streaked face, seeking her soft, moist lips. A surge of passion ignited the wild flame which sped through both of them, making them draw apart, breathless and shaking.

"Come on Rowin, let's head back and get warmed-up inside at the Agulhas Tea Room. Hot chocolate and fresh scones would be great." Rowin nodded her head in agreement and the pair dashed back to the Jeep. They were both feeling wet and chilled. The rain, by now, torrential. This was one of the worst storms of the winter, which had been comparatively mild.

Christian found a small round table in an alcove window and placed their order when the young waitron arrived. Soon, both he and Rowin had warmed up. As Christian watched Rowin slowly sip her hot chocolate, he was overwhelmed with the love he felt for her. She put the pottery mug onto the table and took his large hands in her small ones, rubbing them, "Christian, I love you to pieces. Let's go up to "Belle-France" and sit in front of the fire at dad and mom's. They've asked us to stay for supper. Do you want to do this?" Christian replied: "Great idea, but first, I have something for you." Out of his pocket, he pulled a beautiful chunk of aquamarine glass to add to Rowin's collection. As she took the proffered offering, under the glass lay a glittering diamond ring. Rowin gasped, "Christian, is this what I think it is?" He nodded, chuckling, grinning from ear to ear: "Rowin, I adore you. I love you. Will you marry me?" By now, everyone in the already full Tea Room were watching the couple. Rowin held out her hand and Christian placed his ring on her finger, as she replied: "Oh yes, oh yes, I'll marry you. Let's not wait too long. Christian, I am so honoured and so excited. I can't wait to tell dad and Mia and we'll have to call your parents too. I want to tell the entire world." She jumped up, spontaneously throwing her arms around Christian, to the cheers of the Tea Room patrons. The waitron produced a bottle of Grand Mousseaux Vin Doux and two crystal champagne flutes, popped the cork on the bubbly and the engaged pair toasted each other. More bottles were produced and everyone in the Tea Room sipped champagne and also drank to the couple. (Christian had engineered all of this).

On the short drive back to Arniston, Christian very seriously told Rowin he would like them to be married in early September. She was delighted with this idea, adding she would like them to be wed on the beach at Cape Agulhas. They would have only six weeks to plan everything but they were eager to be together as husband and wife.

Christian was finding it increasingly difficult to keep his hands off Rowin and Rowin knew in her heart of hearts if he persisted, she would give in, as her feelings for him threatened to overwhelm her, if they waited much longer. Rowin had made it very clear, she would only 'give herself' to the man she married. Christian loved and respected her for her convictions. Both were impatient by nature and when their passion exploded, it would be a tumultuous thing…

They had come together first, as colleagues and from this, their friendship grew and they were staunch allies in their fight for freedom against apartheid. Time for them, drifted into weeks and months and the long hot summer fueled their feelings. Christian had a soporific effect upon Rowin, from very early on in their relationship and she in turn, had a hypnotic effect upon him.

The year was 1967 – Rowin was almost twenty-four years old – very sure of what she wanted in life and even more sure of what she believed in. If there was such a metaphor as a 'kindred spirit,' Christian was indeed hers.

∾

The year had seen some dramatic changes in South Africa. The still-ruling Nationalist Party government implemented the "1968 Terrorism Act." This allowed the government unprecedented powers to arrest and detain anyone they felt was a threat to their apartheid machinations and harsh regimé, WITHOUT THE FAIRNESS OF A TRIAL. Anyone sympathizing with the fight against apartheid, lived looking over their shoulder waiting to be arrested and imprisoned. They were forced to conceal their feelings for fear of unjust reprisals. These were times of severe hardship and uncertainty, more so if your skin happened to be black.

The 'purity' of the Afrikaner race HAD to be preserved whatever the cost. NOT all Afrikaners believed in what their Nationalist Party preached and implemented. Many sided with the so-called dissidents and subversives and they attempted to do what their consciences dictated.

The Eugene family continued to stand by their ideals, refusing to be intimidated by the constant threats. Thus far, no one from their lands and estate had been arrested, charged or forced to relocate elsewhere. Everyone was uneasy.

Robin had much to do with their family being so protected. He had been shot at twice by his enemies who hated him and was lucky to have escaped unharmed. His position in government was a powerful one but his enemies were many.

His twin daughters – Catriona and Claire had been sent to live in England with their paternal grandparents, after an attempted kidnapping at the school they attended. The girls were left shaken and their mother, Annabel was vehement: the girls had to have a safe refuge elsewhere. The family had no intention of ever becoming tergiversate.

Along with their grandparents, they worked to the good of the oppressed from afar, and were often go-betweens for those Africans forced to flee South Africa, when hunted like jackals. Robin's mother was a genteel Englishwoman and she willingly gave shelter to her granddaughters.

∵

Rowin had written to her two cousins, asking them to be two of her bridesmaids and they had arrived a week before the wedding. This was their first visit back to South Africa.

Mia was Rowin's chief-bridesmaid and their cousins were the bridal attendants – Catriona, Claire, Ruth and Noelle. Christian's sister was Rowin's matron-of-honour and her three year old daughter – Briony – the only flower girl.

Christian's attendants were Rowin's boy cousins – Cain, his best man, with Jacob, Jonathon and Patrick his groomsmen. His brother-in-law from Australia – Gregory Thompson would act as the Master of Ceremonies.

Christian's parents had arrived from Australia two weeks before the wedding. They were staying with family friends in Llandudno, a picturesque beach suburb situated on the Atlantic seaboard side of the Cape Peninsula, not far from Hout Bay and the magnificent Cape Point Nature Reserve area. (Cape Town and her surrounding suburbs, boasted of some spectacularly beautiful spots, breathtaking in their magnificence).

This jubilant occasion for all of the families, would be a complete "gathering of the clans"…

The wedding would be attended by not only family, but friends of ALL races. The Eugenes' would notably, be contravening the law, in allowing, as guests, blacks, whites and coloureds to be at the same venue, without government permission. This would have been categorically refused.

William and his family fully expected the authorities (police), to arrive in full force and divisively put a stop to the "mixed gathering" enjoying the celebratory festivities…

…Apartheid's regimé managed to worm its way into everything…

∾

The gardens at "Belle-France" looked wonderful. It was an early spring and many of the daffodils and arum (calla) lilies were already in bloom.

The wedding reception would be sumptuous. Felicity had done much of the organizing, excelling herself. It would be held in an enormous white marquee-tent under the ancient oak trees. A large canopy led from the tent to the entrance of the manor house, allowing guests to spill over into the house. William and Felicity had held their own wedding reception at "Belle-France," before William had acquired the grand house and renovated it. (The house no longer boasted the huge reception hall which they had used. This had now become a very large reception lounge, with an adjoining comfortable family room. Extra guest bedrooms with en-suite bathrooms had also been added, making the home far more practical for different social occasions The old house still boasted of its original history and charm).

All the rooms in the house were a hive of activity. The happy excitement could be felt by anyone entering through the many doors. More floral arrangements had arrived and half a dozen telegrams had been delivered. The local coloured band had set up their electronic equipment in the marquee and tasted some of the wine whilst doing so.

Felicity had wrapped up a special gift for Rowin and would give this to her after the ceremony. She had been very gracious toward her step-daughter and thrown herself into organizing an affair to remember. She was very good at this and always an excellent hostess. (One occasionally, still managed to catch a glimpse of a mean streak she had within her: the gift was a perfect example of this. Rowin's day might be marred by Felicity's act…)

∾

The twin-dolphin ice sculptures were delivered and moved into the walk-in freezer, ready to be placed in the marquee later. Champagne was on ice. The crayfish thermidor perfection personified. Filet mignons were ready to be cooked, the sherry-brandy trifles decorated with glacé cherries, toasted almonds and whipped cream. The wedding cake was a four-tiered chocolate confection, butter-icing with van der Hum South African liqueur added to it. Christian did not care for traditional fruitcake and the chocolate cake was a compromise, which was exquisite to the tastebuds. There were numerous other wonderful dishes, many traditional South African recipes and the "SIMUNYE" restaurant had done much of the catering, under the supervision of Rowin's Aunt Patrice Eugene.

… Mia's boyfriend – Sven Bjornsen was at the front door of "Belle-France" – delivering a card for Rowin from Christian, together with a shoebox from Aunt Joanna.

Mia took both through to her sister. Inside the box were the most exquisite French lace, handcrafted wedding shoes from Paris. These had been ordered by Joanna for her niece, and subsequently held up for weeks at Customs. The late arrival of the shoes gained an exclamation of sheer delight from Rowin, thrilled to try them on. A perfect fit. (Joanna always loved to buy shoes for her nieces). The back-up pair of shoes could now be given to Nobukwe. She had lost hers somewhere along the way over to "Belle-France" and as she and Rowin wore the same size, a small disaster had been averted…

Nobukwe's outfit matched that of the bridesmaids, but had a short bell-shaped skirt. She would read passages from the books of Corinthians at the wedding ceremony. Nobukwe was happier than she had been in a very long time. She was engaged to Temba, who resided in Lobatse, Botswana. He was a wanted man in South Africa and dared not cross the border to be at his friends' wedding.

Nobukwe, together with Thokozile, had shared Mia's bedroom the night before and the three of them spent most of the night chattering away about old times. Thokozile was singing two solo pieces during the nuptials. She had married Martin Sithole two years previously and she was heavily pregnant with their first child.

She and her husband shared their very tiny house with Temba and she had driven down with friends to be at this wedding. Temba and Sithole were both banned men in South Africa, wanted for subversive activities. Robin van Zyl had been instrumental in gaining them safe passage across the border, first into Namibia and then into Botswana from there. Thokozile and Sithole had asked Rowin and Christian to be their baby's godparents and they felt honoured at the warm, sincere request.

Nobukwe still carried much bitterness and hatred within herself, much of which she successfully managed to hide from those close to her, but her Aunt Hildy knew her too well – she could hide very little from her…

Today, Nobukwe envied her friend. Her own wedding in April would be a very small, quiet affair with celebrations kept to a minimum. She and Temba could not afford to raise any suspicion from the authorities in Botswana or at the border crossing. She would be entering Botswana illegally and would have to reside in Lobatse for six months before being allowed to marry. There always seemed to be so much red-tape preventing one's happiness. Christian and Rowin would be at Nobukwe and Temba's wedding, even if this meant pulling strings to obtains visitors' visas.

Mia took the extra shoes to Nobukwe and she rather abruptly took them from her, feeling they were cast-offs from Rowin, even though they were brand new and never worn. Mia gave Nobukwe a strange look and asked if there was anything wrong. Nobukwe tossed her head, answering: "Should there be?" Mia shrugged her shoulders and Thokozile looked uncomfortable. There was no accounting in their minds for Nobukwe's rudeness and short temper…

∼

Mia went outside to join Sven. The two of them stole away for a few passionate kisses behind the marquee tent. Mia Tansy would not be too far behind her sister, in getting married herself even though she was a lot younger…

∼

Rowin held Christian's card in her hands. He had made the large card himself. He was a talented artist and had painted her a watercolour of the beach at Cape Agulhas. He had depicted Rowin walking along the beach collecting shells, her hair blowing in the wind, with the short skirt of her summer dress billowing… This was a truly lovely painting and captured Rowin's free spirit amazingly.

The words inside were beautiful.

Everyone had warned Rowin and Christian not to hold an outdoor wedding in September, as the weather that time of year was usually very unsettled and quite cool, but the gods were on their side and the day's temperature was a comfortable 70°F with only the merest whisper of a breeze. The couple had set their heart upon marrying on the beach and their dream was about to become a reality…

∴∽

Old Hildy had slept in Rowin's room on the chaise-longue and was the first one to greet the bride-to-be who had slept really well. The two had decided to have a small bottle of champagne before retiring for the night and the bubbly had done its trick. (They had followed the bubbly with glasses of chilled gingerbeer – an old cure-all for a possible hangover). Oh, how they had giggled…

It was just on 7:00 am and Rowin was sitting in the window seat sipping fresh-brewed Kenyan coffee, when there was a tap on her door. Mia Tansy walked in with a letter on a silver tray for Rowin. Together with the letter, was Mia's traditional gift to her big sister – a pale pink rose in a crystal bud base – the 'Fleur' rose. Each girl in the family, including their cousins, had roses named for them and all were registered with the Royal Rose Society. Rowin's wedding bouquet would be her 'named' roses, intertwined with fleur-de-lis, lily-of-the-valley and baby's breath. (Her mother Elizabeth's flowers had been lily-of-the-valley).

Rowin picked up the envelope, wondering whether Christian had sent another card and then noticed her father's handwriting. She smiled quietly to herself and thought: "… dear daddy. How thoughtful you are and how much I truly love you. I know this will be a very emotional day for you, for we've been through so much together and yes, you will always, always be my darling Daddy-love…" and tears came to her eyes and cascaded down her cheeks. This day, Rowin could cry, for these tears were tears of happiness and cherished memories.

She tore open the envelope and began to read William's special words and inside the pages, she found a silver chain, with a heart-shaped silver locket containing two tiny photographs of her mother which she had never seen before: one of her mother as a baby and one on the day of her engagement. Old Noah had given the locket to William to be presented to her on her wedding day, with a tiny note from him as well:

My dearest granddaughter –

You have been like a ray of ongoing sunshine in my life, just as your own mother was.

I know she would have wanted you to have this. I gave the locket and chain to her on the day she was born. It had belonged to my own mother – your great-grandmother who lived in Barrow-in-Furnace, England. Cherish this always.

Please don't forget your old granddad, now that you have a new man in your life.

Love always my child…

Grandfather Noah

Rowin held the locket and chain in her hands for a long moment and it seemed to her, that her mother, whom she had never known, was with her. Rowin felt suddenly, very lost and very sad. Mia and Hildy walked over to her and held her between them in their arms.

Rowin asked them to allow her to be alone for a little while, as she wanted to read her father's letter in private. She drew 'her' rose to her lips and kissed the petals, whispering: "Mummy, please be with me on this, my wedding day, and tonight I will look up at your stars – the Southern Cross – and I'll know you are there. I love Christian with all my heart Mummy, just as you loved my Daddy. Oh Mum, I'm really quite scared and I have a tummy which is doing butterfly somersaults right now…"

∶∼

September 15/1967 –

Dear daughter – Rowin –

You have been the most beloved of daughters and you are my first-born and this is your wedding day. I cannot believe this day has finally dawned. The day when I shall give my girl away to the man she loves. Deep down, a father always thinks HE will be the only man his daughter will ever truly love, but then reality insists that a father awakens from his daydreaming for his daughter has to leave and seek her own destiny.

Today, I give you my blessing as you say your vows together – you and Christian – on the beautiful beach at Cape Agulhas. What a truly beautiful place you have chosen. Rowin you are indeed "a child of where two oceans meet" and I, along with you, know we have the faith that your day will be filled with sunshine.

Before I lose you today dear girl to this man from downunder, I wanted and needed to write this letter to you, so forgive a South African father's soft heart…

I truly believe that your mother – Elizabeth – would

have said the same words to you I am about to do. She is with us today you know. You are so like her Rowin that at times I almost catch my breath and I am transported back to my days with her, which were painfully too few. I do of course, have Felicity now and without her, we would not have had your sister – Mia Tansy – whom I know you are so close to. God has a strange way of working out our destinies doesn't He? Rowin, daughter of my heart:

FEEL with your bare feet – sandals cast aside – white sand on infinite beaches

FEEL the rain and seaspray upon your face and weather the tumult and storms of life

FEEL the neverending surge of the tides as waves rush to find their secret retreat amongst tidal pools where limpets and tiny crabs and tiddlers hold court

FEEL the sandgrasses waving in the summer holding the sands captive with their tendril roots

FEEL your laughter rustle leaves on baobabs shadows casting cool respite from the blazing sun at noon when the heat of the safari is unbearable

FEEL a tandem symphony as you shelter on leeward side of rolling monstrous sand dunes

FEEL the haunting call of the gulls as they slowly soar heavenward where no eagles fly

FEEL the Golden Glory of an African sunset when the air is patiently still for twilight dispels the anger and wrath of the land and its

toilweary people
FEEL your love and never let this diminish
when time and pain mock that which is true
and wise
FEEL your spirit and fly free always to believe
what you cherish and your soul's conscience
tells you is real
FEEL the pulsing rhythm and emotion of
Africa as it throbs through your veins for it is
the very fibre of your whole existence
FEEL your dreams come alive, and believe
there will be laughter in the Tribe and gather
strength to fight the fight which must be fought
for freedom and what you believe in
FEEL your babyhood, into childhood, into
womanhood and God-willing – motherhood
FEEL the deep joy and love of the Tribe for
we are all one (SIMUNYE) under God's sun,
moon and stars of the Southern Cross
FEEL the love of this man – your father and
KNOW the love of your husband for all
time…
Rowin, I have loosened the reins so you may
gallop FREE – free to be – knowing girlie, that
there is always a special place for you not only
in our home but in my heart always.
God bless you and keep you safe
Beloved daughter, my child of Africa – I love you –

Your father – William

:~

… a sob caught in the back of Rowin's throat and she re-read her father's letter. She drew great comfort from his words but there was a deep ache inside of her soul. Her first love was Africa. Would the men in her life understand this? She tossed her head midst the tears and sobs and laughed. This was, after all her wedding day and she was absolutely sure she knew what she wanted and had the confidence of the young, to truly believe in the future she was about to embark upon with Christian Mark Eastwood.

:~

There was a tap on her bedroom door. All her bridesmaids had arrived, together with the two hairdressers who had been chauffeured through to Arniston from Gordon's Bay and suddenly everything was a hive of great activity with the excitement building by the second.

:~

The bouquets had now arrived and the house and the huge marquee tent were beautifully decorated in white with touches of primrose yellow here and there.

The bridesmaids and flowergirl were wearing soft gowns of white organza with underskirts and petticoats of buttercup yellow with the same buttercup shade for the sashes of their highwaisted full-length billowing gowns. Rowin's gown was of a similar style, but more bell-shaped with a flowing train and gossamer veil. When she was dressed, she looked radiant and when her father and Felicity came to see everyone bedecked in their gorgeous gowns, they both gasped. Hildy cried, Nobukwe and Thokozile dabbed at their eyes hastily. Emotions ran high as the bridal party set off in their limousines for Cape Agulhas.

Only Rowin and her father and grandfather Noah drove together and they were the last to leave for the ceremony. Rowin had one request to make of the driver before he took the short road to where the oceans met. She had picked a special bunch of 'Fleur' roses. She had decided she wanted to place these on her friend – Nonqaba's grave – Rowin had never forgotten her young friend. Her hand touched her mother's locket around her neck.

The car stopped on the small hill and Rowin quietly got out with the help of her father and the two of them walked to the small mound with its neat headstone. Rowin quietly and tenderly placed her flowers on the grave, saying: "Nonquaba, also known as Janet, you were my friend and I did not forget to remember you on this, my wedding day. Your spirit will dance at my wedding, along with Nobukwe, Thokozile and myself." Rowin bowed her head for a moment or two and silently whispered a prayer for her friend.

... now it was time to get married ...

∴

...at Cape Agulhas, the short, cobbled pathway leading to the rocky sentinel indicating the confluence point of two mighty oceans—Atlantic and Indian—lay a red, velvet carpet, scattered with rose petals—waiting for the bride to walk upon them to her bridegroom...

Christian awaited Rowin...

...white chairs had been placed on either side of the carpet. Family and friends were already seated.

Two police cars were parked on the road at Cape Agulhas, their occupants idly observing the scene; penning in notebooks their comments for future reference...

...William and Noah led Rowin forward, as the portable organ played "La Mer" (The Sea)...

...this day was so perfectly beautiful...

CHAPTER EIGHT

BARRIERS I—PAIN

… when everything we made together has been broken, I just want you to know who I am. I need you to answer my question. The very least, you owe me an explanation…

The August day had dawned without a single cloud in the sky and promised to be a warm one, unusual for it was still the winter season in the southern hemisphere. The ringing of the telephone had awoken Rowin and as she reached across the bedside table to lift the receiver, its stridently urgent noise ceased.

Christian stirred next to her, reaching for her in his sleep and murmuring her name. She settled back next to him and their two bodies melded together as one, just as they had always done for twenty-three years. His hand cupped her breast and she responded by turning over towards him, feeling his arousal against her. Even though they were both only half-awake, they began their beautiful ritual of lovemaking, sleepily and tenderly at first, slowly and hesitatingly touching and caressing, feeling their passion build to a wild crescendo and climax. They never tired of each other and loved to pleasure one another and explore the wonder and possibilities of their passion. They complimented and completed their thoughts with such abandonment, that it took their breath away. Christian arose first to put the coffee on, before showering, whilst Rowin languished in bed for a few more luxurious moments of contented blissful laziness. She was loathe to arise. The day seemed so perfect, she wanted to soak up every single second of its beginning…

After bringing her fresh coffee and hot buttery croissants on a bed-tray, Christian ruffled Rowin's hair and kissed her goodbye, before driving through to Cape Town. He was to be key-note speaker at a conference on Tropical Medicine Research Policies. Rowin stretched like a lithe black leopard and finally hopped out of bed, showered and got ready to spend the day with her sister. The two women had decided to go through to Mossel Bay for lunch together at the delightful Arrabella Hound's Victorian Tearoom and Restaurant.

After drying her hair, Rowin switched on the small radio in the bedroom. "LA MER" – one of her favourite melodies was playing on the classical station. When this ended, she impatiently turned the radio dial to catch the early morning news. Nelson Mandela's tour to various overseas countries received top-billing that morning. The joy Rowin experienced hearing about South Africa's top personality and hero and the start at long last to the dismantling of the apartheid regimé, made her place her small hands together in thankful supplication. All the interminable years (from when she turned sixteen years old), working alongside other sympathizers of all races and with the banned groups, had not been in vain. She thought to her herself: "... this year of 1990 is a most momentous one indeed, especially that day of February 11th..." Rowin reminisced smilingly...

∴

The day had dawned a cloudless, idyllic, perfect-Western-Cape-almost-end-of-summer-one – dreamy in its quality...

Outside in a prison in Paarl – the Victor Verster Prison – a fairly large crowd had gathered, patiently waiting for the release of a very special prisoner named Nelson Mandela. Among the curiously expectant gathering, were news reporters, television crews and African National Congress supporters. They all began yelling and shouting as Nelson Mandela and his then-wife – Winnie – appeared. They walked together through the prison gates. This man was seventy-one years old. He had spent twenty-seven years incarcerated as a political prisoner. His had been a long, long walk to freedom. He was now, at last, a free man. His release began a new journey for him, for his long walk was not yet done... When he was among the people, he raised his right fist into the air jubilantly. There was a huge roar as the crowd responded. He had not been able to use this salute for twenty-seven years. This dignified man had survived the severe years of deprivation, the attempts at destroying a prisoner's identity and soul. The couple remained but a few short moments with the waiting people and then returned to the car waiting to drive them to the Mother City of Cape Town.

(Nelson Mandela had been transferred form the notorious prison on Robben Island in March of 1982, to the maximum security facility at Pollsmoor, just outside of Cape Town, together with his fellow prisoners – Walter Sisulu, and Andrew Mlangeni and Raymond Mhlaba. Early in December 1988, after a stay, due to illness, at the Constantiaberg Clinic, he was transferred to the prison situated in the beautiful old Cape-Dutch town of Paarl. Victor Verster Prison was to be his last place of incarceration) ...

... Nelson Mandela's motorcade proceeded extremely cautiously along a winding, circuitous back route around Paarl, to avoid any unforeseen or possible incidents. The drive on this lovely day wended its way through vineyards and lush farmlands, where many white families stood alongside the road to catch a glimpse of one of South Africa's most notorious and memorable prisoners as the motorcade passed by. Many of the people were silent, many waved and many raised their clenched fists in what had now become known as the "ANC Power Salute of Freedom." Nelson Mandela, at one point stopped the motorcade to get out of his car in order to greet and to express his thanks to one of the white families and to tell them how very inspired he was by their support.

How very different the South Africa he was returning to was, from the one he had left behind so many, many years previously.

A large rally had been organized at the Grand Parade in Cape Town. This was a huge open-air square in front of the old City Hall. It was from here, that Nelson Mandela would speak to the crowd from the balcony of the building, for this overlooked the entire vast area. The original intent was to approach the City Hall from the rear of the building, but for some reason, the driver instead, plunged the vehicle slowly straight into the sea of waiting people. The crowd immediately surged forward in their excitement, forcing the car to draw to a halt. The people were cheering, jumping onto the car, knocking on the roof and windows, for the outpouring of emotion and love for this man was tremendous. This man – Nelson Mandela – was once again imprisoned – not by high barbed wire and walls of stone or prison bars in a cell – but by the multitude of loving supporters who wanted their leader among them.

∿

The car was entrapped by the crowd for what seemed like an eternity. A dozen or so marshalls eventually came to the aid of the terrified driver and they managed to clear a tight pathway and the driver with the occupants of his vehicle, sped off in the opposite direction to the City Hall …

∿

Eventually Nelson Mandela returned much later. By now the crowds had become very restless and there were a number of angry outbursts, with the distinct possibility of the crowd becoming out of hand. They wanted their leader Nelson Mandela. Where had he disappeared to?

∿

The crowd saw Nelson Mandela on the balcony of the City Hall at last. The crowd went wild. Cheering, many holding banners and flags, applauding, crying, laughing – every emotion imaginable was on the faces of the people of all races …

Nelson Mandela called out in a strong voice: "AMANDLA," with his fist held high toward the crowd. They responded with their joy-filled cheer and in no uncertain fashion: "MGAWETHU." He yelled back: "iAFRICA." They responded instantaneously: "MAYIBUYE." Finally, the multitudinous gathering quietened down somewhat and he, Nelson Rolihlahla MANDELA began his speech, which was from his heart:

"Friends, comrades and fellow South Africans, I greet you, in the name of peace, democracy and freedom for all. I stand here before you, not as a prophet, but as a humble servant of you, the people. Your tireless and heroic sacrifices have made it possible for me to be here today. I therefore place the remaining years of my life in your hands ..."

Rowin and Christian stood in the square, along with many members of her family and friends. All were so moved by the words they listened to and most of them had lost all composure. Emotions ran high. Rowin clung to Christian's hand tightly, for he too, was so moved...

This was an incredible end at dusk to an amazing day in the history of the Republic of South Africa...

Talks, already begun with Nelson Mandela, prior to his release, on the dismantling of the apartheid regimé, would continue, but the present prime minister – F.W. de Klerk was a very cautious pragmatist, unlike his recent predecessor – P.W. Botha – known as the 'Crocodile.' The government were in no great hurry to change things and it would be a while before de Klerk would be prepared to negotiate the end of white supremacy rule. (He was determined to ensure power for the Afrikaners in any new dispensation. Both sides – the ANC and the government would pledge a peaceful process of negotiating and the government committed to the lifting of the State of Emergency).

On February 2/1990, F.W. de Klerk had stood before Parliament to make the traditional opening speech. He did something which no other South African head of state had ever done before: he truly began the dismantling of the apartheid system. He lay the groundwork for a democratic South Africa. He announced in a most dramatic fashion, the lifting of the bans on the ANC, the PAC, the South African Communist

Party, and thirty-one other formerly illegal organizations, the freeing of all political prisoners incarcerated for non-violent activities, the suspension of capital punishment, and the lifting of many restrictions imposed by the State of Emergency. He announced in a strong voice to Parliament: "The time for negotiations has arrived …" (It would take unfortunately, years of parlaying back and forth, a play for time and excuses by the government, with some promises ignored or broken, etc, before the transition to true freedom and the ending of apartheid). The interim years were not painfree nor peaceful. There was much bloodshed …

Certain diehard factions fought hard against the transcendence from the regimes steel-grip. White supremacists and the extremely militant right-wing Afrikaner Weerstandsbeweging refused to back down. The Zula nation's Inkatha, demanded far more say in the machinations of negotiations. The Kwa-Zulu Natal region of South Africa was witness to much vicious fighting and atrocious killings, spurred on by a new group of dissident South Africans.

Finally, in June 1993, a multiparty forum at the World Trade Centre, voted to set a date for South Africa's FIRST national, non-racial, one-person-one-vote election. APRIL 27/1994 was this day. There would be no more stalling …

∼

… Rowin continued to listen to the radio broadcast. The telephone interrupted her concentration. Mia could not make their date – an emergency with her mother-in-law. No sooner had she concluded her conversation with her sister, when the telephone rang again. This call changed Rowin's life forever. She wished she had never taken that call. What had been imparted to her, left her shaken and sick to the pit of her stomach. It left her life shattered and in ruins. Rowin was afraid and frightened, as she ran to the bathroom and retched and retched until there was nothing left inside of her. She rinsed her mouth and washed her face, but could not stop the trembling of her hands. She lay back on her bed and stared up at the ceiling through unseeing eyes.

It was almost noon before she roused herself. She couldn't remember whether she had fallen asleep or had just lain there. The wind had begun to pick up and leaves were swirling outside of her window. The curtains were flapping like sails, almost horizontal at times. She got off the bed and closed the windows and shivered. Waves were beating along the shoreline and it looked quite dark and ominous across the ocean. Obviously, there was a big storm brewing. The sound of the ocean usually comforted her when she was troubled, but nothing could or would assuage her terrible sense of despair and loss.

The day had started off so beautifully …

She called Christian on his emergency cellphone number and asked him to return home immediately. (His morning conference was over and he could skip the sumptious luncheon). He knew from the sound of her voice, there was something terribly wrong and he drove home immediately. The wild galeforce storm had already hit the Mother City and the long drive back to Arniston was unpleasant to say the least …

∴

It was just on 5:00 pm, already dark outside and the rain was coming down in torrents. Rowin was sitting in the dark on a large cushion in front of the fire. Apart from the storm, the house inside was silent except for the ominous ticking of the old grandfather clock. Rowin felt chilled to the bone and wrapped a mohair shawl around her shoulders. Christian was gone (she knew not where and she really did not care). She had asked him to leave and to never return …

Their beautiful day had ended horribly and Rowin felt a numbness around her heart. Inside – she cried out – but would not let any tears fall.

She left the cosy warmth of the fire in the living room and walked to the bedroom. As she reached the threshold of the room, she cried out for her husband: "Christian." She threw herself onto the bed. The bed she had shared with Christian for twenty three years. She had seldom slept in that bed without him. She missed him terribly, but she never wanted him back. She lay at first on 'her' side of their bed and then rolled over onto 'his' side and placed her hands under his pillow, hugging it to her and burying her head in its downy softness. Under the pillow were his pyjama bottoms, which he only occasionally wore. She sat up, pulling them toward her. They smelled of his wonderful musky masculinity and his favourite Ralph Lauren cologne, which she had given him on his last birthday. Rowin imagined she could almost feel the outline of his body next to hers. A sob caught in her throat, but still no tears. There was no one next to her. She Rowin, wife of Christian, mother of his children was entirely alone.

She switched on the bedside lamp. She gazed around the room. So much of this room was so very much 'Christian,' both in décor and design. They had chosen all the furnishings together and it was a combination of his Australian heritage and her African one. (She would many months later change the room to a French theme).

She sighed deeply, feeling weary and exhausted. She had not eaten since breakfast and felt a little dizzy and faint. She could not sleep in this room tonight. Instead she would use one of the guest bedrooms. She walked through to the kitchen and took a pot of soup out of the refrigerator and heated this on the stove. She popped some wholewheat bread into the toaster as well and poured herself a glass of homemade lemonade whilst she waited for the soup to come to a boil. She loved pea and ham soup and felt she needed comfort food tonight, though surprised she even felt like eating at all. She thought of ringing the children, but she was not yet quite ready to tell them what had transpired. Mia Tansy had rung, but she had not taken the call and had allowed her answering machine to pick up the message.

How would she ever be able to tell her children and her sister and her father she had ended her relationship with Christian? She had ended their marriage swiftly and abruptly. Christian had had very little to say to her, other than he would arrange to have the rest of his things picked up. He never answered Rowin's question: "Why?" She could still hear the echo of his footsteps across the rainwet flagstones of the short driveway of their home. He had walked slowly to his car, with his shoulders hunched into his raincoat against the driving rain.

Christian had driven off without so much as a backward glance. Had Rowin seen his face during those last moments, she would have seen that it was contorted with anguish and pain and Christian was crying…

My dear Christian:

Your letter arrived this morning. Old Hildy brought it through to me on the copper letter tray (She's ninety now – what an age).

I must tell you your letter came as a shock and I opened the envelope with trembling fingers. Seventeen years with no contact between us, 'tho you and our children kept in touch. Only once, over all the years, did they impart any information to me about you. I had implored them never to tell me about you. I did not want to know anything.

You 'broke faith' with me Christian, and in all I had trusted and believed in. Why you decided to do what you did, I never understood and I still do not know your reasons. It was far more than broken vows wasn't it?

Show me your tears now, Christian. Those tears you never shed in 1990. Before you leave this life, this earth, I beg of you, tell me why? Tell me you really did care and that you loved me, show me your tears. Our son said to me ten years after we parted: "Mom, dad truly does feel pain and remorse and would give his life to change what he did to you – to us. He has told me, with tears in his voice, one can never take one's happiness at the expense of someone else, for it is never true happiness but merely a sham pretence at happiness. You never turn back the clock. You can admit your mistakes and ask for understanding and forgiveness and perhaps a second chance to make things right."

Oh, Christian, I gave you my heart, but I never gave you my soul, for my soul belonged to my first love: my beloved South Africa. Is this perhaps what went wrong? Was this your reason, your excuse for your lies and cheating? I did try, oh how very hard I tried to be all I thought you wanted me to be. Twenty-three years of marriage together, in all its complexities, the ups and downs, the wild and passionate moments, the births of our son and precious daughter, which brought so much more deep meaning to our amazing relationship. Oh Christian, so many, many memories… We were so passionate – so happy … We shared our youth, our ideals, our dreams and hopes. We watched so many magnificent African dawns and said our goodnights at so many sunsets. Africa's pulsing, vibrant emotion touched us and we believed in so many of the same things.

When you needed to fly free I encouraged you to do so, always trusting in you. You too, let me fly free and to be my own person, for you knew there was a wild, untamed soul within me. My rebellious nature refused to be shackled or coerced into things I could not accept. I could never be controlled by you or anyone. I haven't changed. I am still very strong-willed, probably to my detriment at times.

Never once though, did I ever break my promises to you in all the years we were together, though there were many temptations placed in front of me. You see, I had promised to be yours forever and a day. That 'forever and a day' arrived suddenly on a rainswept August morning, when I discovered your unfaithfulness in all its seeming reality. A telephone call from 'her' informing me that she was carrying your child, so 'she' said. I was utterly bewildered and devastated. Your affair had been going on for two months right under my nose. How stupid and naïve the two of you must have thought me. Of course, later I was to discover she had lied about the baby. There was no child.

I rang you at the Hospital and asked you to come home. Remember?

Whilst I waited for you to arrive, I slowly and very deliberately packed your bags. I felt numbed and I could not even cry. When you walked through the door, you tried to take me in your arms. I pushed you away saying: "Christian, why? Why have you been unfaithful? Please leave now. I don't want you to ever come back into my life. Our marriage is over. Answer me one thing. Why, oh why?"

You never answered me, you simply picked up the bags I had packed and walked out of my life, without so much as a backward glance. All you said was: "I will arrange to have the rest of my things picked up." You returned a week later to Alice Springs where you are still.

On that horrible afternoon, I did not wish to hear any glib words or excuses or lies, but I did want to know "why." At the time, you probably would not have told me the truth anyway. I was devastated, so hurt I sent you away, far, far away from me and the children. Our children and grandchildren are the only ties which still bind us and the memories, those incredible haunting memories...

You were not the only one who went away. I fled to the starkness of the Kalahari Desert, hell bent on punishing myself even more. I searched for answers and I could find none. I was a desert-nomad for over a year. My days without you were dark indeed, so very, very dark for a long, long time. I was so raw, so devastated and I abandoned my children to their thoughts and fate. The loneliness was so very unbearable. I ached for your body to be next to mine, to feel your arms around me, holding me close, to allow ourselves to lose ourselves in our passion. We were so good together. You were the only man I had ever been with when I was only twenty-three years old. How long ago it was...

Anger, rage and fear tore me apart and I howled and screamed my pain into those desert dunes. In my solitude, I soul searched. Oh, how deeply I looked into myself. I found no answers, I knew one thing: I, Fleur-Rowin, never wanted you back in my life. I never wanted to see you again, but I could not deny my love for you remained...

You were gone from me. We were gone from each other. Why was I filled with so much shame? So much remorse? In the Kalahari, I found in my isolation: utter desolation.

I had an urgent, insane need to destroy everything beautiful we had ever experienced and so I finally returned to Arniston. I opened the front door to the cottage and saw reflected in the hallway mirror a face which was not mine. What I saw was so ugly, so utterly horrible. The mirror reflected a stranger's image: distorted, filled with such rage and ugliness and hatred for all those who had over the years, so savagely and blatantly and needlessly hurt me. I stared long and hard and I did not like what I saw…

I had howled and screamed my rage in the desert with the hot winds carrying the guttural animal sounds away from me. I had not cried tears though. Now, the dam was unleashed and I broke down and wept. I must have cried enough tears to fill both the Indian and the Atlantic Oceans to overflowing. Tears and sobs wracked my body in pain and anguish. Cleansing tears, like raindrops during a summer storm settling the dust and grime. Healing tears, which left me exhausted and spent, as I lay on the floor in a crumpled heap – broken. For all which was gone – all which was lost…

Years later, I did forgive you Christian, but it was too late for me. That forgiving I did, did not condone your actions, but in forgiving, I was able to free myself to once more become my own person and to be a 'free spirit' which is what I truly do believe I am. I had lost faith in God, but I do believe He carried me in His arms and I was sheltered under angel's wings for many years. He – Abba Father – still shelters me and my faith in Him has given me the strength to go on with my life. All anger and bitterness are long gone. In my heart, I know our children have never ever really forgiven me for sending you away and I do carry the burden of my actions deep within me. They both said, bitterly, I was the one who really broke up the family unit, even though they knew the reasons and knew what you had done. They still blamed ME… That has always seemed very unfair. Now it is all water under the bridge and after all these years, does it really matter?

Over the years, I rebuilt my life. I built my towers and walls very high. I hid behind them and refused to let anyone enter into my safe world. I had to prove to myself I could and would survive on my own. I needed no mortal to tangle up my life ever again. I felt safe with my barriers strong and in place… I am now sixty-three years old.

… and then I met someone, who found the chinks in my armour, dislodged one or two bricks of my stronghold. Ours is an amazing relationship, very private in the autumnal years of our lives… never, in my

very wildest dreams did I ever expect this to happen in my life. We appear to almost complete one another, yet remain totally ourselves. Perhaps that is what mature love is all about. Suffice to say, it is indeed a very special thing in all its tenderness and fragility. We share so many parallels to our lives.

Christian, you have NOW asked me to come to you in Australia. Your letter was sad, filled with so much desperation. I cannot believe you have only a short time to live. I am so sorry and sad. I will come to you in Alice … Yes, we do need to put to rest the past and maybe now, you will be able to answer my question: "Why, Christian, why?" Please give me – Rowin – the answers to what really happened so long ago. Be kind to me, please. I pray I will not be too late and that I will see you again. Time to finally, lay those old ghosts to rest. Keep good thoughts close to you.

… Love, true love, never ends – but sometimes it has to be put into a Pandora's Box for all time. I hope in opening Pandora's Box, neither of us will rue the day …

I will harken to your call. I will hold you in your physical pain, but I will never ever be 'yours' again, you must surely know this? The old love cannot be rekindled ever.

Try to keep strong. I will be with you in six days time, when I fly out from Cape Town to Perth and then on to Adelaide. Thank Barabara in anticipation for collecting me at the airport. She has been a wonderful sister to you.

Totsiens my dear Christian

With love

Fleur-Rowin … free spirit always …

P.S.   You mentioned you were craving to taste some biltong. What a strange request from you after no contact between us for seventeen years! I shall have to smuggle some through customs

*in my luggage. I must admit, I can't do without the taste of
that dried African beef either...*

p.s. *The children both telephoned and asked me to send greetings.
They will be arriving two days after I do and are bringing our
grandchildren as well to see their grand-dad.*

p.s. *Am I really coming to you after all these years? It seems so
strange. I feel as though I am inside a bubble, floating in the sky
over the sea, and it is about to burst and I will go plummeting
into the salty water. I hope I don't sink but manage to swim to
safety...*

NOTE: *Christian, I wrote a poem when I returned from the Kalahari,
I enclose this with my letter. Rowin...*

BARRIERS I—PAIN...

Stone walls ivy touch distant skies
Sentinel doors chainbarred – no way in
Deep inside within thornbushed courtyard
I wander sadly with neither kith nor kin
Anguished pain's sorrow is buried deep
For all so precious has now flown and gone
No victory shouts for wild brave warrior
Spear's brutal end to our love when done
Unending guilt which now I must carry
Causes an aching wound of damning guilt
Dark endless nights weep where I tarry
For I toss and turn – dream – cannot sleep
Kindred spirit I thought you my beloved
Unfaithful husband I sent you far and away
For so anger-hurt I was fury-filled
Holding our supposed timeless love at bay
No longer am I your joy-filled woman
Passion ceased with deceitful lies
Figure solitary lay I on desert sandbed
Alone under heavens cold pewter skies
Filled with the deadness which surrounds me
Flee must I – from war's carnage hide
Oceans deep – I seek wild Neptune's spray
Send my companion on your surging tide
Spent and weary – broken I run no further
Pray only your forgiveness at Heaven's Gate
Honour-bound remorse I offer to you
I ask – oh let me be not too late...

CHAPTER NINE

BARRIERS II—NOTHINGNESS

... have our lives been futile? is there nothing left to salvage? surely we can find forgiveness for the terrible mistakes we made? ...

The South African Airways flight was 'on schedule,' coming into Perth at sunrise.

Temba and Rowin were both booked on the same flight to Adelaide later that afternoon. Having a good few hours in hand, they hailed a cab which transported them to downtown Perth, dropping them outside the Perth Hilton hotel. The day was already warm and everyone seemed to be waving to them, so they both promptly waved back before realizing the Ausies were swatting a myriad of flies away. Small blackflies were swarming everywhere. They both burst out laughing.

∿

… Deciding to book day rooms at the hotel, they went up the steps to the reception desk. Temba's room was a few doors down from Rowin's on the tenth floor Travel weary, they opted to shower and rest, before meeting downstairs in the lobby. They would late-lunch at the Swagman Pub in the hotel.

Rowin was exhausted. Her refreshing long shower immediately revived her. She dried herself off with the sumptuously soft Egyptian cotton fluffy towels and donned a terrycloth bathrobe and dried her hair with the hairdryer provided by the hotel. She swallowed a couple of aspirin and flopped down on the large queen size bed. The moment her head touched the pillow, she drifted off into a dream filled sleep…

At noon, she was startled by the ringing of the telephone. Hotel reception were on the other end of the line: this was her 'wakeup call.' She turned the air conditioner on, as her room had become very stuffy. (The temperature outside was a very hot 96°F). She felt inordinately lazy, as she donned matching bra and panties, safari trousers and jacket. Tying a silk zebra print scarf around her neck, she added her lion's tooth on its leather thong, black smallhoop earrings, watch and black bangles to the ensemble. Changing her suede veldskoene for black leather sandals, all she had to do was brush her tousled hair and add makeup to hide the dark circles under her eyes. Deciding she didn't look at all travel weary, she went down in the elevator to meet Temba, already waiting for her.

Their lunch of steak 'n kidney pies with potato wedges was delicious and they ordered Australian Swan Lager to go with their meal.

Rowin was glad of Temba's charming, down-to-earth company. After lunch they strolled around taking in the sights, but it was sweltering outdoors.

They collected their hand luggage from the hotel and cabbed it back to the airport, where Rowin placed a call to her ex-sister-in-law. Barabara's cheerful voice on the other end eased Rowin's nervousness. Barabara was already in Adelaide and at suppertime they would connect for the flight to Alice Springs. Barabara mentioned she had another passenger to transport to Alice. This turned out to be Temba, which was no real surprise to Rowin. Rowin then tried to call South Africa, but could not get through to either her father or Paul. She was very disappointed, feeling very lonely, very vulnerable, a knot of fear at the pit of her stomach…

∴

It was after midnight when the small Flying Doctor plane touched down at Alice Springs airport. It was a hot night and everything appeared to be parched and so dusty. Barabara dropped Temba off first, at the Alice Springs Hospital, where the Visitor Suite had been booked for him. He hugged Rowin, whispering in her ear: "Don't worry, everything will work itself out. I'm here if you need me little friend…"

On reaching Barabara's neat, compact house, with its large verandah running along two sides, like many typical homes in the outback: Rowin was overwhelmed with homesickness for her native land. South Africa seemed so far away and she suddenly felt very unsure of herself. She did not feel tired and after greeting Gregory, Briony and her husband Luca, who had come over to welcome her: she and Barabara sat out companionably on the verandah sipping tall glasses of lemonade. The verandah was protected with a mesh screen and mesh screendoor so no bugs would bother them, though many large moths had been drawn to the lights which were on, but could get no further than the screens.

Amongst Barabara's many skills as a doctor, she was also a brilliant psychiatrist. She had put Rowin at ease immediately with her natural warmth and the two had always gotten along extremely well. Rowin wanted to know how Christian was faring and B, as she liked to be called, imparted much information to Rowin. He had a breakthrough on his chemo-therapy treatment and appeared to be doing better, once again able to walk about slowly.

Rowin was heartened by this news. The two chatted on and B slowly managed to draw Rowin out, sensing there was something important she wanted to tell her.

∴

There was so much to say and Rowin's words came tumbling forth, as though she had opened all of her Pandora's Boxes simultaneously…

B got up with tears in her eyes, going over to where Rowin sat and put her arms around her. Rowin had become quite overwrought and suddenly very exhausted. B suggested bath and bed to her, urging her though, to tell Christian everything. B knew her brother had much to impart to Rowin as well. With her arm around Rowin's shoulders, the two women went inside. Gregory had already gone to bed.

Rowin's small room was very comfortable. She showered quickly and tied a large towel around her naked body, sat at the compact writing console and began to write to Christian… She would ask B to give this letter to Christian before she met with him.

Rowin lay back on the pillows and said her prayers. Afterward, with a deep sigh, she turned off the bedside lamp. She had not drawn the curtains, and moonlight streamed across the room, almost magically touching her face. This brought thoughts of her beloved grandmother Elsie to her. She and old Noah had eventually married, but time was short for them and both were gone before that year was out, dying within weeks of each other. Rowin had missed them with a deep aching void in her heart. They were two of her favourite people. Rosemary and James O'Neill Eugene, followed their two friends eighteen months later. Mary Huddlestone had pre-deceased her former husband Noah – but he and Elsie were by her side at the Wynberg Hospital, as she struggled to speak and ask for forgiveness for all she had done in her life. She pleaded with Noah asking him to tell their granddaughter – Rowin – how very much she regretted setting her up for adoption, asking for forgiveness as well. (They had left this world so long ago).

∴∼

Rowin had the desperate urge to speak with her father. He was in his nineties and his mortality loomed suddenly before her. "Oh, Daddy-love, I wish you were here with me. I am filled with conflicting thoughts about my meeting with Christian tomorrow. Daddy, if I am truly honest with myself, which is what you taught me to be, I still love Christian and I have never, ever really stopped. But now there is Paul and I care so much for him as well. Can we love and be in love with two people at the same time? I haven't seen or been with Christian in over a decade and now my heart is pounding and my thoughts are churning and there is no Kalahari Desert to run to. I feel trapped. I feel like a seagull, about to crash land, and be mortally wounded by the waiting sea eagles … Oh, Daddy – help me. You were always there to pick up the pieces, but perhaps even you will despise me now. Perhaps what Felicity said so long ago is true: I,

Fleur-Rowin – am as black as sin …"

Rowin began to sob into her pillow, stifling the sound, so as not to disturb B and Gregory. She finally ceased her weeping and got out of the narrow bed and poured herself a glass of water. Even this was tepid, for the night's heat was as stifling as it would be the next day. She bathed her face, sprinkling cologne onto her wrists and forehead and returned to bed. She forced herself to relax and to meditate deeply. The Australian nightsounds seemed so intrusive …

It was a while before she dozed off into a fitful, restless sleep and she was haunted by her old nightmares from childhood.

She awoke startled by a noise outside. It was sunrise and the kookaburras were outside her window. She had for a moment forgotten where she was.

She arose quietly, deciding to wash her hair and chose what she would wear very carefully.

B and Gregory were up and about, for they were early risers. The sausages and bacon were sizzling. B believed in a hearty breakfast to start the day. She tapped on Rowin's door, inviting her to join them for orange juice out on the verandah, where she had set places for the three of them.

∴

Rowin did not think she could eat – she was extremely nervous about her meeting with her former husband. She surprised herself by tucking in and felt much more relaxed and better for having eaten.

At 8:30 am – B and Rowin set off for Christian's bungalow on the other side of Alice … She had given B her letter for Christian …

Christian:

I am here in Alice Springs at last. I have asked B to give my letter to you before we meet. I am filled with fear and trepidation. There is just so much we need to say to each other.

I am also filled with thoughts of the past. I have talked at length with B and imparted something to her, which very few people know about. She feels it is imperative that you are told and that you are strong enough to receive my letter. I will understand should you decide not to see me, especially as we have had no contact for all these years, until you wrote to me.

Please, Christian, read all of the pages I have written. I shall wait in the car, whilst you read the letter, knowing what I did so long ago, is huge … If it is your decision not to see me after all, I shall return to South Africa before the children arrive.

Oh, Christian, this is one of the hardest things I have ever had to do …

Love

Fleur-Rowin

Cynthia Elizabeth Sully

Christian: I have a secret I have carried in my soul for seventeen years. We have another child – a daughter of sixteen. She was born out in the lonely desert when I ran away from all my pain and anguish – only I couldn't run away from it, instead I took it all with me. Sithole and Thokozile raised this lovely girl for me. She grew up in Botswana and now lives in Italy. She and I do meet as often as we can. When she has completed her art degree in Sienna, she will be coming to join me in Arniston. She has forgiven me for denying her all the years, but the initial pain of seeing her little face was unbearable for she is so like you. She is a lovely person – warm and loving. Her sunny nature is a joy to behold. How could I ever have given up this child of my love? She knows all about you and wants to meet you. Will you see her before time runs out? None of my family know of my heartbreak and when our other children arrive in two days time, I would like you and I to tell them together that they have a sister called Christina-Rowin.

Oh Christian – can you ever forgive what I did?

Rowin

(I am so filled with such terrible remorse and pain).

BARRIERS II — NOTHINGNESS

Dreams gone to dust – fragmented pieces
Her love has fled and their child is gone
Rains of season pour down wildly
Walls and tower now tumbled stone …

On lonely ground – heart bleeding lays
Set bare and naked for all to see
Brief perfect happiness, oh where are you?
Is loving their child not meant to be?

War torn and weary, feet stumble onward
Nowhere to shelter on long journey home
Bare trees waving are her cold welcome
Numbed pain buried, she returns all alone …

They said – fly high, find and love him
With her broken heart tender and still bruised
All she feels is numbing, savage agony
For you fled her side, when you were both confused …

Buried deep – her love still lingers
Each day her voice sings a song anew
Across oceans waters – longing sadly
For the child she loves is a part of you …

…written for Christian on the way back from the Kalahari and
Botswana – Arniston and Australia seemed a million miles away
(*Fleur-Rowin's journal entry …*)

ⸯ

… her fourteen week visit over, Rowin was now on her way back to South Africa. She thought back to her initial meeting with Christian.

ⸯ

She had waited in B's car for almost half an hour. She felt hot and her throat was parched. Dust seemed to be everywhere. Closing her eyes, she leaned back against the headrest, rubbing her aching forehead and temples, attempting to alleviate her pain and tension. B had eventually called out to her through the open living room window: "Rowin, please come in now. Don't bother to lock the car. Chris is ready to see you…"

Rowin, shaking from head to toe, could hardly breathe through her anxiety. She thought she would faint as she quickly leapt out of the car, slamming the door behind her. She ran up the verandah steps, trying to regain her composure, as B met her at the open front door. She put her arm around Rowin's shoulders and whispered: "Rowin, it's alright. Christian was extremely shocked and it took a while for him to calm down. Here, drink this iced lemonade before you go in to him." Rowin gratefully sipped the refreshing drink.

She had not uttered a word and continued to shake nervously.

Both women entered the room. Rowin and Christian stared at each other, as B quietly tiptoed out and drove away in her car…

ⸯ

Christian stood up slowly from the comfortable chair he had been sitting in. He looked thinner and gaunt from the ravages of his illness. He was still a very handsome man and had aged well. He appeared very tense, a worried frown on his face.

Christian seemed so very vulnerable, as he held out his arms to

Rowin. She walked slowly toward him, her arms outstretched as well. They hugged each other for a seeming eternity, finally breaking away. Christian sat down heavily in his chair – exhausted, still holding onto Rowin's hand. "Fleur-Rowin – you are as lovely as ever. I can't believe you are here. I am overwhelmed with emotion. I thought I would be much calmer. We have so much to talk about, so much to say and none of this can be hurried. Before you say or do anything though, I want to reassure you about one thing, which is vitally important, please, please, know Christina-Rowin is welcome in her father's home, she is our daughter. I must see her before I die. Yes, Rowin, I must see her, I must. I am still reeling from your news. Oh, my dear, it must have all been so very hard for you. Words cannot ease the heartache and pain you must have endured. I am so sorry, so very, very sorry. I am sorry for so much. When I lost you, I lost myself. I owe you the truth and I will tell you everything. Know that I have never stopped loving you. There have been no other women in my life, since that night I left you during that lashing, wild storm. Our children were adamant – you wanted nothing from me – you wanted to know nothing about me. In the end, just weeks ago, I wrote to you. Oh, why did it take me so many years to humble myself and beg you to come to me? Why has it taken this dreadful illness to bring me to my senses? And now, you've found happiness with someone else. But you came, Rowin you came. Rowin, Rowin, you are with me…"

By now, Rowin was sobbing. She knelt down in front of Christian and put her head in his lap. He had deep compassion etched on his face. He gently stroked her hair. The two of them sat for a very long time and still, Rowin had not uttered a single word…

Christian lifted her face and looked deeply into her tearfilled eyes. A sob caught in the back of her throat. "Christian, I am here, yes indeed, I am here. You must not exhaust yourself. We will talk about everything over the next two days, before the children get here. I need to know one thing now, will you tell Sebastian and Raine-Fleur, with me, about Christina-Rowin?"

Christian nodded his head, suddenly very tired and murmured: "Rowin, give me an hour to sleep and then we shall go from there and decide what to do for the best…"

Christian held onto Rowin, as she walked with him to his bedroom. She was rather surprised to find the room had been decorated exactly like their bedroom at the Arniston cottage (which she had subsequently changed).

Christian lay on top of the bed, swallowed some pills and asked: "Rowin, I don't want you to go. Please stay with me." She looked across the room at the comfortable chaise-longue. He noticed her gaze and she looked back at him and lay down, instead, next to him putting her arms around him, she held him to her, as a mother would have held her child…

Gently, she rubbed his forehead and bent to kiss him. He sighed deeply, the medication already taking effect. Rowin's thoughts were in turmoil. Christian, ill as he was, older now, much older, still had the power to make her melt at his touch. They lay quietly together, and Rowin; emotionally and physically exhausted, dozed off into fitful slumber…

∶∽

Christian awoke many hours later and without thinking, carefully rolled over onto his side, sliding out of Rowin's arms. He put his arms around her, as she stirred, but did not awaken. He watched her as she lay in his arms, her face in repose was beautiful and peaceful and he ached to kiss her slightly parted lips. He was in a great deal of pain, but did not want to spoil the moment, nor break the spell of daydreaming for what might have been…

Suddenly, he groaned. Rowin awoke with a startled look upon her face. "Christian, what is it? What can I do? Tell me." The look of absolute agony, touched her somewhere deep inside and she held him and rocked him against her.

Rowin was all confusion, her thoughts in tumultuous waves of agonizing memories of all they had meant to each other in the past. A past which was so long ago, yet ever present, for the Pandora's Boxes had been flung wide open...

:~

Rowin had made a decision. She would collect her things from Gregory and B's home and move them over to the house belonging to Christian. She would use the en-suite guestroom. She wanted and needed to be close at hand for this man. She was filled with compassion for him. It was not out of a sense of duty, nor out of pity. She loved him and had told him so. He had invited her to stay indefinitely, for his home was a large, sprawling bungalow. He had also confessed that he loved her.

Her thoughts of Paul were fleeting and remorseful. One person would be unhappily, terribly hurt. Would this be Christian or would this be Paul? Rowin was in a huge dilemma.

Christian's time was so short. Should she give them both this bittersweet interlude, midst the pain of his debilitating illness and then return to Paul? No, Paul would never understand and one could never take one's own personal happiness at the expense of another. Interrupting her thoughts, the persistent ringing of the telephone. It was her father. Her prayers had been answered. "Daddy, daddy, at last. It is so wonderful to hear your voice. Yes, yes. How is everyone? Oh, yes, Paul had been out to stay for a few days. Lovely. Yes, what? What did you say? Nobukwe has called Paul to set up a meeting with him? What in heaven's name is going on. I haven't had any association with her since, gosh, goodness knows when. How strange, no I never asked her to call Paul at all. Nobukwe, as always, is up to something. Don't want to talk anymore about her. Tell me about everything else and then I will tell you what I have decided to do at this end. The children arrive tomorrow night. Oh my, how I miss you and Mia Tansy............."

∴∾

Rowin replaced the telephone receiver and the look on her face was one of such intense anger.

Nobukwe had been Temba's first wife. (Theirs had been a sad marriage, for Nobukwe was an angry, bitter woman. She could not let go of the tragedies in her past and these, coupled with other issues finally became too much for Temba).

Christian's affair with another woman had destroyed his and Rowin's marriage.

Nobukwe was the woman Christian had had an affair with. Only Rowin, Christian and Nobukwe knew of this. Temba never knew. He had divorced Nobukwe because she could not give him the children he so longed for. Rowin had absolutely no intention of ever imparting the information to Temba. He would never know of his first wife's infidelity. It was all in the past now and would suffice no one, should the secret be revealed. Temba remarried many years later and had four children and deserved all the happiness in his life. How ironic, that it should be Temba replacing Christian at the Alice Springs Hospital…

… What was Nobukwe intent on doing now? How had she known about Paul's romantic liaison with Rowin? All this, Rowin pondered over. There were no answers to be concluded.

∴∾

… Christian, over many hours of deep conversation with Rowin, told her all about his long-ago affair with Nobukwe. He made absolutely no excuses for his aberrant behaviour. He had chosen to break all the rules when Rowin was away on a mission for CAAN. Nobukwe had been there. She had tantalized him, flaunted herself at him, seduced him. Her husband, Temba, was on the same mission as Rowin and Nobukwe had intimated that Temba 'had a thing for Rowin' and as she was Rowin's 'friend' – she knew all about what Rowin 'did' on these missions with some of the men. Christian, by this time had quaffed many glasses of wine and beer and was pretty much intoxicated. Before he knew it – Nobukwe had stripped down to her naked, voluptuousness and begged Christian to make love to her. He was by this time, remembering Nobukwe's words against Rowin and had become insanely jealous of what she might or might not have been doing. He threw all caution to the wind and he and Nobukwe savagely took sexual pleasure from each other.

Christian had awoken the next morning, finding himself in Nobukwe's bed. She had laughed at him and vowed she would never let him go. He was hers now and never would be Rowin's again. Christian felt ashamed and filled with belated remorse.

Christian, sick at heart over what he had done, needed desperately to get out of Nobukwe's apartment. She refused to let him go. If he stayed and would occasionally come to her, she promised not to tell Rowin of his indiscretion. He did visit her on several occasions, but never again had sex with her. She became frustrated and angry. Her marriage was over and Christian was still with Rowin, until she hatched up her evil plan.

Eight weeks after their sordid interlude, Nobukwe announted to Christian that she was carrying his child. He did not believe her for a moment. She threatened to tell Rowin and one day, this is precisely what she did… The rest was history with so many people hurt and lives disrupted through a moment of his indiscretion.

∾

… Rowin looked at Christian. She felt sick to her stomach. If only she had given him the chance to tell her everything. Perhaps, somewhere down the road, she would have forgiven him and they could have attempted to put their lives back together as a family. The woman who would bare Christian's baby, would be Rowin. This was the daughter, he had yet to meet – this "late lamb" – born to Rowin, when she was forty-six years old.

"Rowin, I know you will never forgive me. What I did was uncalled for. I know you could never be unfaithful in our marriage. You ask me to forgive you, for not telling me about Christina. There is nothing to forgive. You did what you thought was the best solution at the time. It is through MY actions that all of this happened. Oh, how I prayed for a miracle to bring us back together. It had to come from you. Not from me. You, rightfully, turned your back on this apology for a man and now, oh God help me, it is too late for us."

Rowin sat very still with her hands folded in her lap with the saddest look upon her face. She felt very old, very weary, very hollow inside…

She walked over to Christian and gently took his hands in her small ones. Kneeling down in front of him she quietly said: "Christian, I forgave you a long, long time ago. Forgiving did not mean condoning what had happened, but in forgiving, I felt I was free of you. I will never be free of you my dear, for love simply never ends. Here we are, both in our sixties, yet we have to admit, in all honesty, we both love and care about each other. What happens now? I don't really know. I have told you all about Paul and I must say, I rather enjoyed seeing that spark of envy and jealousy in your eyes. First we have to get through telling the children about their unknown sister. We have to see how you do, as you so very valiantly battle this tenacious cancer. I will stay with you for as long as I can. I will have no contact with Paul and I will ask my father to relay any messages and explanations to him. He probably will not be patient and will demand that I make up my mind as to the future. What the future holds, I simply do not know. There has been much to absorb and work through, but I love you. Yes, I do love you Christian. There can be no intimacy between us. This would not be fair to either you or

Paul, or indeed to myself. Restraint has to be the order of the day. I will hold you when you need to be held. I will lay next to you when you are wracked with pain or simply need the comfort of a warm body next to you. I can only do these things because I truly care about you. Oh, God, I need Your strength to love this man. God, please help all of us. I pray too, for mine enemies, especially my former friend, Nobukwe."

… and then she cried. Christian held her in his arms, such a look of abject pain and deep emotion on his face.

Rowin's pain was Christian's pain and Christian's pain was Rowin's.

∴∽

As Rowin waited for the aeroplane to land in Perth – everything which had happened, became her "companion" on her journey home to Africa. The children and their families had stayed for six weeks and Christian's health seemed to improve, then plummeted when they left. Rowin decided to extend her stay…

He became very dejected at times. He was now in remission.

∴∽

Back in South Africa, Rowin's father had suffered a terrible fall, requiring hip surgery. She felt she needed to be with him. She felt torn in two. She had promised Christian she would come back to him, but in the recesses of her mind, she wondered whether he would be there…

∴∽

Christina-Rowin arrived out of the blue, two days after Christian and Rowin had told their children about her existence and the mystery surrounding her birth.

This had not been easy to do. This family skeleton had proved almost too much for Raine-Fleur. She was shocked and without a word, had walked out of the room, driven off in a flurry of dust, only returning at suppertime. She walked up to her parents and in an angry voice: "Well, what is done is done. What absolute bloody fools you have been. I am so very angry with you. How could you have done what you did? Why could you not have sorted your differences out and held our family together? Do you have any idea how much Sebastian and I suffered through your total selfishness? Do you?" She put her hands to her forehead, suddenly drained: "When do we get our chance to meet Christina? And yes, I am delighted to know I have a sister. I want, I assure you, to see her."

Sebastian had said very little up until Raine-Fleur had returned and then out of sheer frustration muttered: "Yes, now it's my turn parents. I have actually known about Christina for quite a while, so has granddad. After great-grandma Mary died, she left her entire legacy to Christina, together with a letter to me, telling me all about her and instructing me to send money each month to Sithole and Thokozile for my sister. I sent money to Christina when she moved to school in Italy as well. All done legally through a lawyer and with granddad's help. Your friend mom, Nobukwe, had somehow discovered your Kalahari sojourn journal and she told great-grandma Mary the story, hoping to blackmail her and perhaps you, so great-grandma paid her to keep her mouth shut. Granddad felt you would come to him, when you were ready, so he and I kept your secret for you. Are there any more skeletons in the closet mom? Dad? I love you both and this all doesn't mean I think any the less of you. Sixteen years has been a long wait to meet this sister. Now it's time to do so, don't you think?" Rowin was stunned by Sebastian's revelation…

She ran from the room and stood out on the verandah until she had regained her composure.

The responsibility her son and father had taken upon their shoulders was great indeed. She was indebted to them. She felt so ashamed – so mortified…

∵

… Rowin collected her luggage at the Perth Airport terminal, walked over to the booking clerk and requested her onward flight booking. With determination in her step, she knew, this time she would do the right thing… She hoped she would not be too late. Could there be forgiveness for her imperfections and mistakes? …

.

CHAPTER TEN

BARRIERS III—JABULA

... *strength, hope, laughter. It takes but one small step to begin your journey. Do not let fear of the unknown hold you back. Happiness is a gift found right within you. Find joy and jubilation and walk the long journey home, for 'home' is where you are loved the most ...*

The taxi drew to a halt. Rowin paid the driver, tipping him well. He carried her luggage to the front door of the house. Thanking him, she let herself in. No one appeared to be around, for she had arrived unexpectedly. (She had informed no one of her travel plans...). She breathed deeply and felt very calm and at peace. She walked through to the bedroom and looked at the bed. A monumental stillness descended upon her...

Silently, she began to undress, removing all of her clothes. Her naked body was reflected in the old-fashioned dressing-table mirror. She smiled to herself. Momentarily, butterflies invaded her stomach and she quivered, as though on the edge of a precipice...

Rowin climbed into bed. The crisp sheets felt cool to her nakedness. She was tired but happy, ready to face whatever life would throw at her.

Whispering silently, she prayed quietly and felt a silent peace wrap her entire body like a silken, gossamer veil: "Abba-Father, I know I have Your blessing. I know too, I have Your forgiveness for all the follies and sins I have committed in my life. I am almost sixty-four years old and You have given me such an incredible life. There has been so much depth to it, so much pain too. Thank you Father for all that was and is good in my life. I have such faith in You. I know you are the only One who can answer my prayers. Thank You. Thank You."

Fleur-Rowin turned over and fell asleep instantly. There were no nightmare dreams from the past to trouble her. (She had pinned a note to the bedroom door).

:~

... life is a circle, it begins at conception, then the mystery of birth, and at the end death – the ultimate celebration of that life into eternity...

:~

Africa, Africa, child I call to you. Child of where two oceans meet. You took a shell, you took a stone with you. You kissed all four walls of your room in Arniston. You are part of the Tribe. It does not matter that your skin is white. It does not matter that her skin is black. Your blood is red. You see the same things, you hear the same things, you do the same things. You all matter in the long, tall order of things ... so, dream on my child, remember – "home" is where you are loved the most and

"FAMILY IS WHERE YOUR STORY BEGINS"

Cynthia Elizabeth Sully

BARRIERS III—JOY

Look – now even higher still
I build my tower and strong wall
Will I hear you brave new love
When you challenge me and call?

Beloved, wild soldier-warrior
Hero – proud – on huge black steed
Dare I let my barriers down?
Must I to your passion heed?

Your once strong hands caress me gently
Like no others' warm embrace
Beloved – see I your command
Touch so gently your tearstained face

I will cast down all my weapons
Sabre, fighting stick, spear and sword
I hearken to my pounding heart
Capture me, enter me, hear my loving word

Warmth, tenderness, with wildness
My passion offered willingly to you
Come – ride mounted now, together
O'er African plains in morning's dew

Gallop down to ocean's urging waters
Abandoned movement upon wild seas flow
The minutes of the days, are now ours
For upward and onward we will go

Oh, break not my heart, this I beg of you
For ne'er will it ever mend again
It flutters in its tender fragility
Its soul – a very precious thing

Fleur-Rowin with my love always…

… this was pinned to the door for him to discover…

The landrover drew to a halt. The driver climbed wearily out, his morning had been long and arduous. Shrugging his tense shoulders, he stretched his arms above his head. There was a distinct heaviness to his step as he entered the house, carrying a stack of books, which he placed on the hallway bureau, together with car keys and his safari hat. Yes, he thought to himself, a long cool shower should get the kinks out of his body.

He proceeded towards his bedroom, noticing a large, foolscap sheet of paper pinned to the closed door. This he removed, slowly reading the words written upon it. He felt his heart skip a beat and there was a sense of profound joy within him. Was he imagining all of this? He silently pushed the bedroom door open. Rowin lay upon the bed – hair tousled, tiny smile upon her lips, right hand cupping her shoulder, the sheets between her legs, exposing her still shapely thighs, deeply suntanned. The lion's tooth on its leather thong around her slender neck, just as it always was… He undressed swiftly. Naked now, he climbed into bed beside this amazing woman. He breathed deeply, for he felt somewhat unsure of himself. The house was cool, although outside, the sun was blazing down in its noon hour intensity. Rowin sighed in her sleep. She had come to him. His wait had not been in vain…

∿

On reaching Perth, Rowin had turned around and returned to Alice Springs – returned to the love of her life. Christian held her to him tenderly, lovingly and she stirred and opened her eyes to gaze sleepily into his. It was then he noticed a gold wedding band on Rowin's finger. His old wedding band was on his pillow next to her. This was all he needed to know SHE had decided their destiny for him. "Christian, I want to be with you for however long we may have together. Will you marry me? Will you return to South Africa with me? There are new treatments, new specialists. I believe we can beat this thing. We must leave soon though, for my father needs me too. What do you think my love? Are you willing? I can already sense you are able?"

Christian threw back his head, laughing delightedly: "My dear, dear Rowin. You never cease to amaze me. Yes to all and everything. Can I love you now or do I have to make an honest woman of you first?

Rowin smiled impishly: "Chris, you'll have to wait. Let's get a special marriage licence this afternoon and then ask Temba and Barabara to 'stand up for us' and witness our commitment to each other. We will marry in haste but we will not repent at leisure. You are in possible remission right now and we have to ensure your health continues to improve. Christian, Christian, I love you so much. We will make new memories together, to last us forever through those rainy days…"

"Rowin, I adore and love you."

∴

Christian and Rowin drove to the small town hall. After talking to the clerk in charge of all licensing, they paid the fee for a special marriage licence. Next, they rang Temba, Barabara and Gregory at the Hospital. All three were delighted at the news.

At the Post Office, they sent overseas telegrams to William, Mia Tansy and Sven, Sebastian and Joseé, Raine-Fleur and Andrew, and Christina-Rowin, who had accompanied her siblings and their families on their return to South Africa. (Christina was staying at Rowin's cottage in Arniston, with granddad William…)

The telegrams all read:

"WE'RE GETTING MARRIED FRIDAY IN ALICE – WISH US HAPPINESS SEE YOU ALL IN A FEW DAYS MUCH LOVE F-R & C"

They could have e-mailed or telephoned everyone in South Africa but they wanted the 'excitement' of sending telegrams, to announce their happiness. (How could this tale *not* have, for once, a happy ending?)

∶∿

On the drive home, happy and contented, they discovered a telegram stuck in the front door. This was addressed to Rowin. Immediately her thoughts turned to her father, fearing and dreading the worst, she opened the orange-coloured envelope and drew out the single sheet of paper and read this out aloud to Christian –

> "*R – got weary of waiting for you. Am blissfully happy.*
> *A new and wonderful woman is my wife. Nobukwe*
> *and I married today. Never forget you. How could I?*
> *Love always – PAUL*"

Christian and Rowin were flabbergasted. Fate had played a strange hand in planning the ultimate destinies for all four of them…

∶∿

Rowin and Christian were married quietly. Temba's wife Ijuba stood with him, along with Barabara and Gregory, to witness the joining together in matrimony, two people very dear to them all.

A Judge friend of Christian's had performed their nuptials in his garden, on a sunny morning and as he pronounced them husband and wife, a beautiful dragonfly settled on Rowin's shoulder. This was indeed, a good omen in African folklore. Temba called out: "Fleur-Rowin – you are hereby given a new name. It is the Zulu word – **UZEKAMANZI – Dragonfly**".

Rowin read one of her poems to her new husband after the ceremony. He was no longer her "was-band." She also read the words her beloved father had written many years previously. (He had e-mailed them to her in time for the marriage).

:~

A week later, they returned home to South Africa. Mother Africa had beckoned her children home and she held them close to her large bosom yet again…

:~

… she had gathered sea urchins along the beach for her mother and had woven them into a wreath for her to wear in her hair. The three – Sebastian, Raine and Christina, stood with family, friends and William in a wheelchair, to witness Christian and Rowin re-pledge their vows. The middle-aged couple stood barefoot at the spot where two ocean meet at Cape Agulhas. There was a light breeze and the day was filled with sunshine and Rowin once again, carried her own specially named roses.

The waves, which were magnificently huge, as the high tide reached its crescendo, rushed ashore, sending a fine spray inland, as the surf pounded against the jagged rocks: the child of where two oceans meet, had returned home. Rowin and Christian left new footprints in the soft, white sands… It was a poignant moment – almost bittersweet in its intensity… forty years ago – they had stood here…

:~

… they sang – **Nkosi Sikelel iAfrika**
GOD BLESS AFRICA

… secant line's radius of circle through one end of arc had met tangent to the other end; ratio of this to radius… life had almost come full circle…

:~

what does life hold in store for South Africa and its peoples? Only time will tell – this day – nothing could spoil its perfection of love, for love never ends – love IS the greatest gift of all…

… next morning, Rowin walked to Nonqaba's small grave, to place her wedding roses on the mound. A small, white lamb, was sitting next to the headstone.

AFRICAN DREAM
YOU REST NOW – WISELY ON THE GLOBE

A temperamental heat-filled sun
    bakes your red earth
Desert kisses have drowned your
    pain and sorrows
Peace washes over your sandy beaches
    as the seas rush to your shores
Stony secrets of your hills hear
    far distant singing of the
    Southern Cross and Sirius
Be happy – jabula kusasa – on all
    your tomorrows
Mother Africa – may you weep no more
    as the euphoria of joy wipes
    your tears
Listen for the laughter of the Tribe
    as distant drums beat on a
    moonless night
And woodsmoke burns on an open fire
    When lion roar on a savannah plain
Strength and hope and new dreams be
    your companions now
As peoples of rainbow colours learn
    forgiveness
    as love keeps no record of wrongs
    love does not delight in evil
    love rejoices in truth
    love does not boast
    love will persevere

love will always protect
love is not easily angered
love does not worry
love does not boast
love is patient
love is kind
love never fails – never fails
faith – hope – love
and the greatest of these is **LOVE**

AMEN – so be it ......

Fleur-Rowin's poem for Christian ...

Let us grow lovely growing old – so many fine things do –
Laces and ivory and gold and silks need not be always new
And there is healing in old trees – ancient streets a glamour hold –
Oh – may not we – as well as these – grow lovely growing old?

William's Poem ...

FLEUR-ROWIN'S DREAM
FOR THE FUTURE IN SOUTH AFRICA

All war is over now
I have come home to you
Ebon velvet night's
Suspended silence
Enfolds the day
Phosphorescent glow
Teases waves
On moon's silver ribbon
Fades into morn's dawn
Welcomes love's touch
For there will be joy in morn's dew
Love unites them
It never ends
All is well with my tribe
Strength
Hope
Laughter
on
their
lips
Freedom
their
Shield
Peace their song
All war is over now

God bless Africa
Amandhla

... and there was a peace to be found in their forgiveness ...

and Christian and Rowin read these words together on the beach where the Atlantic meets the Indian, in front of all their friends and family ... and old Hildy Biko wiped the tears from her eyes ...

EPILOGUE

Paul Blakeney had left a package for Rowin to find on her return from Australia. In his enclosed letter, he attempted to explain at length, his association with Nobukwe – now his wife. He also enclosed all Rowin's letters and poems to him. He apologised for his change of heart. His letter was somewhat callous in its wording, as he attempted to explain his actions. He had placed Rowin's white nightgown in the package as well.

∿

... Paul had not yet received Rowin's letter. Her letter had been honest and forthright. She had been far more diplomatic and gentler in her approach of her reasons and explanation for her own marriage...

Nobukwe had found Rowin's letter and had been tempted to read and then destroy it. Resisting temptation, she had given the letter to her husband. Paul was not particularly surprised Rowin and Christian were once again together. Nobukwe's thoughts were otherwise. She was angry and bitter and resentful. Rowin had her happiness and did *not* want Paul after all... She thought to herself: "I hope Christian dies soon, then Rowin will be all alone. I hate her. I hate her family. It's time for me to inform them that Rowin's stepmother is *my* half-sister. I am old Henry Eaton's bastard daughter. They owe me, yes, they owe me." Nobukwe was still eaten up with malicious bitterness and jealousy. Paul knew nothing of any of this...

∿

... as Paul looked out across the ocean toward Robben Island, he had a huge moment of doubt. He was not sure he truly loved Nobukwe. Their association seemed merely one of a sexual nature... Never given to impetuosity, he had been extremely pressed by Nobukwe, to marry her, after only having known her a few weeks... His children had not accepted, nor liked her. This was not due to the fact she was a black woman, for they had no racial prejudices and were not biased in accepting a woman of colour into their family. Nobukwe had not been warm and caring, as Rowin had been. Nobukwe was cold, conniving and very possessive of their father… Had he made a grave mistake after all? He realized too late, Rowin was the one person he had truly loved and cared about. What could he do now? Leave Nobukwe? Wait for Christian's demise? No, he would make the best of the situation he was in, but what of Nobukwe? He really did not know this woman he had married… **Theirs was not connubial bliss…**

... South Africa, as we move toward another year what is happening, for the people do not sing a joyous song...? There is deepseated fear... There is much disillusionment. Shantytowns springing up everywhere, as the housing promised is but a dream. No electricity for South Africa's population, with daily government mandated powercuts to keep the country going. No work – no food – people on the brink of starvation and deep poverty.

The crime rate has risen alarmingly since 1994: over **200,000 Black people** and **40,000 White people have been murdered thus far...**

Weekly, thousands and thousands of illegal immigrants cross South Africa's borders from other neighbouring African countries, seeking sanctuary in a country which promises so much more than their own. South Africa, on the whole enjoys a very high standard of living compared to other African countries, but South Africa cannot cope with its own people in providing for them what was promised when the untenable apartheid regimé ended. The situation is becoming desperate, with marauding bands and gangs, seeking to make a living, by using their own people and terrified refugees as their targets in order to live.

Thaba Mbeki, South Africa's ANC Party/Government President, is no longer leader of the once powerful ANC. The ANC are divided, seeking a more powerful leader and have nominated Jacob Zuma (who has much scandal, including rape charges, attached to his name). Thaba Mbeki's "gentler, middleclass leadership" most ANC supporters, feel has no backbone. Zuma's followers show a strong leaning to the left. Elections are looming and the writing appears to be on the wall... The winds of change are once again beginning to blow. Will they reach galeforce proportions? Will South Africa crumble in the process? There is much corruption midst various politicians and it would seem that old adage rings true:

"the rich get rich and the poor get poorer"

All peoples, indeed all tribes, walk very cautiously as the elections approach for no one knows in which direction the wind might change. One cannot direct that wind, but one can adjust one's sails…

Tradewise, the country prospers, relying heavily on its tourist trade as well but the South African rand currency fluctuates daily and interest rates are high. To obtain a credit card, has become a major issue, but the drums continue to beat… and the countryside is still so beautiful with a timelessness found nowhere else…

Mother Africa weeps once more for the plight of her children, for the terrible scourge of HIV-AIDS is huge. In the old colonial days, she was called "Darkest Africa." Is this continent becoming dark again? Can we, the rest of the world, stand by and watch Africa suffer, doing little to help on an ONGOING basis? Is this what OUR democracy is all about?

Will Fleur-Rowin Elizabeth Eastwood take up the challenge of the battlecry and fight to help her Tribe in South Africa? She is a woman of courage, a wife, mother and grandmother. She has made many mistakes in her life but deep down, her ideals of right and wrong have never wavered… She is no longer a young woman but this will not deter her…

Pray this night and on all nights for the people of Africa. South Africa is a "rainbow nation" with many tribes, many diversified cultures, but under the stars of the heavens, we are all brothers and sisters, linked from a time immemorial, whatever our colour or creed… Ponder deeply on these words and stand up and be counted at the end of the day for it is such a wondrous thing to "give" rather than to receive…

~

… William's ashes were scattered on the Indian Ocean side of the Cape Peninsula at Fish Hoek Beach, one of his favourite spots. This was his wish. He rests now, at peace… He had yet another dream fulfilled. He met and spent time with his grand-daughter Christina-Rowin. The two had a wonderful rapport. William had been instrumental in persuading

Christina to fly from Italy to Australia to meet up with her parents and siblings, whilst they were all in Alice Springs. There was also a very special bond forged between Raine-Fleur and Sebastian – with their sister. This pleased William immensely.

∴∼

Rowin and Christian's relationship with all three of their children, became very close as the years sped by. There was so much to make up for. There was no bitterness, only amazing loving forgiveness for all the wrongs of the past, for love never ends. Only sometimes, it is put on hold, tucked away somewhere in a place where dreams are made…

∴∼

Every Saint Patrick's Day – Rowin drives through to the beach at Fish Hoek. She stands upon the large rocky outcrop on Jager's Walk and gazes out to sea – remembering her father and says: "… Daddy-love, you are always in my heart, until we meet again: size sibonane futhi…"

… TEMPUS UMBRA …
CARPE DIEM
time is a shadow
seize the day

TRANSLATIONS

TRANSLATIONS

ad infinitum		without limit, forever
afrikaans	A	language of the farmer/pioneers
amazolo	Z	dew
apartheid	A	racial segregation
baas	A	boss
biltong	A	dried strips of seasoned meat (beef, kudu, ostrich)
boer(s)	A	farmer/s
boerewors	A	farm sausage usually spicy
braaivleis	A	meat barbeque over wood/coals
bulala	Z	kill
Cabo Tormentoso		Cape of Storms/Torment
ca'gn		tribal Bushmen
Die °kaffir op sy plek	A	the °nigger in his place
Die °koelies uit die land	A	the °coolies out of the land
Die wit man moet altyd baas wees	A	the white man must always be boss
dompas	A	dumb pass
dorp	A	village
gogo(s)	Z	grandmother(s)
habeas corpus	Z	writ requiring a person be brought before a judge or into court
hamba kashle	Z	go in peace
hlala kashle	Z	stay in peace

ibhele	Z	bear
imvu-yamanzi	Z	seal
inkosikazi	Z	mistress
in medias res		in the midst of
intombi	Z	girl
isigwebo	Z	judgement
jabula	Z	jubilation/hope
julle mense is °kaffirboeties Ons sal julle doodskiet	A	you people are °nigger lovers. We shall shoot you dead.
kuphuke ingilazi	Z	the glass is broken
lobola	Z	brideprice (paid in cattle)
manyana	Z	tomorrow
mbira	Z	handheld musical strumming instrument likened to a mini African piano
mielies	A	corn/maize
ngedukile	Z	I have lost my way
ons eie volk, ons eie taal, ons eie land	A	our own people, our own language, our own land
padraos		stone crosses
poqo		independent
riempie	A	leather thong(s)
sawubona		greetings
simunye		we are one
size sibonane futhi		until we meet again
soi-disant		pretended

suikerbossie	A	small indigenous sugarbush
suikerbos ek will jou hê wat sal you mama daarvan sê?	A	sugarbush (young woman), I want you, what will your mother say?
swart gevaar	A	black danger
taal	A	language
thanda indoda	Z	lovely man
toto	Z	child
totsiens	A	goodbye
trek	A	long journey
trekker/s	A	pioneer/s
trekking	A	journeying
ukhulu	Z	grandmother
ulwandle	Z	sea
umakhulu		grandmother
umanqulwana	Z	ladybird/bug
uvemvane	Z	butterfly
uzekamanzi	Z	dragonfly
veld	A	bush
veldskoen/e	A	anklelength bushboots made from suede animal pelts
verkrampte/s	A	diehard/s
WAENSHUISKRANS	A	ARNISTON – the only town in South Africa with TWO official postal names
waenshuiskrans	A	wagonhouse cave/cliff
wemshile wame – thul 'u laleli – intombazane		speak to me softly – stay silent – listen small girl

° Derogatory terminology used against people in the context of a racial slur

A Afrikaanas
Z Zulu

THE "TRIBE" FLEUR-ROWIN ELIZABETH EUGENE BELONGED TO

William James EUGENE	her FATHER
Elizabeth-Amiel (Huddlestone) EUGENE	her MOTHER
Felicity (Eaton) EUGENE	her STEP-MOTHER
Mia Tansy EUGENE-BJORNSEN	her HALF-SISTER
Sven BJORNSEN	HUSBAND
their children	Timothy BJORNSEN Susannah BJORNSEN
Christian Mark EASTWOOD	Rowin's FIRST LOVE
Paul Nicholas BLAKENEY	Rowin's SECOND LOVE
Rowin/Christian's children	Sebastian Adam EASTWOOD Raine-Fleur EASTWOOD
Rosemary (Garôute) EUGENE	Paternal GRANDMOTHER
James O'NEILL EUGENE	Paternal GRANDFATHER
Mary (Shale) HUDDLESTONE	Maternal GRANDMOTHER
Noah William HUDDLESTONE	Maternal GRANDFATHER
Elsie (Embley) EATON	Step-GRANDMOTHER
Henry James EATON ('PA')	Step-GRANDFATHER
Joanna/Peter ROBINSON neé EUGENE	her father's SISTER (no children)

Cynthia Elizabeth Sully

Beth/Ari BEN JORDAN neé EUGENE   her father's SISTER

their children   Cain BEN JORDAN
                 Ruth BEN JORDAN
                 Jacob BEN JORDAN

Annabel/Robin VAN ZYL neé EUGENE   her father's SISTER

their children   Jonathon VAN ZYL
                 Catriona VAN ZYL and
                 Claire VAN ZYL (twins)

Richard/Patrice EUGENE   her father's BROTHER

their children   Patrick EUGENE and
                 Noélle EUGENE (twins)

ABOUT THE AUTHOR

Cynthia Elizabeth (Collins) Sully born and educated in Cape Town, South Africa – grew up with her sister Myrle – within the shadow of the Cape's magnificently brooding and awe inspiring Table Mountain...

Cynthia's family heritage reaches back generations to Ireland's: County Cork – England's: Barrow-in-Furnace and Lancashire and France's: Alsace-Lorraine region.

Her heart has resided in two places since moving to Canada in 1978 with her then-husband, son and daughter. South Africa draws her back like a magnet with ten visits back thus far... She has also visited Brazil, Argentina, Uruguay (twice), with short trips to France and England and has resided in Australia twice.

She is an interior design consultant and her many interests include gourmet cooking (specializing in Cape-Dutch-Malay cuisine from South Africa). Many of South Africa's traditional recipes may be found in her first published book (part of a biography), entitled – *SNOWFLAKES TO SEA URCHINS* – *'twas the night after Christmas*... (ISBN 1-4251-0095-3), a book well-received by the public at large...

Her books are obtainable directly from her (call or fax: 604-946-7439 or mail: B302/4821 – 53 Street, LADNER (Delta) British Columbia V4K 2Z3 CANADA... or TRAFFORD Publishing www.trafford.com.

"SAWUBONA"
Cynthia on the day she left for Cape Town 2007
(her book already partly written)

ISBN 1425176615

Edwards Brothers Malloy
Oxnard, CA USA
February 10, 2014